DEAD COLD

REANIMATED DIARY
BITS AND PIECES ANTHOLOGY

Published by: Genesis Creations Entertainment

Published by:
Genesis Creations Entertainment

PublishingonAmazon.com

For more information go to:

www.genesiscreations.biz

www.publishingonamazon.com

Keith Carpenter

rottenzimbiesmail@gmail.com
www.keithcarpenter.biz

Table of Contents

Dead Cold and

Reanimated Diary

Written By

Keith Carpenter

Cover Design By

Matt Ficner

Edited by

Daniel Chandranayagam/Bonnie Vent

Anthology Contributions by

R.R. Alexander

Wayne Hood

Thomas M. Stoops

Matt Ficner

Keith Carpenter

Introduction

I have been a fan of the zombie genre since I was a teenager. The Romero films always mesmerized me with their ability to entertain the horror lover in everyone while at the same time, making important social statements that reflect something in our society that many people would rather ignore. For me what makes the Zombie the scariest fictional "monsters" in both film and literature is that they are, for all practical purposes, us. The thought of that loved one that you have cherished and adored as an important part of your life, dying just to come back from the dead with one desire..... to eat your flesh. That thought alone is enough to scare the hell out of the bravest soul.

Four years ago, after collaborating on a zombie movie script with a friend, I got "bitten" pun intended, by the zombie writing bug. The novel you are about to read, which was originally called "Freeze Dried" was about a world I created in my mind. It was a world where the zombie plague is started, not by terrorism or radioactive fallout, or even toxic waste etc, but by Corporate Greed. Those big corporations, who have a very clear responsibility to the general public, but choose to take chances with the lives of millions to save a buck and lower the corporate "overhead".

When you peel back all the zombies and blood-guts and gore, you'll see that's what this story is about. After I wrote this novel, I was still teeming with ideas that clearly took place in the same world I had just created, so I hope as the reader, you enjoy the extra goodies that the book has to offer over and above the main storyline. It's a novel, a diary and an anthology all rolled into one. Over the years as a fan of the genre, I have learned that there are literally millions of fans just like me and the internet has been a wonderful medium in which to meet many of them. The anthology of stories at the back of this book is largely made up of stories written by some of those people I have had the honor of meeting on various zombie related websites or just as a result of their having read my work. It was my goal to give them a platform to debut their work, so I hope you zombie lovers out there enjoy the read and please feel free to give me your feedback.

Thanks

KC

rottenzombiesmail@gmail.com

DEAD COLD
By Keith Carpenter

I s it a dream or a nightmare? It's like my conscious thought is flickering in and out like a television screen with a short in it. Is it time? Are they here for me? It seems like I was just put under ours ago! Oh god how I hope it is time... to wake up and be free of this frozen coffin.

The light, like a flickering screen was dim but clearly real and it pierced through my closed eyelids like a bolt of lightning. Something popped and exploded in my face. There was a buzzing sound like a light bulb blowing out and something burned my face like sparks hitting my skin. The hissing sound of an air-tight door opening almost burst my eardrums and that's when I realized I wasn't dreaming. It was not some figment of my imagination or some ghost of an image leftover in my head, it was something I was really seeing. I was awake and this was not a dream. What the hell was happening? Why was I seeing anything at all? Was it time? Had they found a cure and awakened me from what was supposed to be a long if not permanent sleep? I didn't hear anyone around. Where were the doctors? Why wasn't someone helping make this transition easier? There should have been technicians all over the place, helping me revive correctly and monitoring what was going on. My eyelids were sealed shut with a layer of smut that had to be peeled open and all of my senses were dulled but what I smelled didn't smell like the cleaning solvents used to sterilize a hospital room. In fact the putrid stink that was invading my nostrils smelled more like a mixture of rotting meat and cow shit. Then everything seemed to be shifting. Up was down and down felt like up. SMACK! I felt myself hit the floor with a thud.

The moment of consciousness I had experienced was rudely interrupted by a sharp pain in the side of my face… then once again… consciousness faded away.

I woke again, I'm guessing only moments later, and realized I had fallen out of the safety of my metallic coffin and landed face first on the floor. I could feel my cheek sticking to the cold wet ground. It was stuck there by a thick layer of blood and saliva that was oozing from the corner of my mouth. My face was pressed against the floor tile and my cheek bone horribly bruised if not broken. There it was again, the overwhelming stench of that rotting meat and shit. It was even stronger now. I forced one eye to open, pulling apart the thick layer of goo that was holding it shut. I gave it a moment to focus and suddenly I could see where the stench was coming from.

OH MY GOD… I gasped and my other eye flew open ripping out the eyelashes that were glued shut with goo. It was a cadaver… the upper half of a human torso and it was lying not three feet from my face. I had to hold back the urge to vomit. The body was horribly decomposed and the intestines, especially the large, was strewn out across the floor and ripped open like an overstuffed sausage casing. The smell of shit was coming from a thick layer of dried human feces that had obviously been oozing out of the dead body's intestinal tract for as long as it had been lying there rotting. Then I noticed it, a really bad sign. I didn't recognize the body but it was wearing the remnants of a doctor's lab coat. What the fuck?

The room had been vandalized. Steel medical tables had been upended all over the place and surgical equipment was littering the floor. The other coffin-shaped cryo chambers lined up against the walls were badly broken. Some were left lying open or in some cases still sealed shut with the oval shaped glass portholes broken, exposing a rotting putrid corpse inside. I grabbed the metal handles on the sides of my cryo chamber and pulled myself up and saw that Chamber 73, which was next to mine, had a decayed grotesque corpse glaring at me from behind the glass. Blood was spattered on the inside of the glass as well as on the outside, all over the chamber. My guess was that this poor fuck had woken up and been trapped inside, only to suffocate to death. Seeing this made me suddenly feel lucky, at least luckier than number 73. The blood spattered on the outside of the chamber was more evidence that something horrible had happened here; probably the same thing that left that stinking rotten corpse dead on the floor.

I looked around. My vision was clouded and limited. Suddenly, out of the corner of my eye, I saw the corpse in chamber 73 move. I spun back around to look at it but it was gone. Rubbing my tired, dehydrated eyeballs, I tried to put it out of my mind and chalk it up to my imagination. Who knew how long the corpse had been propped up in there? It was only a matter of time for gravity to take its toll and cause it to collapse in a pile at the bottom of the chamber. I ignored it and turned to face the door when I heard a faint thump. Was my mind playing me for the fool? I had just awakened from a very deep sleep and I was well beyond fucked up. It had to be my imagination. I shook my head and slowly turned back toward the glass porthole and sure enough there was nothing there. The old rotten corpse in chamber 73 had surely collapsed and fallen down out of sight, no big deal.

"Jesus". I mumbled under my breath.

I had to pull myself together. This was definitely not what I had expected to wake up to. Especially after spending 2.5 million bucks to freeze my sick body in cryogenic stasis till the fucking doctors could find a way to cure me. I was supposed to be resuscitated only after they had cured me. I wasn't even supposed to have to see the inside of an operating theater... it was even specified in my fucking contract.

I had the overwhelming desire to yell at someone. Hell I wanted to break someone's jaw, but reality was that I was doing good to wiggle my toes. I would have loved to have sued the fly by night outfit for every penny I spent on my contract and then some...but with my luck my lawyer had probably been dead for years, so the thought quickly dissipated. I called out and listened for an answer. I wanted to know how long I had been in that damn freezer, but the answer never came. Honestly by the looks of the place nobody had been there in a long while. I slid weakly back to the floor where there was a layer of dust covering everything. There were some hand prints in the dust that weren't mine and several bloody trails that led away out of the room, but in my dizzy stupor I couldn't hear or see a damn thing... the prints must have just been remnants of whatever had happened while I was asleep. Hell, God only knew how long that might have been too.

Once my eyes were adjusted to the dim glow that was coming from the open door, I began to drag my semi-paralyzed body across the floor. I was pretty determined to get out of that room as soon as I could. The smell of Stinky Stinkerton's torso was about to make me puke and having not eaten anything in who knows how long, that wasn't going to be a pretty sight. Once a guy starts the dry heaves, the next step is to start puking up bile and that was the last thing my dry parched mouth needed. As I dragged myself across the cold dusty floor, I could feel my legs coming back to life. I was doing an army crawl, kicking up a dust cloud behind me. I finally got into the hallway to what had once been a nurse's station or some sort of information desk. The halls were dark in both directions and there was not a sound to be heard. Light was still a rare commodity so it was hard to recognize where I was. I called out several more times just to hear my hoarse croaky voice echo away into oblivion with not a soul to hear it. I couldn't for the life of me imagine what had happened here. All I knew was that the multimillion dollar company 'Eternal Slumber Inc.' was now a in shambles and what was supposed to be a blissful slumber for me had ended in this abrupt awakening to God knows what. All I knew for sure was that it was not part of the plan and it sure as hell was not in my contract.

I sat with my back against the wall and massaged my aching legs. The floor was cold and hard against my naked body and my flat bony ass was getting sore sitting on the rigid tile. I sat, rubbing the stiffness out of my thighs when I noticed that there was still a thin plastic catheter tube sticking out of the end of my penis. It hurt like hell to pull it out, but I had to do what I had to do. It was a helpless embarrassing feeling to have urine dripping out of me onto the floor but at that point I was really just happy to be alive and I knew I had bigger things to worry about. I threw the tube down the hall and leaned my head back, taking a deep breath. I just couldn't believe what I had woken up to. I just wished it was all a horrible nightmare and I would wake up but I knew in my soul that wasn't going to happen. Suddenly I heard a beep. It was coming from me. I looked myself over and noticed the digital wristband they had put on me when I was sedated. It was still working, monitoring my blood pressure as well as my heart rate and to my luck and surprise it actually had a read-out of the date. It seemed I had been rudely awakened on August 5th 2015 and I remembered that I had gone into cryo on the auspicious date of January 11th 1999. It was auspicious because it was a year to the day my wife left me for another woman. You're probably thinking why auspicious if it was the date something bad happened. Well I hated the bitch and was glad to see her go and when the divorce was final she ended up with nothing... well except my son. Anyway in my still somewhat dazed and confused condition I started to try to do the math. I had been asleep for about sixteen years… and boy I felt every minute of it. I couldn't help but wonder what the fuck had happened between then and now and why 'Eternal Slumbers' headquarters had been ransacked like this. I wondered to myself if it was some terrorist attack or some sort of nuclear war that had happened while I was out? At that very moment I really didn't care what it was, I was just trying to get my wits about me so I could deal with the fact that this was my reality.

Finally I tried standing up again. I knew if I could only find Doctor Benson, the man who sold me my 'Eternal Slumber' policy, I could get some answers as to what had happened. I thought I remembered his office being just down the hall near the lobby so my new goal was to make it down there. As I rose to my feet, I caught my reflection in a nearby mirrored door. JEZUZ H. CHRIST were the words that escaped my lips as I saw the emaciated skeleton of a naked man standing there gazing back at me with his hollow sunken eyes. The life support system in the cryo chamber had obviously worked good enough to this point that I was still alive, but whatever nutrients it was supposed to be feeding me had run out a while before the chamber had opened, waking me up. Was I lucky to be alive? I thought to myself. I honestly didn't know, but my next thought was to get the hell out of this building and access my accounts and get myself checked into the nicest hotel I could find…. My favorite had been the Ritz Carlton but I was nowhere near New York. Oh yeah and get myself a nice big deep dish pizza. The clothes I had taken from the corpse of a nearby janitor hung off my body like limp drapes. They were bloody and smelled like the rotting corpse they had come from but they were better than nothing and I didn't feel much like strolling through town naked.

I wasn't sure what to think as I made my way down the hall toward the entrance to the building. What in the living hell had happened here? There was blood smeared on almost everything and decaying body parts were strewn around like confetti after a New Year's Eve party. If there had been some devastating event happen in the building, where were the rescue workers? Where was the police department? Why had the authorities let pieces of dead people lay around rotting for so long? I mean hell, I'm not a doctor or a pathologist even, but it was obvious even to me that from the level of decomposition in all these bits and pieces of bodies, they had been there for weeks or even months. And to hell with the authorities, where were the families of these dead people? I could have understood if the cryo chambers blew up and showered the place with body parts, but it was obvious that these people were not all 'Eternal Slumber' clients. Some of them were janitors and nurses and even bits and pieces of what looked to be children. Something very wrong was going on and I wanted to get the "heads up". I slowly made my way to the waiting lobby that had once been adorned with plush carpet, high end leather furniture and a rose colored crystal chandelier but it was now all in shambles. Torn, broken and pretty much covered with blood the place was completely unrecognizable. It all made my mind race back to my last day awake on earth… the last time I had seen this lobby and the reason I even went there.

"I'm sorry Bill, but it's a tumor and it's inoperable and there just isn't the technology to cure it now." Sander Breckenridge was my doctor and my childhood friend and he didn't want to be the one to have to deliver this news to me and I knew it.

"So what are my options, San?" I knew the answer in my gut but I asked it anyway.

"Well by my estimation and all I can do is estimate, you don't have much longer before there is an event." Sander did that same

nervous pen twitching thing he did when we were in science class back when we were eleven and twelve.

"By 'event' you mean some sort of embolism or something? Like my brain exploding?" Sander sat quietly and nodded his head in affirmation.

"I'm really sorry Bill but there is absolutely nothing I can do for you at this point. If I were you, I would get my things in order so you don't leave your family with a mess to clean up."

"Well my wife can go to hell, but I do want to make sure my son gets what's coming to him. You know I have the money, San; I will pay anything or go anywhere to get this fixed. I don't even care if I have to see some voodoo witch doctor in the darkest jungles of South America, I just want a cure." Sander sat long and thought hard then he said something that I could tell he was hesitant to say.

"Bill there isn't a cure now, but that doesn't mean there won't be in a few years and I know you don't have a few years, so I'm going to suggest something that's going to sound crazy. There is a company that caters to only the.... well... exclusive client... only clients with a lot of money and even more optimism. It's not a cure but it is a possibility for a cure later on. It's a cryogenic alternative that might allow you to be put to sleep until a later date when there is a cure for your problem...."

That conversation rang in my head like a church bell. It had been sixteen years and I thought maybe if I could find Sander he could turn me on to some new and 'way out' surgical procedure that would fix me, FAT CHANCE, if I knew then what I know now I would not have wasted the brain power thinking about it.

The only thing between me and the door now was a short section of hallway and the lobby. The end of the hallway leading to the lobby had caved in and there was rubble from the ceiling lying all around. It wasn't impassable but it was damn close. There was a partially blocked door on the right, at the end of the hall. For a moment I thought I heard someone or something moving around in there. I called out but the sound quickly stopped. In my weakened state, I tried to climb up over the rubble and look inside the room. It was impossible to go in there as the rubble was blocking it almost completely. There was a crawl space between some wooden planks that was big enough for a child to squeeze through but even in my emaciated state of 'thinness' I wasn't going in there.

I was on top of the rubble straddling some broken planks when suddenly I got a whiff of something even more putrid smelling than ole Stinky Stinkerton back in the lab. I tried to poke my head in and see what was in the room when suddenly out of nowhere a withered, writhing claw of a hand lunged out at me. It was human from what I could tell but it was only partially covered with skin. There were emaciated, rotting strands of muscle and sinew stretched across the blood dried bones. At first I wasn't completely sure but it was a hand alright. It could only penetrate so far into the hallway through the rubble but when I got a look at what it was attached to, I almost passed out. Gathering my wits about me, I grabbed a piece of metal ceiling frame and bent it, breaking it off. Just as the hand grabbed my baggy bloody shirt, I came down hard on it with my make-shift metal weapon. After three good whacks, as I tried with all my might to make the damn thing let go of me, I heard a horrible cracking sound. The disgusting withered forearm bent awkwardly in two in a way that no arm should. The bones were sticking out of the little bit of rotting flesh that was left as the writhing hand opened and closed and dangled out of control.

As I climbed down the other side of the rubble just yards away from the front door, the ghoul that was trapped in the room began to moan and scream and squeeze his head through a small opening between the door-jam and some of the fallen rubble. It was obvious to me that the opening was way too small for his head to fit though but he was so determined to get a hold of me, that he just kept trying. I cringed and backed away… pressing my back against the wall as I watched the human monstrosity press his head through the opening. It was almost like watching someone squeeze raw meat through a grinder…. Or like some large round bloody banana with its skin peeling away. The monster's scalp, or what was left of it, split in the middle and slid off on either side, exposing a putrid rotting muscle covered skull with two bulging eyeballs looking right at me. It was like seeing a bloody rubber Halloween mask with the ears still attached on the sides, being peeled off someone's head. As he forced his head through the opening, a piece of metal caught his bottom jaw, ripping it right out of the socket, leaving it to dangle to one side. It was the most horrible sight I had ever seen and then I saw it. I didn't want to believe it because it meant that any hope of finding out what had gone on here was gone. As the horrible bloody meat puppet continued to squeeze his much too large body through the eye of a needle, I caught sight of his jacket. There on the ripped and bloody lapel of his once white lab coat was the name tag that read 'Robert Benson M.D.'. I fell to the floor. It was like someone hit me in the stomach. What the hell was going on in this fucking place? I didn't know if I was dreaming… caught in some horrible cryogenic nightmare or if this was all really happening to me. I just watched as the poor excuse for a human being destroyed himself trying to squeeze through the rubble. He would lunge and then stop… as if resting. Lunge and stop, over and over… with no hope of making it through. He was so determined to get to me. What did he want? Did he recognize me? How could he still be alive? I was sick to my stomach thinking about it and trying to figure it out. Part of me wanted to just lay there and die. I felt like dying… hell I was half starved to death already and honestly not that far from the great mortal threshold into the afterlife anyway.

I leaned back with my head against the wall not really knowing what I was waiting for. Maybe I was secretly hoping the tumor in my head would suddenly explode, sparing me all this horrible reality. I slowly opened my heavy eyelids and looked up, when I noticed something else. In the upper pocket of Dr. Benson's lab coat was what looked like a small hand held tape recorder. Knowing there was really nothing I could do for the old fool now, I said my apologies and grabbed the same metal bar I had used before and with all my might I planted it right into the disgusting old doctor's brain-case. The moaning and screeching stopped and Doctor Benson's entire body went limp.

The recorder was caked with dried blood and the back was gone exposing the two double A batteries. It seemed to be in tact though and I found if I pressed the batteries in with my thumb the player would work. The memory card was cracked and sticking out of the recorder, but pushing it back in place seemed to do the trick. Hoping the worn out recorder would actually work, I pressed the play button and that is when I heard what I was guessing was the good doctor's last words as a normal human being.

It's April 12th 2015 and this is Doctor Robert Benson M.D. Managing director for 'Eternal Slumber' Inc. At approximately 5:45am this morning we had an incident in cryo chamber 23a. It seems that the client Mrs. Agnes Morehead flat lined while in cryo stasis. All of her vital signs ceased for no apparent reason and she appeared to be completely dead. Our doctors tried to resuscitate her to no avail and her corpse has been stored in the morgue. As she has been in cryo for almost twenty years, she has no next of kin, so she will remain there until we are able to dispose of her remains properly. Our experts seem to think the chemical we inject into the blood to help stabilize the freezing process may be the cause of this most unfortunate episode.

It's April 14th 2015 at 10:30am and this is Doctor Robert Benson M.D. It was brought to my attention this morning that there was another incident in the wee hours of the morning before my shift started. Mrs. Agnes Morehead, who had expired two days ago, was being stored in the basement morgue when her body began to show signs of resuscitation. Although she seemed to be animated and alive, her vital signs remained nonexistent. I am completely puzzled as to what happened and her still animated body has been strapped down on one of the autopsy tables in the basement until we can find out what is going on.

This is Doctor Benson and its April 15th. While trying to subdue the restrained but extremely violent Mrs. Morehead, one of our orderlies was violently bitten on the arm by Mrs. Morehead. I am not sure what the hell is going on but the orderly, a certain Bradley Snyder is showing signs of extreme fever and disorientation. If his situation doesn't change soon he will probably not live through the night.

This is Doctor Benson and its 11:45 pm on April 15th. The basement has been blocked off until we can rectify the problem we are having. I have decided not to notify the authorities until we can get things under control. To be frank the company doesn't need the bad press. It seems that Bradley passed away a few hours ago and then began to re-animate similar to Mrs. Morehead, only this time much quicker. From what I understand three more orderlies were trapped in the morgue with the two subjects and they too were attacked and killed. As of this moment they too have reanimated and now we are faced with the problem of exterminating them.

It's 3:00am and they're loose in the building. I have locked myself in the office and I think Mrs. Morehead and the four re-

animated orderlies have begun to kill the entire staff. All I can hear is screaming and people ransacking the laboratories. I don't know how, or if, I'll ever get out of here....

I've been bitten... It's been five hours since they tried to break into my office. That bitch Morehead grabbed my arm and took a chunk out of it. It's the 18th of April and I've been cooped up in this damn office for three days. It's a good thing I had this mini-fridge in my office stocked with food. I have used up all the antibiotics I had in there but they don't seem to be doing any good anyway.

April 22nd and the chaos has spread everywhere. I'm still cooped up in my office and my breathing is labored. The door has been blocked by rubble from a cave in caused by the creatures ransacking the building. I don't have the energy to move the heavy beams and rubble and I don't think I have much longer. From what I've seen when I do pass I'm going to be revived to rise from the dead as one of those horrible things. I have been able to get the news broadcasts on the computer and it seems since the infected escaped the building on the 15th the infection has spread all over the city. I fear if something isn't done there is no stopping the spread. If something is not done the entire northern hemisphere could be infected by late June or early July.

It's the 27th of April and I have been trapped in my office for just over a week. I have not been able to move or stand for almost 48 hours. I can feel it taking over my body. My head feels like it's going to explode... I'm sorry for this... I only have myself to blame for not alerting the authorities when it all first started to happen... it's my fault... my fault...CLICK!

Day 1-----His body lurched forward into a sitting potion in one single jerk, like those people who suffer from sleep apnea do when their body decides to start breathing again, but he didn't seem to have the luxury of breath. He sat there a moment; something was wrong. Every inch of his body hurt and the pain was like nothing he could remember having felt before. He began to rise from the wet damp ground where he had been lying in a pool of his own blood. His arms and legs were limp as if they had all gone to sleep but there were no pins and needles, just dead weight trying to prop itself up, trying to make itself walk again. He had no memory of who he was, where he was or how he had gotten there, but he was there and everything around him was a haze; a blur of an unfocused reality that he didn't seem to be a part of any longer. As he began to move, he realized something was plastered to his chest just under the gaping open wound in his neck. It was stuck there by the blood that had dried and it was attached to a chain that was around his neck. He tugged at it and noticed it was some sort of necklace. Probably something someone meaningful had given to him but he could not remember where it came from. It was a tooth of some kind. A large sharp tooth with something etched into the enamel. It was covered with blood and hard for his dried up eyes to make out but it must have been important to him so he left it alone and his attention went back to that terrible urge he was having, the distinctive hunger that he still could not identify. He tried to call out to anyone who might hear him, but nothing came out. Nothing audible at least, it was just a moan of agony and pain as one foot shuffled in front of the other allowing him to slowly move. He could feel air escaping from his throat, escaping from his neck, through that open gaping wound; gurgling blood as the last air escaped his lungs... he was hurt. How badly he didn't know. Something was calling him, drawing him away, something that he had once had but now seemed to have lost. There was an overwhelming desire in him to find it but he wasn't sure what exactly IT was. The thing that drew him was overpowering, he had to have it. Nothing else mattered anymore. The desire was like a flame in his inner most being, a hunger for something that would sustain him and keep him going. He wanted it, he needed it but he didn't even know where to get it.------

Hearing his voice re-living the experience was almost like living it myself. Now I understood what had happened and just how long he had been rotting in his office, a living dead remnant of what was once a great scientist... a living dead corpse. I yanked out the memory card, stuck it in my pocket and threw the worn out recorder through an opening in the rubble and it landed with a thud on the office floor, breaking into pieces. Hearing the doctor's words only made my mind race. I could only guess what had happened next. It had been months since his last entry and a lot could have happened since then. Had this horrible infection spread very far? Was it possible that it was stopped and now things were being put back to normal? I could only hope that the doctor and this isolated building were all victims of one horrible isolated incident that was nipped in the bud before it had gotten any worse.

Now knowing what I was up against I made my way slowly across the waiting area toward the door. Could some of the other staff members have "survived" the devastation and ended up as meandering undead cannibals like the unfortunate doctor? If so it certainly was in my best interest to be on my guard. In the weak emaciated state I was in, I would not have been much of a challenge for them but I was hoping with every fiber of my being that I would not have to find out. The only light in the room was made by the last few rays of sunlight that I was guessing came from the dusk of a setting sun. I had no reference of whether it was morning or evening or if I had to worry about surviving my first horrible night after my rude awakening. God only knew what would be out there once I opened those doors but I had no choice but to find out.

Getting out was no easy task. Apparently one of the final survivors of the undead riot had locked the doors to the waiting area. Nobody was getting in and I certainly wasn't getting out... at least not without a key and where I was going to find it was anyone's guess. I tried a few times to push open the doors but it was simply impossible. The place had been built like a fortress, with a very upscale security system and steel doors that would keep out a charging elephant. It was obvious that without a key I was not getting out of the building.

My body seemed to get weaker by the second and I knew if I was going to survive long enough to find the key I would have to find something to eat. I knew there had been a café just down the second hall that led away from the waiting area. On my first visit sixteen years ago, I had actually eaten there with Doctor Benson while he went through his sales pitch to get me to sign up. From my recollection from back when I got the "grand tour" I seemed to remember there being a pretty large pantry as well as a walk in refrigerator and freezer. With any luck I thought it might have been possible to find some edible food that had survived the last few months.

As I made my way down the second hallway I found myself skittish and jumping out of my skin at the slightest sound. After going through what I did with the good doctor I guess I had every right to be. I still didn't know what to expect when I did finally get outside, but finding some sort of reliable weapon was a good idea either way. The doors to several of the offices had been blocked off by what I am guessing were staff members trying to protect themselves from the raving ghoulish lunatics that had attacked the building months before. I slowly approached the first door and put my ear to it in case of any sign of movement inside the sealed room. There was nothing. I didn't hear so much as a peep. When I got to the second door I put my ear to it and I could hear a faint scratching sound. I couldn't decide if I should dare to try and open the door to see what was there. I was pretty certain it couldn't be anything good.

It had been four months since the incident and if there was something still moving in the room the chances are it would be just like Benson. Who in their right mind would have stayed around if they were not infected… and if they had why wouldn't they have put the good doctor out of his misery months ago? I was going to put the scratching sound out of my mind and move on when it suddenly occurred to me. What if whoever or whatever was in that room happened to have the key to the only way out of the building? It seemed as though I was going to have to go in there and find out. I decided I would do just that but it didn't mean I had to do it first. I decided to go and find the café and at least get something in my stomach. If I did end up having a confrontation with some unwelcome inhabitant I wanted to at least have a bit more strength.

The café was just as I had remembered it except now it was completely trashed and covered in four-month old, dried blood splatter. Up until this point I had not noticed any lights on in the entire building, so I had assumed the electricity was out. I wasn't expecting to walk into a walk in freezer that was still cold but possibly there would be a pantry full of dry-goods that were still edible. I was making my way quietly across the café's sitting area when suddenly I heard something off in a dark corner of the room. The sound was familiar and sounded a lot like someone dropping a fork or knife from a table top. As I slowly and cautiously turned my head I could have sworn I saw something move in that dark corner. In my peripheral vision I could tell there was a table in that corner and maybe it was my mind playing tricks on me but I swear I could make out a body in the darkness, if it had moved… I knew exactly what it had to be and exactly what I was going to have to do. Every muscle in my body tensed up.

I slowly turned to face the sound and my fists automatically clinched. My heart almost stopped as I hear the noise again and this time I knew without a doubt that something in that dark corner had moved. As my eyes adjusted to the darkness of the room, I could certainly make out the silhouette of someone sitting at the table. I whispered "Who's there?" but there was no answer. Then I heard the sound again. It was unmistakable now. It was the sound of a small metal object hitting a larger metal object. As if someone was plunking the side of a metal cup with their fork or spoon. "Who the fuck is there?" I yelled… but there was still no answer.

Not even a moan or screeching sound like the doctor had made. For the first time in the last hour I had been awake, I realized that my throat was parched and sore and I could barely speak. I had called out earlier right after waking up but I didn't notice then what bad shape my vocal cords were in. Still the lone shadowy silhouette didn't move an inch but I heard the sound again. Just then I noticed that on the wall nearest me was a light switch. I really didn't think anything would happen if I flicked it. I mean come on, it had been four months since the place had been ransacked and the likelihood of there still being electricity was probably pretty low, but then it occurred to me. This place was a high tech laboratory that specialized in freezing people in cryo stasis for years. Certainly they had to have some back-up generators or something.

Not taking my eyes off the figure in the corner, I slowly moved toward the switch. I was ready for anything or at least in my head I was. In reality I was still standing there alone and hungry and extremely weak with no weapon to speak of, but I was ready. I flicked the light switch up and to my complete surprise the entire room was flooded with light. Two of the florescent bulbs on the other end of the ceiling blew out due to the sudden surge of power but a single long bulb in the center of the room was enough to see what I needed to see. There in the corner sitting in a chair was a rotting withered corpse of a woman with long black hair. She was wearing what had once been an expensive suite jacket with the "Eternal Slumber" logo embroidered on the front pocket. In her left hand was a metal cup with a metal spoon in it and her other hand was completely gone.

After a couple of seconds I saw what had been making the noise. Suddenly out of the woman's sleeve came the most disgusting mangy rat I had ever seen. It scurried out of her sleeve and across the cup, knocking the spoon against its edge. That stupid rat and the fucking cup is what had made me want to piss my pants. As I examined her from a distance I noticed there was a gaping hole in her chest and it seemed several more rats had made their nest in her dried rotting chest cavity. I guess it shouldn't have surprised me. I mean what better place to be infested by rats than an abandoned building full of bits and pieces of rotting corpses. From everything I had heard rats were supposed to love that sort of thing.

After about 30 minutes of eating frozen fish sticks and canned spaghetti my stomach was aching from too much food, too fast. I grabbed a huge cleaver from the kitchen as well as whatever I could, that was nonperishable and shoved it into a backpack someone had left hanging in the employees break room just off the kitchen. It wasn't a shotgun like I would have preferred but hey it was something and it would do in a pinch. Now it was time to go back to that room and see what was making the sound. Hopefully who or whatever it was had the key I needed to get out. When I made it back to the door the scratching sound had stopped. I was suspicious that whatever it was had heard me and was now trying to lure me in with its silence.

I slowly grasped the door handle and pushed it downward. As the door slowly creaked open I heard the scratching sound again. To my relief, once the door was open I could see what it was. There was another door, a large metal one, inside the small closet sized room and next to the door was a telephone receiver that was hanging limp from its cord and it was scratching against the wall. It had been for some time as there was a groove worn into the paint where it had been swinging. The sign above the metal door said "Pet Heaven" in big white letters and had a picture of a cute kitten's head next to the text. It was a bit cheesy but cute at the same time.

What I wouldn't have given to see a cute cuddly kitten at that very moment. The door had a security lock with a digital panel next to it, but the entire panel had been smashed and it didn't look like there would be any problem getting in. I asked myself why I wanted to go into 'pet heaven' but honestly the curiosity was just too much. As I approached the metal door I realized that I could hear a new sound. It was unobtrusive and very faint and certainly didn't sound like anything threatening. It was like a soft beeping sound that was sporadic and without any specific rhythm. With the panel smashed the door opened with ease into another somewhat darkened room.

There were what seemed to be emergency lights that dimly lit the edges of the large room. It was all very familiar but different than what I had seen before. It was another room full of cryo chambers but these were very small. Pet Heaven was obviously designed to cater to the over indulgent pet owners who would rather spend millions of dollars having their pets frozen rather than put down. I could only guess that these pets, or what was left of them, were in the same boat as myself. Most of the chambers were off and many of them were empty but the ones that were not, had dead mummified pet remains in them.

Suddenly the faint beeping stopped and there was a strange sound almost like gas being released. I noticed in the corner of my eye, some movement so I turned to see what it was. As I turned I caught sight of a small door opening on one of the cryo chambers. There was a soft whimper and I noticed some movement inside the chamber. A million thoughts ran through my head but I finally realized the reality of what was going on. The last remaining pet that was still alive was being revived from its cryo chamber. I heard the whimper again and this time it was mistakably coming from the pet in the cryo chamber. From where I stood I could only see a small flash of matted fur but there was definite movement.

Not knowing what to expect, I slowly approached the chamber. I heard the whimper again. It was like that of a puppy that was dreaming. You know what I mean, when they jerk and twitch and whimper in their sleep. That's exactly what it was like. I went over and looked in and there in front of me was one of the most welcome sights I had seen in a very long time. It was the most adorable beagle I had ever seen. He looked to be a bit long in the tooth but he was adorable laying there sleeping in his chamber. I had personally always had a passion for beagles and this was almost like some sort of reward for my surviving. Now I just might have a companion to help me through this horrible ordeal… that is if either of us lived long enough.

I stroked the dog between the ears as he slowly revived. I couldn't help but wonder if he was going through the same things I had gone through… the blurred vision and muscle spasms and severe cramps in my extremities. I tried to make his revival as comfortable as I could and once he was fully awake he rewarded my kindness with a great big sloppy tongue across my hand. I must have spent an hour in the room holding the dog and massaging his muscles to help him get on his feet. It wasn't long before he was fully aware of his surroundings and jumping around like any excited dog that just made a new friend.

After examining the chamber, it was number twenty one of about forty of them lined up against the walls. It looked completely intact and I could only guess it had opened due to an electrical error caused by the state of the entire system. But seeing it in such good shape, made me wonder how many other people might be frozen in this place completely undamaged. How many other rooms full of cryo chambers could there be. It was something to keep in mind once I found out what the hell was actually going on, but for now I wasn't going to waste any time investigating it. I was ready to find that damn key and get the hell out of the building.

Finding 'Rufio' *(which was the name written on a small plaque on his cryo chamber)* was a real stroke of luck. He was sweet and pleasant and could possibly come in really handy later if he was able to sniff out any more of those re-animated puss bags if there were anymore. Maybe the doctor had been a fluke and lived so long by some weird coincidence. Surely any more of those things would have been rendered harmless by now. I mean how long can a rotting corpse move around? I was taking into account the rate of decomposition as well as rigor mortis. I mean even if a dead body could get up and run around… for how long? It just didn't make sense and it had been four months since the other infected specimens had escaped the building.

I guess I was really hoping deep down inside that I would get out of the building to find a normal world where things had been handled correctly. Maybe I was just the unfortunate victim or leftover experiment forgotten in some quarantined building that had been ignored. Well I knew if I didn't get out of there I would never find out.

Feeling much better after stuffing myself with food and finding my new companion, I decided to investigate something that had been nagging at me ever since I had listened to Doctor Benson's recorder. I made my way back down the hall to the nurse's station where I had originally waited on the floor, for the feeling to come back to my legs. I wanted to read some of the files and if there was going to be a working computer terminal that would possibly be the place to find one. To my surprise and delight, I found a working monitor and one of the computers that had not been smashed. There was still power available so the computer actually booted up after a few moments and the monitor sprang to life.

Benson had said something in his diary that kept bouncing around in my head. He had said that the scientists thought that Mrs. Morehead's situation had been caused by some sort of chemical they injected in the blood to help with the freezing process. I read the notes of Zack Kramer the head researcher and lab administrator and found that that particular chemical used on Mrs. Morehead had been somewhat of a new breakthrough and had been used on her as an experiment to see if it would be suitable to replace the more expensive alternative they had been using since the company had been established.

In his notes he stated that he personally felt that the chemical had been solely responsible for the incident with Mrs. Morehead and he even went on to mention that although she had been the first one to receive a dose of the new chemical, there had been thirty more clients injected with it between the time Mrs. Morehead had been injected and the time she had flat-lined. It suddenly dawned on me that if she had died and become re-animated due to this chemical four months ago, that meant there were another thirty potential victims of the chemical that may or may not have already reanimated. With my curiosity peaked, I logged into the cryo chamber stats and found that the chambers of all thirty clients dosed with the new chemical had been smashed and they were empty... with the exception of one. It was cryo chamber 73. I knew I had heard something moving in there and now I knew why. I made a mental note to stay the hell away from it and certainly not open it.

Suddenly Rufio, who had recovered remarkably from his rude awakening, began to look down the hall in the opposite direction and growl. I leaned over the counter to see if I could see anything but it was quite dark. I patted him on the head and told him to chill out but his growl turned into more of a throaty bark. I didn't have a leash so I had no control over what he did. I could only hope he didn't run off and get himself into trouble. Suddenly just as I feared he took off at a full run down the hall. I yelled after him and tried to follow but he was much faster than I was.

Rufio stopped dead in his tracks but continued to bark. It's almost like there was something he didn't like up there but he was fully aware that he wanted to keep his distance. I came up behind him and squatted and hugged his little neck. "Take it easy, big guy" I whispered in his ear. His growl was so vicious. I knew there had to be something up the darkened hall from us but I couldn't see it yet. I continued to try to appease my little buddy by rubbing his neck and gently whispering in his floppy ear but then I heard it too. It was moaning accompanied by a strange jingling sound. All at once there was a loud thud on a nearby door and the knob shook as if someone was trying to open a locked door. The moaning got louder and Rufio's growl got even more ferocious. Before I knew what had happened the door burst open, almost off its hinges and into the hallway staggered a huge silhouette of what had once been a man.

"OH MY GOD" I mumbled under my breath.

I recognized him. On my first visit to Eternal Slumber, Dr. Benson had introduced me to Phil Kowalski their six foot four, three hundred and twenty pound head of security. I remembered him to be a hearty fun loving jokester with a great sense of humor. Very pleasant guy to be around when he wasn't dealing with a security issue, but now.... now... well this was a different story. Standing in front of me, staring at me with his two swollen hard-boiled eggs he had for eyeballs that were sticking out of his rotting half mangled face, was the most horrible sight I would have ever imagined seeing in my worst nightmare. His huge rotting muscles were still tangled around the exposed bones that held him upright. He was still in his tattered and torn uniform and dangling from a tangled fist full of hair was what looked like the remains of a severed head.

Rufio darted out toward the monster, but I grabbed his tail at the last minute and flung him backward behind me. I know it had to hurt, given the yelp he let out, but I figured it was better than the alternative. With my newfound friend now whimpering and cowering behind me, I slowly reached into my backpack and took out the huge meat cleaver I had taken from the kitchen. Phil's eyeballs were so swollen and bulging from their sockets that they could not move. They were fixed looking straight ahead. He had to completely turn his head to look around and that movement appeared to be somewhat labored so I knew this would be an advantage for me.

He was a huge hulking corpse of a man but I knew with the amount of time he had been dead he would be a slow moving gargantuan. I leaned down and put my mouth next to Rufio's ear and whispered "STAY" and he seemed more than happy to do so. Still looking at me, the monster leaned against the wall. It was as if holding up his own weight was an amazing task in and of itself. Then with a putrefying grunt he lunged forward and tried to grab me. I had the presence of mind to dodge his bow but I lost my balance and toppled to the ground. I rolled just in time to miss a huge steel-toed boot coming down where my head had just been. He was a bit faster than I had anticipated.

As I got to my feet, I swung my cleaver and actually caught him right at the wrist. It was the one attached to the hand that was clinching the severed head. As the head, hand and all, flew by me, I got a sick feeling in my stomach. I actually recognized who it had been. The severed head belonged to Sarah, the head nurse (no pun intended) that had been working there forever. I had gotten to know her a bit before I was put under. I remembered her so well because she was one of those people with a soothing personality that could make anything seem like it was going to be alright. She was in her late forties when I met her and now it ended like this. It almost made me want to get this big rotting puss-bag even more.

They say before you die your entire life flashes before your eyes… well I found myself re-viewing every kung-fu movie I had ever seen. I was trying to think of moves that I could use to bring this guy down, but between the state of my body and my lack of knowledge of actual kung-fu, I was feeling quite hopeless. Phil made another lunge at me and I simply stepped aside. It occurred to me that one of my old school time bully moves might work here so I put my foot out as he went sailing by from the momentum of his own body and I simply tripped the monster of a man.

He went down face-first on the floor with a thud. I jumped on top of him, holding my breath of course as he smelled like a meat freezer left unplugged for a month, and I planted my cleaver right into the back of his skull. Red bloody goo sprayed out of his head and all over me as he groaned and tried to lift himself up... but then he collapsed and went limp and was finally no longer a threat. With a whimper and those big puppy dog eyes looking at me, Rufio came over and put his front paws on my leg like a dog does when he wants to be held. I reached down and snatched up my pal and pressed my nose against his.

"You were a good boy." I told him. "Just next time don't try to be such a tough guy."

I was about to walk back down the hall when something caught my eye. I looked down at Phil's belt. That's what had made that strange jingling sound. There on the big dumb corps's belt was a huge ring full of keys. I had just found my way out.

Day 6-His muscles ached and were so stiff he could barely move. He had wandered around for days trying to figure out what drew him and compelled him onward. People all around him screaming and running and being knocked down by others just like him. Those other people smelled different. It was a smell that penetrated his putrefying nostrils from a hundred yards. It was a wonderful smell. Maybe that's why the creepers like himself were devouring them like rabid animals, eating their flesh... FLESH... that was it. He finally realized what was drawing him onward... what he smelled... What it was that he needed. He wanted to join them and tear into the flesh of the other people who ran scared and hid in the shadows of the buildings and garbage bins that lined the alleys between them. He began to realize he was dead. He had awakened from death into a world where he was drawn by the desire to consume that which he didn't have, warm bloody flesh. He went into the street and saw a faceless man slumped over a wrecked car attacking a woman who was helpless; screaming for help that would never come. There were hundreds of creepers just like him and they all desired the same thing. They all wanted nothing more than to peel the flesh from the bone and devour it like ambrosia from the Gods. It had been days since he awakened and he had yet to satisfy this hunger inside of himself. Now that he realized what it was he was eager to eat. Eager to devour the very flesh that he knew would sustain me. Then he heard a cry. It came from inside the car where the faceless man was eating the woman. He slowly crept into the car and saw there in the back seat ... a baby buckled safely into its car seat. His cloudy eyes could make out its small squirming figure. He reached out his hand and touched it. It was warm and soft..... and... and... delicious.------

When I left the building it was dark out. It was really hard to tell how much the incident at Eternal Slumber had affected the out-lying towns because the ES headquarters was actually about fifteen miles out of town in the rolling hills of upstate New York, between Lake Pleasant and Indian Lake. Troy and Albany were the largest cities nearby and then was the big Apple several hours drive from here. I could not even fathom this thing having spread that far. I mean surely the National Guard would have mowed down a few twitching corpses before they got that far. I was a little familiar with the area from my many visits previous to my being frozen. Rufio and I walked for several miles before we came to a small farm house that I vaguely remembered seeing before. I remembered on my last visit, having seen the farmer on his tractor in the field. It stuck out in my head because at that time I was thinking it may be the last time I ever saw such a sight.

The place was dark and peaceful looking but then again it was the middle of the night. Rufio sniffed the air and went bounding around the house as I stepped gingerly onto the front porch. I reluctantly rang the doorbell and waited to see what would happen. It was one of those old timey ones that was like a bicycle bell and didn't need electricity, so I couldn't tell if the power was on or not... all I could do was to wait. Best case scenario would be the farmer coming to the door with a shotgun pointed at my face. Worse case would be.... Well you probably got the picture by now. After having to dispatch Zombie Phil, I really was hoping for the shotgun. I stood for a few minutes and then rang it again. I thought I heard something stir inside but I simply wasn't sure. I could hear Rufio barking around the other side of the house, so I decided to go check it out.

When I got to the side of the house Rufio was sitting there in the grass barking at a window with, of all things, a cat sitting on the inside window sill taunting the poor pooch like cat's love to do. The big fat cat looked very healthy and like it had not missed any meals and I found this very encouraging. Perhaps Benson had been wrong and the building's security had actually kept the crazed corpses he talked about in his audio diary, inside the building. Maybe he just thought they had gotten out and ravaged the countryside. It did make sense. He was delirious and locked away in his office, making assumptions based on what he heard.

I stood there for a moment convincing myself that everything was fine… convincing myself that the house belonged to some deaf old farmer that didn't hear the doorbell because he or she had taken out their hearing aid. I mean the fat cat was surely a sign of everything being normal, wasn't it? Suddenly there was a gust of wind and I heard a slam around the back of the house. Rufio and I both ran around to the back to see what it was. It seemed to be the screen door on the back porch. It had been left open and the wind had blown it shut. As I got closer I saw that it was askew and off of one hinge. It was just sort of hanging there swinging back and forth. The screen was torn but that wasn't that unusual in these old farm houses. The farmers are usually so busy they can't get to fixing all the little odd jobs around the house. Just inside the door of the porch were two more very well fed cats, that didn't look happy to see me.

As I approached the door they looked up at me, hissed and ran into the house through the cat flap that was built into the back door. I motioned for Rufio to stay, which he did, and I went up to the back door. I knocked on it with one good knock and it slowly creaked open and that's when it hit me. That all too familiar smell. If I never smelled the stench of rotting meat again it would be too soon. I walked into the kitchen of the house where there were a total of about five cats. All avoiding me like the plague.

The entire house was dark but there happened to be a full moon and the light was pouring through the windows and lighting the place up enough for me to see pretty well. I looked around the kitchen and everything looked pretty much in order but like it had not been touched in a long time. There was dried food on dishes in the sink, broken cups that had obviously been knocked off the counter by one of the cats with nobody to pick up the mess and the refrigerator door was standing open and everything inside was way past spoiled.

I pulled out a chair and sat at the table for a moment. There was a phone sitting there so I picked it up and tried to use it, hoping by some slight chance it would work. No such luck. I wasn't sure what to do next. My hopes of the rest of the world being fine and this incident being isolated were starting to dwindle more and more. I was starting to feel the fatigue of my ordeal and even though I had slept for sixteen years I was starting to get tired. I noticed a piece of paper on the table with writing on it so I began to read it.

A strange man came into the yard today. Harold went out to see what he needed as he appeared to be hurt, but when he tried to help the man, he attacked Harold and ripped out his throat. I screamed and he turned and saw me standing on the porch, so I ran inside and locked the door. Within minutes there were more of them. I could not believe that three of them just started to rip Harold's stomach open and eat him while he was still squirming on the ground.

Soon there was a group of them surrounding the house. I couldn't get to Harold to try to help him but soon I noticed that he was alive and walking around amongst the others and they were all, including him, trying to break into the house and get to me. Harold, I don't know what happened to you and I want you to know I love you and would never do anything like this but I just have to. It's that or end up being attacked by those crazy people that killed you. I love you dear, please forgive me. I love you..... I LOVE YOU!

I was puzzled by the note. I was trying to figure out what it was really saying when suddenly one of those big fat cats jumped up on the table next to me and scared the hell out of me. I looked at the cat and everything seemed normal except for the fact that it had dried blood coated in its fur all around its mouth. It started to purr and rub itself against my arm then without any warning whatsoever, it tried to bite me. I was lucky it didn't break the skin but it tried to sink those fucking little kitty fangs into the flesh of my arm. I had never had a cat do anything like that. In a motion that was pure reflex, I swung my arm and smacked the cat, sending it flying across the room. It landed on the couch, let out an awful howl and darted into the hall.

I followed it with my eyes and that's when I saw why the cats were all so fat and well fed. Hanging in the hallway, dangling just about four inches from the ground was the body of an elderly woman. It was obvious that she had hung herself from a sturdy light fixture. She was withered and grey and badly decomposed but the most horrible part of all was that all the flesh on both legs, from her ankles to her knees had been gnawed away by what I assumed were her five faithful little kitties. God I knew there was a reason I hated cats. I had always been a dog person but this sealed it for me.

Morning came pretty quickly. I awoke in a nice soft bed with my pal Rufio snuggled up next to me. If I didn't know there was a horrible infection spreading across the planet I would have thought it was just another beautiful day outside. The night before I had cut the old woman down and put her body in the basement along with her five disgusting cats. I figured they deserved each other and I wanted to use the house as a sanctuary to get some rest without having to worry about her fucking cats turning me into kibble. I opened a can of spam and some beans I had brought with me from the café and I had a pretty nice breakfast. Rufio didn't mind joining me for breakfast with some canned cat food that I found in the pantry. I figured dog chow or fancy feast…. What the hell was the difference to my furry pal.

One of the many indulgences I had treated myself to in my wealthy pre-frozen life was the fact that I had taken flying lessons and gotten my pilot's license. The town of Speculator wasn't far away and I knew there was a small airport near there, because I had landed my plane there before. It wouldn't take long to get to the airfield if I could find a working vehicle. My plan was to snag a little twin engine Cesena and get my ass to the city where things may have actually been set straight. I knew if I didn't find transportation, I would be falling back on plan 'B', which meant 'hoofing it' and I didn't like that thought at all. I was still exhausted and feeble and every muscle in my body ached like crazy. At this point it was only my sheer determination to find a place that had not been infested by zombies that was keeping me going.

It was a bit hard to believe but there were no vehicles at all at the famer's house. Maybe the elderly couple was too old to drive and they had a family member who carted them around, but either way I didn't see any other farms nearby so I knew I would be hoofing it for a while. It was times like this that made me really miss my Bentley and my driver slash bodyguard Hanz, who used to be my faithful companion and chauffeur. He would have been the perfect ally to have in this situation. He was older than me but he was a strapping muscular mountain of a man standing at a good six foot six. The reality that those days were not only long gone but took place more than sixteen years ago was almost impossible to accept but I would have given anything to know where Hanz was now and whether he was alive or dead.

Poor little Rufio was starting to limp a bit and I felt like it must have had something to do with his rapid thaw that was affecting his muscles. I picked him up and carried him for a few miles until the fatigue was beginning to wear on me as well. The little guy and I were both victims of an incurable illness that would eventually kill us but for some reason that just wasn't the heaviest thing on my mind. Yeah I had a tumor that could explode any second and he had... God knows what, but pushing forward was the only thing I could think about.

As we got closer to the small town of Speculator, the winding country road I had been walking down began to show signs of the plague that had evidently swept through the countryside. Up the road between me and the horizon were as many as three abandon cars that were crashed in some way. One was wrapped around a tree. Another was flipped over in a ditch and the last one I could see way up the road was just sitting on the road but it was completely burned out. From what I could tell all three of them were worthless to me.

I had to fight off the irresistible urge to explore them and see if there was anything interesting inside but the last thing I wanted was another run in with one of those walking corpses. I decided my best bet was to keep on moving down the dank road. All morning the sun had been an elusive stranger and had never really fully come out from behind the angry storm clouds. I just knew there would be a heavy downpour while I was still out in the open making my way down the road. I mean it was just the way my luck always seemed to work, so I was on the lookout for anything that looked remotely like shelter.

I passed the first two vehicles without incident and was cautiously approaching the third that resembled nothing more than a charcoal frame, when there was an ear-splitting clap of thunder. Following Rufio's lead, I ducked into the burned out shell that had its roof still intact. Suddenly there was another loud clap of thunder then almost as if on cue, a blanket of water began to fall from the sky in stinging raindrops the size of bullets.

What was left of the car's interior was charred and burned and barely recognizable. The seats were a mixture of piles of black ash with bits of left-over foam and springs sticking up through the soot. On the far side of what had been the back seat were the remains of what appeared to be a snoopy blanket or sleeping bag. It had obviously belonged to a child due to the barely recognizable cartoon character pattern that it once proudly sported. The front seats were far more devastated by the fire than the back. They were so badly burned that you could not tell the badly charred seat frames from the burned skeletal remains of their former occupants.

The only way I knew there had even been occupants in the front seats when the car burned was because of the recognizable remains of two adult skulls but the rest of the bodies were reduced to nothing but spindly black charcoal frames. The dank smell was strong but there was little or no hint of the stench of rotting flesh. It seemed it had all been burned away. Rufio rolled up in my lap as I huddled up next to the burned sleeping bag remains. The huge raindrops were blowing in from every direction and there was really very little protection from the torrential downpour.

The constant splattering sound of the water hitting the hard pavement had a lulling, almost hypnotizing effect on me. I found myself starting to doze off as Rufio lay sleeping on my lap. For the first time since my rude awakening, I was almost in a state of complete relaxation, when suddenly I felt something move. My eyes flew opened and I looked around when suddenly Rufio shifted his weight while sleeping. I thought to myself that must have been what I felt. I lay my head back and listened to the non-relenting rain when suddenly I heard something. Rufio obviously had heard it too because his little head sprung upward and his ears perked. I felt the movement again but this time I realized it wasn't coming from Rufio. It was like a stiff wiggling feeling that was coming from underneath me.

I slowly turned my head as I caught something moving in my peripheral vision. It was like the ashes were writhing and beginning to stir. Rufio began to whimper and tried to climb up my chest as if he was terrified of something. With the rain pouring down relentlessly, I hadn't heard the sound before but now I could make it out. It was a sort of hissing moan that was originating from underneath me. Suddenly a jolting movement in the ashes under me caused me to bump my head on the rusted roof framing. After a second it happened again but with much more intensity, then something plunged up out of the thick crusty soot. Rufio squealed and jumped into the front seat with the corpses just as I jumped up and banged my head on the roof again. The sleeping bag that had been charred and burned along with the seat cushions was ripping open and something like the remains of a charred child's arm was wiggling and writhing and making its way out of the ashes.

I remember trying to think of the logic of something that had been lying there so long rotting, still being mobile and able to move, when before I knew it, it was on top of me.

The charred decomposing child was very much 'alive' if you could call it that and had sprung from under the soot and had me pinned to the burned out metal door that was unfortunately sealed closed from the heat of the previous fire. I will never forget the smell of the writhing rotting tongue that wiggled like some morbid swollen caterpillar trying to squirm its way out of the mouth full of rotting broken teeth. What had once been someone's beautiful blonde child was now reduced to a mindless mass of rotting flesh that was bent on depriving me of my life.

I was still a bit weak and I could not believe how difficult it was to hold the decaying youngster off. He or she, whichever it was, had buried its sharp bony fingertips into the sides of my skull and was pressing in on me obviously anxious to take a bit out of me. The snapping putrid jaws of the child reminded me of my neighbor's bulldog, minus all the slobber. It's amazing what goes through your head at a moment like that. I found myself so exhausted that I was seriously thinking of just giving in, when suddenly Rufio came to my aid. With a threatening growl he jumped in the back seat with me and began to gnaw at the putrid child's leg but it was to no avail. The determined zombie youngster didn't even flinch.

With my head pressed against the broken window frame of the car-door, I could feel the youngster's bony fingers digging in deeper. Its strength was unbelievable. Almost like it had been laying there under the soot saving up all its strength for the first poor sap that came along... ME! Mouth a-gap and tongue flailing back and forth the putrid youngster moved in for the bite. It pressed its broken teeth against my forehead as if to take a large chunk out of my brain, when suddenly it stopped. It backed away for a moment and looked at me with its hollow shriveled eyes, that didn't look as if they could have possibly actually seen anything, but they were focused right at my face. The monster pressed in again and did something that I found very unusual. It seemed to sniff me. Almost as if it smelled something unpleasant, which would be quite a feat for a zombie I would think. Now reality is one thing and movies are another but I suddenly remembered all those Romero living dead movies I had watched back in my college days and I remembered that if there was one thing zombies loved it was brains and it seemed that this is what the putrid youngster was actually sniffing.

It was such a surreal moment. Here I was thinking about zombie movies and there was one planted on my lap with its bony fingers digging into my skull, sniffing my brain… and where was my camera? My immediate death was not my concern actually. I guess having a cancerous brain aneurism about to explode in my head caused me to make survival a much lesser priority. Suddenly as the zombie youngster sniffed me with a rotting puzzled expression on its decaying face, it dawned on me. Somehow that zombie child could smell it. It could smell the cancer in my brain. As much as it desired to eat my brains, it was thrown off by something it considered unpleasant, thus making my particular brain much less attractive.

Suddenly it came to me, like a familiar old friend, my strength came back. I grabbed the rotting rug rat by the shoulders and flung it off of me. It let out an ear splitting squeal but I grabbed it and threw it out the window into the pouring rain. It hit the web pavement with a thud then scrambled to its feet and lumbered off into the tree line.

"Jesus Christ, Rufio, looks like I'm a fucking zombie reject."

I grabbed the pooch and hugged him tight. Never would I have ever guessed that the very thing that threatened my life was actually the one thing that would save it. Not only that, but now I was stuck in a fucking zombie holocaust and I was damaged goods. I suddenly felt like some sort of anti-zombie super hero. The one thing those fucking corpses wanted was the one thing I didn't have, a fresh healthy brain. I kissed Rufio on the nose, picked him up and crawled out of the car, standing to my feet in the downpour. I scratched Rufio behind the ears and headed down the road I was ready to face whatever was out there... fuck the rain!

The cool rainy morning air had quickly turned into a scorching hot sunny afternoon. I had walked down that fucking road for what seemed like days but it had only been four and a half hours. I found myself occasionally looking down at Rufio and thinking to myself how lucky I was to find him. What a great companion. He was like having a zombie detector with me. Once in a while he would let out a little gutsy growl and look off into the trees, where I would catch a glimpse of something moving in the distance. I might be zombie proof but I had no desire to tempt them, plus what would happen if I met the one zombie on the planet that couldn't smell or hell even worse liked the taste of cancerous brain matter. It wasn't worth pressing my luck. The abandoned cars on the road got more frequent but I stayed the hell away from them. I hadn't seen one that even looked remotely usable, so I steered clear of them all.

It was obvious that noon had come and gone and I was still walking when suddenly there it was. The sign I had been hoping to see. "Speculator Municipal Air Field". Those words were like heaven to me at that moment. The thought of nicking a plane and flying out of this hell hole was my one and only dream in life... well at that moment anyway. I snatched up Rufio and began to speed up to a slow trot for the first time. My head was throbbing and the constant reminder of the fucking golf ball sized bomb in my head was ever-present. The windy road eventually opened up to a large open field with one of those aluminum hanger buildings standing out by itself in the middle of nothing. There were a few planes sitting around but most of them were destroyed or completely burned out. The building itself, from what I could see from afar, was still pretty much intact but with the way things looked I was going to approach with extreme caution.

The way things had played out since I had awoken made me ready for just about anything. As I got closer to the building I could see a car sitting out front. It looked very normal. It was sitting there with the trunk still opened as if someone had just taken luggage out of it and walked into the building. If I hadn't known better I would have expected them to come back out and close their trunk... but as expected they didn't. I slowly made my way up to the building. It looked safe enough but then that familiar smell accosted my nasal passages. It was that all too familiar smell of someone who had died a few months before and was probably still wandering around waiting to rip out my throat.

The sign on the door said "Davis and Davis Aviation. Inc." The glass window on the door had an obvious hand print of blood smeared across it. I slowly sat Rufio down and motioned for him to stay. He happily complied and I went for the door knob. Just as I touched it I heard a sound inside. It was the distinct sound of someone dropping a metal tool on a concrete floor. As if a mechanic had dropped his wrench. The door opened with a low creak and I was able to crack it enough to see inside. The room was dim but I was still able to see pretty well. I slowly went inside of what I figured was the aviation companies office. There were log books and stacks of paper all over the place as well as a cash register that had been emptied out long before I got there.

Suddenly there it was again. The sound! It came from the other side of a door that I gathered opened into the hanger area. I slowly approached the door and looked through the window. I could see a plane that looked to be in great shape. And underneath it I could see a pair of mechanics legs. He or she was standing on the other side of the plane working on it… from the way things looked. If it hadn't been for that smell that lingered all around I would have assumed it was a living person and called out for help but my common sense suggested I wasn't going to find a normal mechanic on the other side of that plane… but I could always hope for a miracle.

Suddenly Rufio started to bark outside. He was still sitting obediently by the front door where I had left him. "Oh God" I thought to myself. I could just imagine a horde of those undead things making their way straight to the building and I would be hopelessly trapped. He barked again and I saw the legs of the mechanic move. They spun in place as if the person had turned to face the direction Rufio's bark came from. I had this feeling that I just may have found a living breathing person. The mechanic's legs didn't seem to shuffle like they probably would have if I were dealing with a zombie.

I made up my mind. I was going to open the door and call out to the mechanic. I was holding tightly to my cleaver just in case the mechanic wasn't a living breathing person… but just then Rufio barked again. It was the same bark that I had heard before. The one with that guttural 'Doggies in trouble' sound to it. I ran to the front door to see what was causing Rufio to bark and there in the middle of the giant parking lot was that skinny emaciated, charred little faceless child that I had thrown off of me in the car. You know the one that didn't want to eat my brains. It must have followed me all the way from the main road, which seemed impossible as it had been a four hour walk, but there it was and it had brought a few friends.

Far in the field just outside the tree line was a small cluster of undead. They were meandering mindlessly across the field straight toward the hanger. It was inevitable that they would come, but had I lured them here unknowingly? I ran back to the window just in time to see the back of my mechanic pal as he opened the small door that led from the hanger to the outside. I still couldn't tell if he was a person or a zombie. It was time to find out.

"God damn you zombies…. Get the hell away from here!"

I was stunned. I couldn't believe I actually heard the voice of another human being. It suddenly dawned on me that it had been over sixteen years since I had had a conversation with another human. I opened the front door and ran out to greet the mechanic but just as I got out into the parking lot I was met by a tattered old man in a greasy mechanic's jumpsuit who was aiming a shotgun right at my face.

"Who the hell are you and what the hell are you doing snooping around my hanger?"

The old man looked down at Rufio, who by this time was at my side barking up at him.

"I'm just a normal, non-zombie type of guy who is looking for some help." I said with a bit of a tremble in my voice.

"There ain't no way… there ain't been survivors around these parts in weeks. You're one of them government spies or some sort of rif-raf like that."

The old geezer put the end of the shot gun barrel right up to my face.

"Why I otta blow your 'Zombie Experimenting, Top Secret Government' ass right off-n my tarmac... Goddamit!"

The old man was well aware of the corpses that were meandering their way closer by the second. He didn't seem to be as concerned with them as he was with me. I could understand the novelty of seeing a real living person but the problem was from where he was standing he didn't see the crispy little zombie child slinking up behind him, getting closer by the second.

"Mister I know you are upset by my presence but one of those horrible little monsters is coming up behind you and I think you might want to deal with that before you worry about who I am."

The old man didn't even flinch, look back or seem the slightest bit concerned that I might be telling the truth. He just clicked the hammer back on his ten gauge shotgun and cracked a smirk. The crusty black little zombie was getting dangerously close to the old man. I was afraid if I lunged at it or tried to help him he would pull the trigger and send my face flying across the pavement. Rufio was going crazy.

My eyes were locked with his. The old man was not crazy but on the contrary was probably a lot more alert than I was. I wasn't sure what to do as the crispy little grotesque child twisted its way up to the old man's pant leg. I was so afraid if I opened my mouth I would eat led but I also didn't want the old man to get a chunk bitten out of his leg. My mind was racing as to what to do when suddenly, in one fail swoop, the old man flipped the shotgun backward over his shoulder and pulled the trigger. Bits of charred zombie child went flying across the pavement. It was actually a relief to see the poor thing put out of its misery.

"You had better God damn be who you say you are, mister."

The old man spat a tar black chewing tobacco loogy onto the ground where it blended right in with the other bits of charred black zombie that were littering the pavement.

"Now c-mon with me les'n you've got a death wish."

Day 50-His craving was relentless and never satisfied. It had been many weeks since his awakening. His skin now drawn over the bone like layers of decaying leather, made every movement harder to achieve than the next. The baking sun was agonizing as it only made the process of decay seem to speed up and cause him to feel like he was literally falling apart, which he was. Hoards of other creepers just like him pushing and shoving in every direction, only seeking out the living to only eventually turn them into what they were, the walking dead. The arm of a man he had devoured that morning at sunrise was dangling from his left hand. He had it in a death-grip, holding onto it thoughtlessly as he made his way toward that every present destination, where or what it was he didn't know but his rotting decaying brain was leading him somewhere... nowhere... like a living dead mannequin pressing onward toward hell. The city never seemed to end. One trashed street after another, one avenue of smashed burned out cars after another and only once in a great while did he get a whiff of that delicious aroma. The smell of ambrosia mixed with the recognizable aroma of sweat and body odor. People... living breathing people... but where were they? A tendon snapped in his neck as he quickly craned it to the left. He saw something move in the distance. Suddenly there was a feeling of pressure in the side of his head. Something had hit him. He looked and saw in an alleyway between two tall buildings a teenage boy hiding behind a smashed car. He jumped out from behind the car and began to yell at him and he threw something at him. It hit him again just like before. It was the same feeling of pressure smacking into his flesh but there was no pain. It only made him angry. He began to shamble toward the ballsy teen, arms outspread and fingers clawing like eagle talons. He wanted the boy... he wanted his flesh... he needed his brains.------

The nonchalant attitude of the old man had come from many days of putting one in the skull of any zombie that meandered onto his property. He had become good at what he did and callused to the results. What was once a kind gentle grandpa who would have never even thought of blowing someone's brains out had now become a protective killing machine. You could see it in his intense cataract laden eyes. His name was Norman Carlson and he had survived the effects of the spreading plague by staying hold up in his airport hangar.

Just seconds after spreading the charred child all over the pavement, Norman led me back into what seemed to be a normal airplane hangar. It started to get really interesting when he took me to a back room no larger than a broom closet and moved a stack of boxes aside to reveal a large metal door.

"This place used to be some kinda government military base until the cutbacks in the 80's. You know when Reagan cut back funding from almost every conceivable government program possible? Well that's when the base became nothing more than a civilian airport."

Norman explained that he didn't own the airport but he was just the manager and head mechanic and had been for twenty years. The door opened up to a staircase that led to a maze of underground corridors, all of which branched off into rooms of almost every shape and size, most of which were locked.

"Never really had any use for all this space down here. We used to just keep the damn place locked up until those fucking zombies started taking over."

Norman led me to one of the bigger rooms. Inside it was set up like someone's humble home. I was startled when I saw a young boy of about 10, sitting at a table. We both jumped a bit at the sight of each other. The boy looked up at Norman as we entered the room. His eyes got wide and a smile cracked his youthful face. Norman had been living down there with his grandson Taylor for the last few months. They had been the sole survivors of their immediate family. Rufio snuggled in my lap as we sat and chatted about everything over a spam and pork-n-bean dinner. Norman told me the story of how things had progressed from his perspective. He told me that when the shit hit the fan his Son Ben had loaded up his wife and two kids and tried to make it to the airport, but on the way there their car had met with an accident when it was attacked by a mob of living dead. From what he could gather from Taylor, who escaped by the way, his mother, father and sister had been badly mauled by the zombies and run off the road, hitting another car, blowing up, burning his son, daughter in law, and granddaughter alive.

"I'll never forget Becky squirming in her snoopy sleeping bag, trying to get out of the flames...."

Taylor mumbled as he stared into his spam and beans.

It was almost like a morbid puzzle, Norman, his family, the burned out car, the charred zombie child. I didn't dare tell them how I had put the pieces together. How would Norman have reacted if he knew that charred black ghoul he had blown to bits was his granddaughter?

"There's one more thing I think you should see."

Norman said, jolting me out of my series of deep morbid thoughts. He handed Taylor a rifle, motioning for him to come with us and opened the door that led back into the dark corridor. We walked down all the way to the end, where he stopped and grabbed the latch of a rusty old door.

"Yer first reaction is gonna be to throw up, but try to contain yerself. I don't need any more messes to clean up around here."

Norman proceeded to open a makeshift lock by pulling a metal rod out of the padlock flap that held the door closed. The door slowly opened with a long metallic whine and a cloud of stench, like none I had experienced up to this point, hit me in the face like a pillow. It literally sucked the oxygen right out of my lungs it was so strong and what made it different from the whiffs of death I had smelled so far was that this was fresh.

Norman covered his nose as he led me into a room shaped like a half moon with a high ceiling. There was a thick layer of glass that separated the room from what appeared to be the bottom of some sort of large metallic pit that was opened at the top.

"This is my only problem down here."

Norman pounded on the glass.

"This old silo made back in the 50's was covered up with wooden planks and such, but those rotting fuckers seem to stumble their way in every few days. They fall from about 100 feet straight up there."

He pointed at the dim light that shone down from the top of the silo. The bottom of the metal silo was stacked at least five feet thick with corpses. Some moving and some rotten to the bone, but the way the place was designed, there were air vents that connected the room to the silo so the stench of the rotting flesh was overwhelming. Stumbling back and forth over the top of the layer of bodies were about fifteen to twenty zombies that were very much alive and well… or as alive as a zombie can be. They were pounding on the glass, smearing a variety of body fluids across it, doing what they could to try to get to the fresh meal on the other side.

"See my concern?" Norman groaned. "We should be safe as bugs in a rug down here but this place keeps me on edge day and night. I have no idea just how strong that glass is and how long it will keep those bastards out."

I went over and examined the control panel built into the counter top on our side of the glass. Based on what I saw it seemed that the silo had possibly been used to test some sort of small explosives like hand grenades and other small hand to hand combat explosives.

"I think as long as we keep the door secured we're pretty safe." I assured Norman. "Plus how long can those ghouls stay mobile. I mean they will eventually get too rotten to move."

I looked up toward the top of the silo, where the dim light of dusk was shining through.

"What we really need to do is block off that opening at the top. That way we won't get any new visitors and the old ones will eventually become incapacitated."

After a long night of tossing and turning with the obvious zombie nightmares, I woke the next day to something that smelled very inviting. Norman had gotten up and was cooking some spam and eggs for breakfast. With the odd chicken wondering around the air field he was about to keep a decent stash of eggs around.

"You had the dog long? Norman asked as he flipped my egg. "Seems a dog's a good thing to have around, they can smell them bastards way before you can."

My head was pounding but I managed to nod and smile at the sight of the delicious looking spread he placed in front of me. Rufio was very excited about the smell but his excitement subsided when Norman poured some old dry kibble into a bowl for him, but I tossed him a nibble once in a while.

Spurred by Norman's questions about Rufio, I spent the rest of the morning telling Norman how I had come to be there, telling him about being frozen and having a tumor and how I found Rufio. I told it all, leaving out the part about the burned out car and the charred zombie child. I told him I had searched for the airport in hopes of getting a plane and flying to the city to see if things were any different there. Norman's excitement grew upon finding out I was a pilot. It seemed in all his years working at the airport he had only worked up to head mechanic and never actually learned to fly.

"Damn lot a good it does ya to be able to fix the damn things if you can't fly them."

Breakfast was over and we had formulated a plan. I would help Norman secure the opening to the silo and in return he would give me a plane to fly to New York and see if things there were any better. At the very least maybe we would find a secure pocket of survivors with some sort of military protection. I would only do a flyover to see what the status was and then I would fly back to the airport. We argued a bit bout which should come first. Norman was eager to get the silo opening sealed and I wanted to at least take the plane for a spin to see what sort of shape it was in. I felt the silo could wait a day or so but Norman was insistent.

We spent the rest of the afternoon gathering scraps of sheet metal we could use to cover the silo opening. Our plan was to go fix the silo after dark, which didn't matter much as we had both come to the conclusion that the eyeballs in those zombie's dried up skulls didn't really work anymore. This meant that they mostly hunted based on smell and some strange zombie sense they seemed to have. We figured that walking around with flashlights at night was not going to attract them as much as the smell of our flesh and this was the basis for the most disgusting idea I had come up with yet… zombie camouflage.

Norman and I gathered up four nearby ghouls that had been lying rotting in the afternoon sun. They had been brained by one of Norman's shotgun blasts a few days before and were… needless to say RIPE.

We emptied out what was left of their intestines and slimy body fluids into a large five gallon bucket and chopped the mess up into chum. It was the most putrid mixture I could have ever imagined. Once the bucket was full of the stuff, I took two pairs of mechanic's coveralls and pushed them down into the gory soup using a broken baseball bat, until they were completely covered by the chum as to soak up every bit of fluid they could. Then like some morbid mass-murdering maid, I hung them up on the cloths line to dry.

"Grandpa, do I have to wear one of those?"

Taylor asked with a gnarly grimace on his face. Norman just chuckled, assured the boy he didn't, handed him a 45 revolver and told him to stay put in the bunker while we went out to do the deed…. And it was time.

The sun was disappearing behind the hills and it was rapidly getting dark. I must have heaved a dry heave about three times as I slipped into the damp meat suit that smelled of rotting zombie ambrosia. I was sure that not only would the coveralls camouflage us but they would probably send anything within sniffing distance running like hell. Norman and I each took a shotgun and a hand grenade each. He had found them in a burned out military truck a few weeks before and stashed them away for just such an occasion. I took some rope and made a make-shift sled out of the largest piece of sheet metal and piled the other pieces on top so I could slide it along behind us as quietly as possible. I knew that most of the zombies eyeballs were dried up and shriveled like prunes but rather their ears still worked… well I didn't want to take a chance.

Making our way through the woods toward the silo opening seemed pretty uneventful at first. It seemed that our designer meat suites were working. I heard a few walking corpses through the trees but they didn't seem to be bothered by us at all. We made our way along the path we had chosen when suddenly Norman, who was leading the way, stopped dead in his tracks.

"Shit-bag at twelve o-clock!" he whispered.

There in our path standing directly between us and the silo opening was a zombie. He was tall and burly with a military uniform on and a broken rifle strapped to his back and he seemed to be staring right at us but he wasn't moving. He cocked his head and raised his face to the night air as if he smelled us… or smelled… not us but our meat suites. He had a strange confused expression on his mangled jawless face. His dried up tongue dangled from the opened gaping hole where his jaw had been ripped away and it was flapping back and forth as if he were trying to taste something in the air.

"Brawwwlllggg" The zombie gurgled as he whipped his head slowly back and forth.

He took one slow methodic step in our direction. He looked at Norman with his beady little shriveled up eyeballs. I told myself there was no way in hell he could actually see anything through them, but he certainly seemed to know we were there, he just didn't seem to know what the hell we were. He cocked his head again and reached out toward us as if to touch what it was he smelled, but we were still out of arms reach of him. Then when he didn't feel anything in front of him, his face turned and he glared directly at Norman and lunged forward with an ear-splitting howl. I felt like a super hero or something, because without really even thinking about it, I pushed Norman out of the way, grabbed one of the smaller pieces of sheet metal and swung it through the air, catching the dead soldier just at the neck, slicing his head off clean, dropping him like a sand bag.

"Well whoopty fucking doodley dee... where the hell did you learn that move?"

Norman lifted himself up and shook the leaves from his damp putrid jumpsuit.

"I ain't never seen anything like that."

I just put my finger to my lips as an indication that I wanted Norman to shut the hell up and I motioned for us to keep going. Honestly, I didn't have a clue how I knew to do that. It just felt like a natural reflex.

A few more minutes of walking through the woods and we were there. It was the silo opening. We couldn't see it at first but the smell led us right to it and the faint echo of moaning undead could be heard coming from deep beneath the ground. I shined my light around and saw that the once sturdy wooden cover of the silo had a gaping hole in the middle where the rotten wood had broken. I was guessing by the weight of some zombie who tried to walk over it, but it was certainly fix-able and I wanted to make quick work of it. The thought of Taylor and Rufio alone in that bunker was a bit un-nerving to me.

Norman and I worked quickly. He helped me spread the sheets of metal out to cover the entire opening all the way out to the edge to make it ever that much more secure. I had brought a small ball-pine hammer with me as well as a can of roofing nails that I used to tack the metal to the existing wood. I remember my heart thumping every time the hammer went down onto the nail. I was afraid the banging sound was going to lure every zombie within earshot down on us like flies on a cow paddy. I hit the last nail on the head and stopped to listen. No moaning… no rustling of bushes in the distance or twigs cracking… maybe they hadn't heard me with their rotten withered ear drums. It seemed everything was going to be fine until Norman got a wild hair up his ass.

Before I knew what was happening, Norman had bent back a corner of the metal just big enough to drop a hand grenade down into the silo and he was holding one there ready to go.

"What the hell are you doing?" I asked as I grabbed his arm.

"Well if new ones can't get in, I'm going to take care of the ones that are there now!"

I yelled and pushed him back but I was too late. He had already dropped the live grenade down into the silo.

"You said that glass was strong enough to test small explosives…." Norman whispered angrily.

"No… I said I THOUGHT it was… there are no guarantees!"

Just as the words left my mouth there was a loud explosion deep in the bowels of the silo. And then my stomach sank. There it was... followed by the sound of the grenade exploding was the distinct sound of breaking glass.

"Oh my lord, what the hell have I done?"

With no regard for his own safety, Norman jumped up and ran through the trees back toward the bunker. I jumped to my feet and followed him as quickly as I could, but it was as I feared. There they were, as if drawn by the sound of the explosion, undead corpses meandering all around us, coming toward us as quickly as their stiff rotting legs cold take them. What seemed like a ten minute walk to the silo had turned into what felt like a hour long run back to the bunker. I ran into the hanger and slammed the door shut behind me. I had finally caught up with Norman, who was hunched down at the door to the underground bunker.

"I can hear those bastards in the hallway."

Norman said with his ear pressed against the door. I assured him that there couldn't have been many of them left after the explosion, but he wasn't listening. He cocked his shotgun and opened the door. Smoke was everywhere, lingering in the hallway. Neither of us could see a thing.

The moaning was loud as if the explosion had really agitated the zombies. We hunched down and slowly made our way to the bunker where Taylor was supposed to be waiting but when we got there he was nowhere in sight. We made a quick sweep of the room but Rufio was gone too. By now I could not only hear the sound of an occasional moan coming from the corridors, but I could also hear a flourish of pounding and wailing undead coming from up at the hanger door.

"Norm you really screwed the pooch on this one you bastard."

I said as I sidled up behind him, holding tightly to my shotgun. We slowly made our way toward the silo room when I heard Rufio start barking. The closer we got, the gorier things were. I noticed an occasional body part strewn along the hallway and then several feet up I saw the source of the moaning I had heard. There on the floor was half of an upper torso of one of the silo zombies that was still barely twitching. It was lying there half of its head and chest missing and it was still trying to reach out for us.

Rufio was close. I could hear his barking much louder and he was pissed off. As we rounded the corner where the silo room door was, there were two zombies trying to get to something in the corner of the hallway. Rufio was hunching nearby barking at the two zombies but they were paying him no mind at all.

"Grandpa, help me!"

The weak voice of Taylor came from the corner. He was completely obscured by the two zombies that were obviously trying to get at him. Norm and I lunged at the zombies, he grabbed one and I grabbed the other. Taylor was hiding behind a broken piece of the control room panel that had been blown into the hallway by the explosion. It seemed it had saved his life. My zombie swung around and tried to take a bite out of me, but I was too quick and it got a face full of shotgun instead. Just as it fell to the floor I hear Norman let out a loud cry. His zombie had gotten the better of him and had him pinned against the wall and had taken a huge bite out of his shoulder.

I came down hard against the creature's skull with the butt of my shotgun sending him flying down the hallway a few yards. Taylor jumped up and ran to his granddad who was bleeding on the floor as I made my way to toward the putrid shit bag who had just taken a bite out of the only family this poor kid had left. My heart was beating in my chest with distain as I approached him.

Suddenly I stopped. For a split second I didn't see a horrible wretched monster but I saw the poor teenage kid that had somehow been the victim of this entire mess. He was a pretty fresh kill. His youthful rotting flesh was still very much intact and he was rolled up in the fetal position as if whimpering in pain. Wearing jeans and a football jersey he looked like looked more like someone's victimized son than a flesh eating zombie. I walked closer with this overwhelming compassion welling up in me. Almost like I wanted to reach out my hand and help him too his feet and apologize for smacking him in the head.

The sound that was coming from him was almost like a whimper, like a puppy in pain. I could not see his face but I could see the huge gash of peeled back skin where my shotgun butt had laid back the flesh revealing a small swatch of skull underneath. His feet were kicking as if he were trying to get closer to the wall and away from me, his attacker. What a mind fuck, I was actually feeling sorry for this kid who had just tried to make a meal of an innocent young boy and his grandfather. Suddenly the whimpering stopped and he turned to look at me. One eyeball gouged out and the other no more than a raisin floating around in a gaping open socket. A strange expression came over his face, almost like he was thinking 'GOTCHA!' then like a flash he lunged at me and almost grabbed my leg when I kicked him in the head and pointed the shotgun at him. He shook his head as if to get his wits about him then he stared at me with is little raisin eye and snarled like a rabid dog. BLAM! All I saw was smoke rise from the barrel and I heard the sound of his brains painting the wall behind him. It was over, he was dead and I was alive.... For how long I didn't have a clue, but for the time being we were safe.

Even after we got our gory meat suits off the stench of rot was everywhere. The hallway all the way from the silo room to the bunker was painted in crimson chunky soup. I hated to ask him to do it but Taylor took a broom and swept all the body parts into the silo room and locked the bent up door while I tended to Norman's wounded shoulder.

"God damn high school kids…"

Norman laughed, making me chuckle as well. It just didn't seem right but it was sort of funny.

"You know I'm a goner, don't ya?"

Norman whispered to me while Taylor was occupied with his sweeping. I ignored the comment and continued to wrap up Norman's shoulder. He looked over to see if Taylor was watching and then grabbed my arm and shook me.

"Goddamit, listen to me!"

He pulled me close and proceeded to tell me that he wanted me to take Taylor and the plane and get the hell out of there. I insisted that he was coming with us but I knew as well as he did that he was right. It was only a matter of time before he became one of those things and tried to kill Taylor and I. Norman was damn persuasive. He was one of the hardest headed old geezers I had ever met and after a few moments of argument it was decided. I was going to lie to Taylor, telling him he and I and Rufio were going to take the plane for a spin but we weren't coming back. That's the way Norman wanted it and I agreed to do it but there was still the problem of how to get the plane out of the hanger door with the horde of meandering corpses just outside.

Day 51-He had been eating all night and now it was dawn. Looking down on him, gnawing on his intestines, he would guess he was about sixteen years old. The boy had turned to throw a third chunk of brick at him and probably would have hit him in the head again if he hadn't tripped on a car tire and fallen down. He hadn't thought about it or remembered it until that moment, looking at the boys flesh but he too was a teenager when he died... He was a week short of his 20th birthday. Something in him regretted having to kill to survive, but the feeling of sheer bliss that the flesh of the living gave him when he consumed it, was well worth it all. Plus he didn't ask for this, to be killed and brought back as a hunk of walking death. In some ways he was doing this kid a favor by speeding up the inevitable cause he would eventually have become one of them.... sooner if not later. And he would come back... for sure. They always do when the brain is left intact. And as hungry as he was he could not be bothered to crack open the boys skull and eat the brains. The work involved is almost like the difference in tucking into a nice juicy meat pie and trying to crack open a coconut.

I woke up to a thumping sound. My first thought was that they had gotten in through the hangar doors, but then I hear the crotchety old voice of Norman cursing under his breath and mumbling. I shut my eyes, hoping to get at least another hour of sleep. Down in the stuffy bunker there was no way of knowing whether it was daylight or not but my internal clock felt screwed up as it was. It felt to me like it was very early morning. I dozed for a moment and rolled over then heard another sound, farther off this time. It had to have come from the hangar. "Norman." I whispered so as to not wake Taylor up. He didn't reply. I glanced at the clock whose glow-in-the-dark hands were just about out of glow but I could tell it was 5:45 am.

I slid on my pants and quietly snuck out of the bunker, leaving Rufio snuggled up next to Taylor. They were safe and sound but I wanted to find out what that sound was and where Norman had gone. When I got to the hangar I noticed the doors were tightly shut and still bolted from the inside, but then I noticed something.... It was moonlight. I looked up and saw that a small roof-hatch that was positioned just above an old cat-walk that led to the ceiling of the hanger was opened and the moonlight was spilling in. Even though I had never noticed the hatch before I knew that it had to have recently been opened because there was no way in hell Norman would leave something like that unsecured. There were too many resourceful ghouls meandering around to leave us that vulnerable.

As I climbed up onto the cat-walk, I noticed a piece of paper flapping around in the wind. It had been taped to the inside of the metal hatch cover. It was a note left for me by Norman.

"By the time you read this, I will have taken care of our little problem..."

I didn't even finish reading the note when it dawned on me that there was a very obvious absence of moaning and scraping on the hangar doors. I squeezed through the hatch onto the roof and looked out over the moon lit field next to the airport. By this time the moonlight was being replaced by the glow of dawn and I could see pretty well. There he was. The crazy old fool was jogging out into the field about ten yards in front of a mob of at least forty hungry rabid zombies. He was zigzagging across the field taunting them. It almost looked like he was enjoying himself. Getting back at them for putting him though the hell he had been through the last few months. At first I didn't know what the hell he was doing. Why would he be playing tag with a mob of hungry zombies for no reason... unless... and that's when I saw it. His answer to our problem, he was waving it around in his hand as he jogged across the field. "What is it with him and hand grenades?" I mumbled under my breath. Then I saw him stop. He hunched down on the ground like a ball and I heard his voice echo across the field.

"Come and get me you motherfu...."

And just as the mob tackled him like a football quarter back, when they were all piled nicely on top of him he pulled the pin and blew him and all forty zombies to hell. It was actually a great plan, too bad he had to die to make it happen. I stood there for a moment watching the pieces settle into the grass. Only a few bits seemed to be moving or twitching but for the most part they were no longer a threat to us. I was running through my head what I was going to tell Taylor when I suddenly felt something. It startled me for a moment but then I realized it was a hand sliding itself into mine. I looked down and there was Taylor, tears running down his cheeks. He had seen it all and me; well all I felt at that moment was an overwhelming feeling of relief… now I didn't have to lie to the poor child.

Taylor packed up all the food and useful supplies to get ready to fly out while I went out into the field and collected all the bits of Norman that I could identify. I felt the least I could do was give him a proper burial, which we did late that afternoon. It was about 5:45 pm when I rolled the little Cessna out onto the tarmac. It was loaded with as many supplies and extra fuel that it could carry. To be honest I was a little worried we had stuffed in too much but it was worth the risk. I had no idea what we were going to find and I knew the chances of not finding more supplies for a very long time was extremely likely.

"You know how to fly this thing?"

Taylor asked me, making me chuckle. The kid had no idea. I used to fly my plane from Miami to L.A. just to take my wife to her favorite restaurants or pick up a few tubs of her favorite European ice cream, the name of which I never could pronounce right. I ruffled Taylor's hair, assured him that I knew what I was doing and fired up the engine.

"That's my baby."

I said as I savored the melodic hum. Everything was ready to go, except one thing, Rufio. I looked around and didn't see him anywhere.

"Taylor stay here and don't move, I'll be right back."

I went back into the hanger and looked around. The little fellow had gotten thirsty and had his head practically submerged in a bucket that was half full of rain water. I knelt down beside him and rubbed his neck while he lapped up the water, when I caught a blur of red in my peripheral vision. Just as I turned something caught me hard under the jaw. I felt my body being slammed up against the wall like a rag doll. I remember asking myself why I couldn't catch a fucking break. Here we were so close to just getting the hell out of here and this had to happen. Out of nowhere this zombie bastard had to sneak up behind me and catch me off guard and I had nothing in hand to use as a weapon. The other ghouls I had seen up till now had been disgusting but this guy took the cake. It reminded me of one of Austin Power's fem-bots with its face removed but this guy was a hundred times uglier. His face had been removed and in its place was just a gore-covered skull with two bulging eyeballs swollen in the sockets and to make it worse he was one big some of a bitch. I suddenly thought of the boy from the day before with the jersey on and wondered if there had been a college nearby cause this guy looked like he had been the football team's linebacker.

I squeezed out the words 'help me' trying to yell them loud enough to get Taylor's attention over the sound of the Cessna, but it wasn't working. If I was going to survive this, it was going to be all me. Rufio tried to take a bite out of the monster's arm but he was swatted away like a gnat. The gory zombie behemoth slid me up the wall by my throat till I was standing upright. Again, like the charred little child he seemed to be studying me, like he too smelled my not so delicious tumor ridden brain and having second thoughts about eating it, but he didn't seem to be considering letting me go. He was truly choking me to death. Again using real life situations I had lived through I suddenly remembered 8th grade, when I grabbed the school bully Dwayne Cox by the balls to get him to let go of my math book. So that's what I did. With all my might I grabbed the zombie's balls with my free hand and squeezed with all my strength and to my disgust I felt them instantly explode like two over ripe swollen cherry tomatoes. If the zombie hadn't been choking me to death I probably would have thrown up and the worst part is that it didn't faze the monster one bit.

Now feeling my consciousness slipping away I reached down and felt around for anything I could find and to my relief I felt the bucket Rufio had been drinking out of. I took it by the rim and with every ounce of strength I still had I smashed it into the side of the giant linebacker zombie's exposed skull. I instantly felt the release of his grip and he went staggering back a few steps. Just long enough for me to get my wits about me and look around for a better weapon… and there it was. The grandfather of all monkey wrenches and it was leaning against the wall just three steps away. The zombie lunged again in my direction as I did a diving roll to the ground and came back up with the monkey wrench in my hands. It was heavy and clumsy and my first swing missed the monster completely but getting a better grip, I kicked the zombie backward and aimed for the middle of his head and came down hard, splitting his skull like a melon. He staggered for a moment while his brain oozed out like strawberry jam from a broken jar and then I heard the sound of something bursting and I got a face full of putrid gas along with some cold wet spats of blood. For a second I didn't know what it was but then I realized a broken mop handle was sticking out of the monster's chest. The zombie fell to its knees and collapsed exposing the angry little boy standing behind him.

"You're a day late and a dollar short, but thanks for coming to my rescue."

I smiled and wrapped my arms around Taylor's neck and hugged him. He seemed a bit traumatized by the event but I knew in my heart he would have to get used to it if he was going to survive.

With the runway clear of zombies, we were in the plane and up in the air in no time. Looking at the beautiful crystal sky and the billowy clouds you would never guess that just a few thousand feet below the world was a nightmare. Through the clouds I could only get glimpses of the world below but the only thing I saw was devastation… everywhere. Would New York be just more of the same? Or by some grand twist of fate could it have possibly escaped the horror that seemed to spread everywhere else like some zombiotic cancer.

I was cruising at just above three thousand feet and the overwhelming desire to sleep was starting to overcome me. I don't know if I was still having side effects from being awakened from cryo sleep just a day or two before or if I was starting to feel the symptoms of having a tumor in my brain, but falling asleep was not an option. It was one thing to have the responsibility of taking care of another life in the form of a cute cuddly dog, but a ten year old boy was a completely different story. I couldn't help but wonder what would happen to poor little Taylor if I were to drop dead of an aneurism. The thought of that young boy left alone in this world full of flesh eating ghouls was more than I could imagine. I looked over and the picture was so peaceful that it was hard to fathom reality. The boy was in the seat next to me asleep with Rufio curled up in his lap. It looked like something from a Norman Rockwell painting and there we were, smack dab in the middle of hell. I barely had time to take in the sweet irony of the situation when suddenly the engine light came on. The prop started to skip and the plane was obviously in trouble.

For the first time in the forty-five minutes I had been in the air I grabbed the radio headset and tried to raise someone. At first there was no answer. I still couldn't see through the clouds and I had no idea where I was but then a scratching sound came over the radio. It wasn't static but more like someone on the other side was dragging the microphone over a hard surface.

"Hello, is anyone there? This is Cessna 24357 out of Speculator Municipal Air Field. I'm flying blind and my engine is giving out."

I waited for a response and the scratching sound got louder. Then suddenly a loud moaning sound came over the radio. It was obviously a human voice and it sounded like it was trying to make out words, but I knew in my heart of hearts what was on the other end of that radio.

In an angry rage, that woke Taylor and Rufio from their peaceful slumber, I ripped the cord out of the radio and let out a few hand-picked expletives that didn't really make me feel better. As a last ditch effort, I grabbed the controls and tried to pull up on the flaps to make the plane glide longer, but it was obviously going down.

"Tighten your seatbelt and hold on to Rufio!"

I yelled at Taylor as the engine went up in flames. The cloud bank we had been in was now parting so I could see the ground. Rolling hills and farmland was all I could see for miles. New York City was still nowhere in sight.

The Cessna was gliding haphazardly and I was able to control my descent quite well but where the hell I was going to land the bitch was a whole other question. Suddenly in the peripheral of my left eye I saw a flash of color. There a few miles off was a large flat field that had dozens of colorful blobs of fabric laying everywhere. At first I didn't know what the hell I was seeing but then as I got closer I noticed that each blob of fabric was attached to a wicker gondola. It must have been one of those hot air balloon lift off carnivals that was interrupted by… well a zombie holocaust. I tuned the plane toward the open field and eyeballed a spot where there was a long grass patch between the fabric balloons that stretched on for quite a bit. The last thing I wanted was to get the plane's wheels caught up in balloon fabric and flip the plane. The landing was going to be hard enough as it was.

There were about twenty zombies in the path of my plane but the wings and the last few spins of the propeller made short work of all of them. Guiding the plane away from the balloon fabric was a challenge with all the blood and brain matter on the wind shield but it finally came to a stop safely and we were unharmed. It was a challenge but I managed to land the plane in one piece. But soon I realized the challenge was far from over. The sound of the sputtering engine had attracted the attention of more zombies. I knew I could take out the few meandering around the fairgrounds but I could hear the rising of wails and moans on the other side of the fairgrounds. I was sure I had gotten the attention of every zombie that had been within earshot of the landing.

The fairgrounds consisted of three buildings and a large open field, now full of multiple collapsed hot air balloons. The main building was large like one of those Wal-Mart superstores and it had a gigantic parking lot on the other side. One of the other buildings was a public toilet and finally the last building looked like an office. It was definitely the safest looking building and it's the one we high-tailed it to. The door was unlocked and the office was dark with just a ray of light coming through a window that had its shades pulled. I told Taylor to hold Rufio and hide under the desk while I took a look around.

The initial office area was empty with no real zombie tale signs. It looked pretty safe but there was a strange scratching and thumping sound that seemed to come from down a darkened hallway.

"Can I come with you?"

Taylor poked his head out from behind the desk. In a knee-jerk reaction, I shushed him and pointed at him to be quiet. Thinking back I had a somewhat irritated and serious stare in my eyes. The boy just sank back behind the desk. There was debris all along the hallway. It was strange but there were what appeared to be drawings done in crayon, littering the floor. It looked like a collection of children's drawings. I got a sudden whiff of that all too familiar smell. Rot and Shit mixed up in a recipe of living dead terror. I was ready for anything. I had only made it a short way down the hall and to my right there was an open door. I couldn't see inside yet but I could tell it was where the smell was coming from. The scratching and shuffling sound was coming from further down the hall and I was in no hurry to get there.

I slowly made my way to the opened door and peeked around the corner. I was stunned. I didn't know whether to laugh or throw up. It was a kid's play room. A lot like a kindergarten classroom with short tables and short chairs and there lying across the table in the middle of the room was a dead clown. He had been dead for months but his curly orange hair and multi-colored bell suit were intact except for the gaping hole in his chest and stomach where someone or something had eaten away his intestines and what was left of them were strewn across the floor... again a mixture of blood and human feces soaked into the multi-colored checkered carpet that was designed to look like alphabet blocks.

I started to deduce in my head what must have been going on in this building. It had been a hot air balloon lift off fair and this must have been the place where the smaller kids were gathered and entertained while mom and dad prepared their hot air balloons.

Gutso the clown must have been entertaining the kids when all hell broke loose. But that brought up a much more disturbing question. Where were the kids?

My attention immediately went back to the shuffling scraping sound down the hall. It was actually a combination of several sounds. A low moan as well as a shuffling sound but the one that seemed the closest was the sound of something moving with a back and forth squeaking motion. When I slowly crept back into the hall, I could still see Taylor poking his head out from behind the desk. I put my finger to my lips to make sure he didn't make a sound and I turned again toward the shadow laden hall that led to only God knows what. On my hands and knees I slowly made my way along. Up ahead in the darkened hallway I could see that there was a door on the right that opened into what looked like some sort of nursery nook. It reminded me of the nursery of my former church, where people would leave their baby for a sitter to watch. It had a open doorway leading into a room with colorful cartoon characters painted on the walls. As I slowly peeked around the corner of the doorway I saw the corpse of a woman propped up in the corner. She had a small bundle tightly clinched in her withered rotted arms. Her bottom jawbone was gone exposing an open gaping esophagus that had been partially ripped out of her body. The organ was wizened and soaked in dried blood and reminded me of a vacuum hose. The sight of the woman hadn't startled me as I was quite used to it, but the smell was overwhelming. The room was in shambles as if there had been a huge scuffle there and obviously the woman had lost. I looked around and noticed four baby beds, one of which was toppled over, leaning against the wall. Another had been smashed and was basically in pieces but the two remaining were intact. Something in me wanted to look inside the two remaining beds but then I heard it again, the soft sound of squeaking movement accompanied by a soft scratching. I looked around and at first I didn't see anything. I couldn't tell where the sound was coming from. Then I heard a muffled gurgle and the scratching seemed to get louder and that's when I noticed it. The baby bed closest to me was moving ever so slightly.

"Psst, is there anything in here?"

Came Taylor's voice from behind me. My heart flew into my throat as I spun around to see him peeking in the door, tail wagging Rufio by his side. I quickly grabbed Taylor and pulled him close. Again I made with the 'shushy' finger sign and pointed at the slowly creaking baby bed.

"You don't think it's a..."

"Zombie baby?"

I whispered. First Taylor made a funny face like he had just sucked on a lemon, but then he gave me a look like I was a big wimp or something, and made for the bed with his shotgun in hand. I wasn't sure what to do. On one hand he was just a kid and if anyone were going to put the zombie baby out of its misery it should be me, but on the other hand he had already grown a pair and he was becoming the brave little kid he needed to be in this sick new world. I let him go.

The scraping and squeaking got more intense as Taylor made his way closer. I was a bit worried for him but I kept telling myself it was a baby, how dangerous could it be? I mean what was it going to do, gum him to death? Taylor snuck around the bed and crept slowly up the side. When he got high enough to see over the edge into the crib, a look of disgust came over his young face and I didn't expect what happened next. Without warning Taylor took the butt of his shot gun and began to pulverize something inside the crib. I was having images of some poor zombie baby being bashed to bits when Taylor smiled at me and said...

"Don't worry it was only this!"

With that he held up the pulverized remains of a Chihuahua sized rat and an old baby bottle with remnants of dried rotten milk in the gnawed up nipple. Once we were over the shock of the situation, we both giggled softly under our breath. The situation was sick and extremely gruesome, but it was also so fucked up and laughable. I tilted my head back against the wall and took a deep breath of relief, when suddenly Rufio began growling.

Day 79--The buildings around him were mostly vandalized and trashed. The creepers kept growing in numbers and the living were getting scarcer. It was becoming harder and harder to find sustenance and he could feel his body tightening and slowing and falling apart as he lumbered along. He realized that he kept seeing things that brought back flashes of memory to him. Things that had been part of his previous life, like music and pictures and people. Sometimes he would even see another creeper that looked familiar to him, but what could he do. It's not like they could introduce themselves and shoot the bull about days gone by. His decaying brain just didn't work that way anymore. The flashes were few and far between and his consciousness was negligible at best. Mostly it was just a driving force to find bloody flesh. Suddenly a shot rang out and his left arm wrenched back with a force that ripped open the rotting flesh. He looked up and saw faces looking at him from the broken windows of a decapitated apartment complex. They really should have left well enough alone if they had been smart. He didn't know they were there until they ripped open his arm with their gunshot. He turned and looked at the open stairwell and started towards it with all the speed he could muster. About thirty other creepers heard the shot too and seeing him turn they followed his lead into the building. Suddenly some words entered his rotting brain. Words of wisdom his father had said to him before.... "You should never kick a sleeping dog."

I had gotten so caught up with the sound coming from the rat in the cradle that I had completely ignored the other sounds that had been coming from down the hallway. I made a move to shush Rufio but as I turned I saw something in the corner of my eye. Then I saw something else and then another something and before we knew it, there were about five emaciated rotting zombie children ranging from about age four to about seven coming through the doorway from the hall. They were slow and cumbersome but almost all of them had their lips ripped away exposing their jagged snapping teeth and everyone knows that's the business end of a zombie.

Taylor had been smart and had jumped into the baby crib that was about four feet off the ground. He was yelling at me and aiming his shotgun at the dead brats one after the other. I had holstered my pistol and slung my rifle across my back and I was having a hard time getting it off as the strap had caught on something.

"Shoot them Goddamit, shoot the little bastards!"

Taylor was almost in tears as the children clawed at the baby crib and snapped at him. I guess after what happened to his little sister it was just too much. Suddenly the biggest of the group, a boy... I think... turned his attention on me and came at me. I was still fucking with my rifle that had gotten caught on a hook in the wall I was sitting against. The youngster had what had once been a bright yellow t-shirt with a picture of some smiling cartoon character on the front. His pants were torn almost off and his right ankle was broken with his foot dragging along behind him, attached only by bits of rotten sinew. The boy's nose looked as if it had been bitten completely off and one of his eyes was swollen shut and the other one was bulging out like a dented up ping-pong ball. He could not have been a day over six years old when he died but even so it was those grimy brownish yellow teeth that were gnashing at me, that made me nervous. The boy threw himself on top of me and I caught him just under the jaw with my free hand. I felt the wall hook break but at this point it was almost impossible to get my rifle positioned correctly, so I grabbed at my gun and pulled it out of the holster. I had an idea that this kid would probably do what Taylor's little sister did and smell my tumor and leave, but he wasn't giving in. His rotting flesh was rubbing up against me and literally making my own skin crawl. I heard a few shotgun blasts come from Taylor's direction as I managed to get my pistol barrel pointed right between the boys eyes. I pulled the trigger and... nothing happened.

"GODDAMIT!"

I yelled as I realized the gun had jammed. I dropped it and literally picked the six year old zombie up with both hands now that I was in a position to stand. As I lifted him above my head, I noticed that Taylor had made quick work of the other zombie rug rats once he got the guts to fire the gun. I, on the other hand, had my hands full with just one, literally. I looked around, not sure what to do with the little pecker, when I realized there was a window very nearby. I heaved the wiggling zombie child with all my might, sending him smashing into the window pane sending shards of glass everywhere. He wasn't dead but at least he wasn't my problem for a while. My adrenaline was literally gushing through my veins. I felt unstoppable as I grabbed that fucking rifle of mine and headed out into the hallway. I didn't say a word to

Taylor but he followed right by my side as I went from room to room, looking for a little zombie bastard who's head I could blow off. When I think back I sort of feel like I was so overwhelmed with everything at that moment. It was almost as if everything had caught up to me at that moment in time. I was an unstoppable crazy man and all I wanted to do was get to fucking New York City. Was that too much to ask? As I began to calm down I realized I had gone through the rest of the building and there was basically nothing there. The decaying children were the only undead occupants of the building, but this was only one on the compound and it was by far the smallest.

Night came fast and Taylor, Rufio and I all crashed in a little nurse's station with two bunks. After my little adrenaline tantrum, I blocked up all the doors and the broken window and made the place safe again. If there was one thing I needed it was my sleep.

"It was pretty gross having to kill those dead kids huh?"

Taylor was feeling talkative after the event.

"Yeah having to kill the big ones are bad enough but when they are small like that, it's pretty disturbing."

Taylor laid there with the moonlight shining through the window onto his bunk. In the light he looked like he was glowing, like some little angel I was destined to protect.

"If I turned into one of those things, do you think you could do to me what you did to them?"

The question was haunting. The very thought of Taylor turning into one of those undead monsters was unthinkable. But I knew that if I did find myself in that predicament I would do exactly what I had to.

"Well Taylor, I think I would just take you and lock you in a candy store to live out your days eating candy. I would never be able to shoot you, because you're such a good kid."

Taylor laughed at the silly answer but it was closer to what he wanted to hear than what the truth would have been.

"Did you ever have any kids?"

Taylor asked punctuating it with one of those yawns that makes you know this will be his last question before nodding off.

"Yeah, kid, I did have a boy of my own. He was only three when I had to go into the freezer. I can only speculate what might have become of him and his mother. But I loved him so much it hurts to think about him."

Taylor rolled over in his bunk and snuggled with Rufio.

"Well if you like…." He said with a tired yawn. "I'll be your kid."

His words trailed off as he drifted into dreamland. It was a sweet thing that he said and I knew he meant it and I guess rather we liked it or not that's about where we found ourselves. We were a family rather we liked it or not… but in the midst of everything, I liked it just fine.

When morning came all seemed quiet for the most part. Taylor and Rufio were still asleep so I decided to take a better look around and see if there was any way we could hot wire a vehicle or something to get us to New York. As I looked around I noticed there was a small closet that opened off of the main hallway. I had not checked it the evening before when I was cleaning the place up. I slowly opened the door to make sure there were no surprises waiting for me and saw a ladder that led upward to the roof. Taylor was stirring so I told him to stay put and that I was going up to have a look around.

The roof was high with no way for the meandering living dead to make their way up. They were all too emaciated and brain dead to climb up and there wasn't really anything to climb up on. There were spent, collapsed hot air balloons littering the massive field as far as the eye could see. Whatever had happened here it had happened fast, so fast indeed that not many of the balloonists were able to make their escape in their balloons. For a moment I wondered if I could salvage one and get it up in the air, but they were all too far away and there were literally dozens upon dozens of those walking corpses. The chance of getting one of those heavy gondolas upright and then filling the balloon with hot air was impossible. The sound of the fans themselves would alert every zombie within earshot. I was completely out of ideas when I noticed something bright at the far corner of the building. As I walked closer I could see that it was part of one of the balloons that had collapsed near the building. When I went and looked over the edge, not only was the balloon intact but the gondola was just under the lip of the roof. It must have taken off and caught on the edge of the building and gotten stalled there until its air leaked out. No telling what had happened to its owner. This was it, our way out of here and onward to New York City.

It took Taylor and me both, along with a lot of tugging and heaving, to get the gondola up onto the roof. The balloon seemed to be in good shape and the fuel tanks were full. Now all I needed was a fan to blow the air into the balloon so I could get it heated up and ready to fly. I had never flown a hot air balloon myself but I knew the principals involved. My old pal Pete Gatsby was a balloon enthusiast and I had actually invested in one of his latest corporate balloons that actually advertised one of my companies, so I went up plenty of times and knew basically what to do. The problem is there is no steering a hot air balloon. You just sort of go where the wind takes you so I had to make sure it was blowing where I wanted to go and that was southeast.

Taylor was a good little helper. He went through the building and found every single thing he thought would be helpful on our trip. He packed food and water and tools and he even found a hand held video game device in the kids play room that he planned to take along to get his mind off the grim putrid reality that was now our lives. I left him to the task and trusted him to use the shotgun if he found himself in a dangerous situation because it was my job now to get us a fan that could fill the balloon. As I looked around the field I could actually see dozens of fans lying here and there. They had been left behind by the balloon's owner when the shit had hit, no pun intended, THE FAN! I could almost pick and choose any fan I wanted but there were two problems. (One) I had to leave the safety of the rooftop to get it and (Two) although they were oblivious to my presence at the moment, the field was swarming with the undead and getting one of those heavy ass fan from the field to the rooftop was another task altogether. I looked around with my binoculars and spied what looked like the fan for me. It was about ten yards away from the front door of the front of the building I was on and to make it better there was what looked like a bundle of tethering rope near it that I could use to help hoist the fan up onto the roof. I looked around at the pathetic zombies meandering in the parking lot. Altogether, from what I could count there were about fifty of them lumbering around in the field and another twenty or so in the parking lot, where my fan was located.

They were all not only oblivious to my presence up on the roof but they seemed to be trying to go about the business they had when they were alive. There were two extremely bony gray-skinned security guards that wondered around the guard house at the parking lot entrance. The broken down concession stand had two corpses meandering around behind the counter, busy with a lot of nothing. One was a young teenage boy about fifteen from what I could tell from what was left of him and the other was a fat man in his late 30's who had now turned into a walking blob of rotting flesh. From what I guessed these particular zombies had probably been behind that counter rotting for about two months. Every zombie I could see was very decayed and some were bloated still with gases and others had rotted almost down to the bone and could barely move. I knew once I got down off the roof I could outrun any one of them but as a group they could easily overcome me if I lost my edge. The idea of climbing down to retrieve the fan was an obviously stupid idea that was beyond dangerous and I knew what I really needed was a plan.

I spent the better part of the day rummaging around the inside of the building looking for anything that would assist me with my plan. In the nurse's station I found a huge stash of rubbing alcohol. There must have been twenty or so sixteen ounce bottles of the stuff. I guess they got a lot of skinned knees and gave a lot of shots in that place, but I wasn't complaining. While rummaging around the place I also found an old wind up alarm clock and one of those big glass water bottles from a water cooler. My plan was coming together and I was pretty sure it just might work.

Morning came way too early as I had stayed up all night getting the balloon laid out on the roof and the gondola in place so I could try to get it aired up and hot as quickly as possible. I knew once that fan went on; any zombie left within earshot was going to be scraping and scratching to get on the roof, to the fresh meat, before it escaped. I laid two long planks from the roof down to the ground on the side of the building opposite the truck that had my fan in it. I filled the glass water bottle with every drop of the alcohol, stuffed a rag in the nozzle and laid it on its side at the top of my ramp. Practically full, it was heavy as hell so rolling it was my only option. I looked down my ramp into the parking lot and drew an imaginary line. I set the alarm clock to ring in one minute and tossed it at the spot at the end of my imaginary line. It was time for my plan. If it worked we'd be up-up and away safe and sound, if it didn't it was back to the drawing board.

Taylor was next to me and was as nervous as I was. He had Rufio in his lap, patting him on the head assuring him everything was going to be alright. Suddenly the alarm clock went off, its annoying bell piercing the otherwise silence of the dead parking lot. Just as I had hoped every zombie in the parking lot turned and looked toward the clock. They all began to shuffle toward the irritating ringing sound. I was hoping the bells would continue to ring long enough for all the zombies to get to it before it stopped. On and on it rang. Within seconds the zombies had gathered around the annoying clock obviously irritated by its ear splitting bell. The clock kept ringing and they kept coming, until almost every zombie in the parking lot was huddled in a mass around the clock.

"Ok boy, here we go."

I turned to Taylor and gave him a wink as the clock's bell wound down to silence. Before the corpses could disperse from their cluster, I lit the fabric plug in the glass bottle and rolled it down the ramp right into the crowd of zombies. With its weight and speed, it actually knocked a couple of the zombies on their asses like huge rotting bowling pins. Gun at the ready, I took aim at the bottle with the flaming end and squeezed the trigger. Just as I had hoped, the bottle exploded engulfing the crowd of zombies in a shower of flame and glass. Burning corpses flew in every direction and this was my chance. I ran to the other side of the building and jumped down, making a b-line for the truck with the fan in it. As I had hoped the keys were still in it, but rather it would start up or not was another thing. I looked around, flaming zombies everywhere and completely oblivious to me. I turned the key once and nothing. I pumped the gas and tried again. It tried to turn over but just didn't seem to have the battery power. I turned off the ignition and turned it back on. The meters and lights all came on as if the battery was ok so I made to turn the key again when suddenly there was a thump. I looked and there in my window was a flaming zombie. He had seen me make for the truck and followed me flames and all. I hit the lock with my elbow so he couldn't open the door and turned the key again. To my surprise the truck roared to life. I let out a joyful chuckle, turned to the flaming zombie, aimed my gun at his head and blew his brains all over the pavement. From what I could see the rest of the zombies were too pre-occupied with their flames to notice me whiz around the parking lot, and park next to the building. I quickly jumped into the back of the truck and hoisted the fan up onto the roof. With Taylor's help I got the fan in place, plugged it in and was filling up the balloon in no time. The parking lot was littered with flaming corpses lying motionless on the asphalt. With a little bit of luck and a lot of wind in the right direction we just might make it to NYC safe and sound.

When the balloon had taken shape and was plump with air, I began to pull the lever sending jets of flame into the balloon to warm the air and make it stand erect. We had tethered the gondola so it wouldn't get away from us but the process was just taking too damn long. I had only seen my buddy to it before I had never actually gotten a hot air balloon up into the air by myself. The jets of fire were loud and I had to yell directions to Taylor so he could hear me over the sound. Finally I pulled the lever back to let the flames die when suddenly I heard it, a very unmistakable sound that I had heard before. It was as I had feared. The sound of the alarm clock and the fan and the jets of flame that warmed the balloon had done just what I thought it might do. A horrid putrid moaning sound echoed across the parking lot. I looked at the entrance to the compound and there at the gate they were coming. It was a mob of undead that had to number in the hundreds. It was almost like they had their own sonar or something else that let all the nearby corpses know that there was fresh meat to be had here at the fairgrounds. I pulled the lever again and the flames shot up into the balloon that, thank God, had risen up and was completely erect. The gondola was already floating a few inches above the rooftop and the balloon was about ready to lift us to safety.

For some odd reason the new zombies were faster than the ones I had just torched. At least that's how it seemed because before I knew it they were all over the truck and some of them were actually grabbing the edge of the roof, trying to pull themselves up. I grabbed Rufio and the pack with all our supplies in it and threw them into the gondola. I was giving the air one last blast of heat when I heard a gunshot. I turned in time to see Taylor, eyes the size of saucers and his smoking shotgun pointed at the edge of the roof. The corpses were like ants, climbing over each other to get up on the roof and it was working. One of them had gotten all the way up and luckily he saw it in time to blow it off the edge. Soon another and another were climbing up. I handed my pistol to Taylor and grabbed him, slinging him over the wicker edge of the gondola to safety. Before I knew it there were about ten corpses that had managed to crawl their way up onto the roof. Finally I too climbed into the gondola and yanked the gas all the way open, sending a ten foot flame into the balloon. I pulled a buck knife out of my pack just as the first zombie grabbed the edge of the gondola. I began hacking away at the tethers so we could float to safety but we has already acquired about four unwanted guests, dangling to the side of our balloon and they all weighed a significant amount of weight. The balloon lifted up until it was about three feet off the surface of the roof. We floated over the edge, pulling about four zombies with us. The problem was that each of those zombies had at least one other zombie hanging onto it, keeping us down and unable to life off properly. I grabbed the shotgun from Taylor and smacked one of the zombies in the face. He instantly let go, but there were still three left to go and they were all on the same side of the gondola, causing us to lean dangerously to one side. One of the zombies, a huge burly bearded lumberjack looking corpse that had been rotting a very long time, had reached his arm down into the gondola and grabbed the handle of our supply pack. I laid into his arm with the butt of the shotgun over and over again but when he finally relented and fell to the pavement, he took the pack with him. All of our supplies were gone. All we had were guns and not a scrap of food. A sudden burst of anger rushed through me and I cocked the shotgun and blasted away at the two remaining corpses, sending them down into the waiting mob below. Finally we were free to ascend but with our supplies gone, it was going to be a very rough journey and only a lot of luck would assure that we would get where we wanted to go.

Day 86- He had been wandering around in the apartment building for a week at least, but time is nothing to you, when you are a walking corpse. He and the other creepers sniffed out at least ten of the survivors that had held up in the apartment building and they had spent the better part of the week ravaging their flesh and eating their brains but there were a few left, still hiding, just waiting to be found by them. The one with the gun had taken another shot at him and missed and that was his big mistake. He didn't really feel emotions per say but he did take out some sort of revenge on him when he smashed his skull against the stair banister and feasted on his warm chewy brains. Somehow it felt really good and he was driven to find the rest of the survivors. He and a group of about twelve of the ugliest creepers you could imagine finally made it to the roof of the building. Most of the creepers he was with had been dead longer than he had and they were in really bad shape. He had a gash in his neck and a torn up arm but some of them had their guts hanging out or their faces half eaten off it was quite gruesome but hey he was one of them so he was used to it. Norman the creeper who was leading the rest of them to the roof got his fingers cut off by the metal door at the top of the staircase. It seems the survivors were trying to push against him to close it and he got his fingers caught in the slamming door, only to have them severed clean off. The three remaining survivors, an old man, a woman and a teenage girl, finally relented and ran for the roof's edge with nowhere to go by the time we got out onto the gravel and tar. "Treat others like you want to be treated" this rang out in his memory for some reason. He was having a random memory all of the sudden. He remembered that he was very young, about four to be exact, when his father had to leave him for medical reasons. But his mother used to always remind him of his little sayings. Sayings like "kicking the sleeping dog" and "treating others like you wanted to be treated" things that meant nothing to him now, but in his life he had held them near and dear to his heart. He was still pretty satisfied with Mr. "Smith and Wesson's" brains that he had gorged on only an hour or so before, so his zeal for the kill was not as strong. He actually thought for a minute that he might just bite the girl in the throat and let her turn so he could have someone to hang out with for a while. Someone his own age so to speak.

The air was cold and the sun was disappearing into the horizon. It had been about six hours since we had made our escape. Taylor and Rufio were snuggled up at the bottom of the gondola sleeping soundly. I could only guess how little 'real' sleep the poor kid had gotten since this whole ordeal started. I had taken inventory of what we had left and it wasn't much. As luck would have it I had a few canned goods still stuffed into my own personal back pack but the pack that had been designated for supplies is the one that bug-eyed stiff had pulled overboard with him. I wasn't sure how long it would take us to get to New York but I didn't think we could all three survive on two cans of Vienna sausages, a can of fruit cocktail and a can of smokehouse flavored Spam. We still had the shotgun and my pistol and enough ammo that I had tucked away in my backpack, but you can't eat lead, so to speak... and in a post-apocalyptic zombie world, is there ever 'enough' ammo?

The compass on the handle of my 'Rambo' style buck knife was telling me we were traveling South East which is exactly the direction we needed to go, but hot air balloons were not known for their speed. Without a map and some sort of landmark we were flying blind and I had no idea where we were. I guessed we were flying about three thousand feet above ground and in the dusk I could see hundreds of small ant like shapes meandering along the fields and roads that stretched out below us; a sprinkling of corpses restless and hungry with nothing but air between us and them.

"Are we almost at the city?"

The tired quiet voice of Taylor whispered from the dark corner of the cramped gondola.

"Hey pal what's wrong? Can't sleep?"

The boy shifted with Rufio still on his lap and put his head on my shoulder. The constant rocking of the gondola was quite soothing and made me feel at peace. The wind was picking up and the gondola seemed to jerk around a bit but I simply chalked it up to the wind and the pull of the cables adjusting. The handle for the gas nozzle had a long tether on it so I was able to sit at the bottom of the gondola and still pull it once in a while, sending flames high into the balloon.

"We'll be there before you know it"

I ruffled the kid's hair and leaned my head against his.

"Do you think there will be other people like us there... I mean normal kids like me?"

Taylor's voice was echoing off a bit as I was feeling lethargic, like I could fall asleep at any moment. I answered him with a grunt as he cuddled up next to me and my eyes rolled back in my head. I was fading away into that place between the waking world and dreamland. But dreamland was a much better prospect so I let myself fade. Deeper and deeper I was going, feeling so safe and secure in the little wicker heaven floating in the clouds. I drifted into that place where tranquility meets contentment, lulled by the slow steady breathing of the ten year old boy cuddled up next to my ear. How was it all going to end? Was it possible for it to end well in a world overcome by a living dead plague? It was the answer to that question that scared me more than anything.

I became conscious but sat there with my eyes closed for a few moments. Something had awakened me but I wasn't sure what. It was the jerking feeling like the gondola was being pushed about, but the wind was not that strong. I cracked my eyes open and saw something peeking at me over the edge of the gondola. It was a pair of hungry eyes that were completely dead. I immediately recognized the 'Wonder Weenie' hat that was pressed down onto the creatures head. It was the teenage zombie that had been behind the concession stand counter at the fairgrounds, what the fuck he was doing here was boggling my still sleepy mind. As the creature grasped tightly to the edge of the gondola, one grubby decaying hand at a time, I could only figure that he must have been in the mob of zombies that were trying to attack me when I lifted off and he must have been either twisted in the tether ropes or holding on for dear life, or lack thereof, all this time. Either way here he was, three thousand feet in the air hanging onto what was supposed to be our little slice of peace and safety. It was odd how the zombie teen's dead eyes could also burn with desire at the same time. It was almost like there was a sort of 'death glow' inside of them. His grotesque face and mangled mouth were twisted in a look that almost resembled a grin, as if he were thrilled to have finally made it to the top of the tether where the 'buffet' was being served. Before I could rise to my feet, he had already thrown one of his legs over the edge of the gondola in an attempt to come inside. Rufio began to growl and bark like a crazy mutt, nipping and snapping at the zombies legs. The shotgun was lying on the wooden floor of the gondola, underneath Taylor in a position that made it hard to grab. I punched the rotting youth in the face in hopes that it would let go and plunge to its death, or final death as it were, but he had the edge of the gondola in a death grip and wasn't about to let go. He reached in and grabbed Taylor's arm and pulled it toward him. I punched the zombie again, which in retrospect I realize was a horrible idea, because this caused the zombie to let go of the gondola but get a fresh grip on poor Taylor's arm, pulling the boy almost completely over the gondola's edge. I scrambled for the shotgun as I grabbed Taylor by the belt. I could hear him screaming and fighting with the zombie teen as I heaved the barrel over the edge and aimed it right at the boy's rotting, dripping face and pulled the trigger. His head exploded in a cloud of red with brain matter and other goo flying everywhere as he released his grip on Taylor and plunged through the clouds below to the unseen ground far beneath us. I hugged the crying boy and tried to console him when I noticed that his arm was bloody.

"Are you bitten?"

I asked him as I looked into his tear-soaked eyes.

"No, I don't think so"

He said as he handed me his arm for examination. He hadn't been bitten but the zombie teen had dug his rotten dirty fingernails deep into the boys flesh. I doused his wounds with some of the alcohol I had stashed in my backpack. The cuts were deep but I could only hope that being scratches and not bites that the boy would have a chance to survive and see another day, without being destined to become one of those horrid things, either way I was going to keep a close eye on him

Hours had passed since we had our incident with the zombie teenager. I was suddenly craving one of those Cohiba cigars my doctor had made me give up a month or so before I was put to sleep. I missed the aroma of those bastards and the way they calmed my weary bones. The thought that there must have been a million of those things lying around the city in hotels and tobacco shops all just waiting to be smoked by me... Oh to risk one's life for a stogie... it almost seemed worth it. I smacked my lips at the thought and looked over. Taylor had finally fallen asleep and was deep into it, somewhere in ten-year-old boy dream land, which I envied. I could only hope he was dreaming of hot wheels and video games instead of corpses trying to rip the flesh from his bones. I would never know but he seemed to be having a peaceful sleep. According to my watch, dawn was probably two hours away and I had gotten a grand total of three and a half hours sleep. My blood was still pumping from the tangle we had with that zombie teen and I had been inspired to reach over the edge and check the other tether lines and pull them all inside the gondola. I wanted to cut them all off but I figured that was overkill, so I just pulled them in so I knew where they were and who or what was using them. It was dark and cloudy and the air was filled with a chill. Once in a while I could hear sounds being carried on the wind, it was the occasional sound of a choir of zombies singing a spine chilling death whale in unison. I wasn't sure how they could sound so close until it hit me. I mean literally something brushed against the gondola. It was the metal spire. It was the tip top of a sky scraper that was towering high above the fog and mist. I peeked over the edge and saw that New York City was right below us. I pulled the tether and sent a huge pillar of flame up into the balloon, so we would ascend and quickly. My feeling of being high and dry and safe from the death grasp of zombies was fading when I began to realize that many of the buildings around us with flat roofs were full of them. Many had noticed our balloon and were reaching out in our direction. Some were so close and so anxious to grab us that they were pushing each other from the building tops, only to plunge hundreds of feet to the asphalt below.

Thought after thought was racing through my mind. What should I do? Should I just float on by or stop and see if we could replenish our supplies? The thought seemed impossible after seeing building upon building with the roofs filled with the walking dead. But if I could find the right one…. if I could find the one building where we could lad and tether off the balloon for a quick escape, maybe we could find some food. Maybe we could find supplies and get some rest and hell who knows; maybe I could find a Cohiba or two. Far below I could see that there must have been some attempt at an evacuation of the city. Cars were littering the streets piled up on top of each other like tonka toys around a kid's toy box. It was a multi-car pileup as far as the eye could see. In the distance the bridge to Manhattan was thick with trashed cars and walking dead. If we were going to land this balloon it was going to have to be somewhere high and unpopulated. The sun was coming up and it was becoming easier to see the carnage that was New York City.

"Are we there?"

Came Taylor's small voice from behind me. I turned and put my arm around his neck and pulled him close to me in a hug.

"We're here, but I don't know if we're going to be able to stay or not. It all looks like more of the same little pal."

Taylor looked down at the rooftops below that were teaming with zombies.

"You mean more of those dead things?"

The boy's voice sounded defeated.

"Yeah... as far as the eye can see."

I thought back to the good doctor's tape recorder and his words, the timeline in which all this had happened. It seemed impossible. In three short months the entire eastern seaboard of the United States was a walking graveyard and all it took was one bite. The thought hit me and I quickly grabbed Taylor's arm and examined it. It didn't seem any worse than a normal scratch. It wasn't festering or infected as you would think it would be if the zombie infection were setting in. I felt the wind and looked where it was taking us. In the distance I could see a familiar building and we were heading right for it. It was the roof of the Ritz Carlton Hotel where I had stayed many times. I racked my mind to think and remember and it seemed that the very top floors of the hotel were pent house suites that were usually empty or had some high profile celebrity staying there and the security measures just to get up to them were unbelievable. I knew there wouldn't be any zombies who would just be wandering up there, they would have had to already been there when the plague started and that meant there would be few if any at all. It would be a good place to tether the balloon and take a look around.

The Ritz grew closer and I could see the swimming pools that belonged to the two top suites. If my memory served me correctly the very top floor of the Ritz had two executive suites. They were both two storey's high with their own spiral stair cases and each had a swimming pool. And to make things ever better they both had designated elevators that went directly to the lobby and didn't stop anywhere else. There was probably no way to get to them from the ground and we were coming in by air. I suddenly felt luckier than I had in days. I made a cowboy style lasso with one of the tether ropes and began to spin it in the air as the balloon approached. The poolside ledges had iron railings that went along the length of the building with rod iron hooks lining the tops of them. All I had to do was catch one of those and we were in luck. I suddenly felt like I would give my left nut for a pistol with a silencer on it. How great would that be?

I told Taylor to get the shotgun ready in case the suite was occupied and I threw that lasso and hooked the top of the railing. It was easy, just like those cowboys I had seen in the movies. I pulled the gondola close enough to jump out and I did, leaving Taylor in the balloon. I quickly tied the tether tightly to the railing and told Taylor to stay put for a few minutes while I took a look around. The balloon was secured tightly and I knew it wasn't going anywhere. At first glance the place looked empty but I'd been down that road before so I wasn't taking any chances. With the pistol in one hand and a swimming pool rescue hook in the other, I started to make my way toward the sliding glass doors of the suite. To my surprise the doors were not locked and they slid open with ease. The interior of the hotel suite smelled a bit stale but there were none of the un-dead aromas I had grown so used to. The place looked untouched and ready to be rented out but that was only the first floor. Just past the living room was a spiral staircase that led to the upper floor where the master bedroom was. I figured it was safe enough so I went back and got Taylor and Rufio to accompany me in the final stage of my security walk-through. I certainly knew at this point Taylor could hold his own with a small number of the stenchers. Rufio scampered around the room sniffing here and there but he seemed un-agitated and didn't find anything to bark at, so I took that as a very good sign. Shotgun in hand, Taylor slowly followed me to the upper floor to the master bedroom. When we got to the top of the spiral stairs I could see that the room was empty and clean. Just like the rest of the suite it looked immaculate for having sat there unused for at least four months. The only dead thing in the room was a vase of flowers that had been placed there to welcome whoever was supposed to have rented the room but the zombie plague happened and the flowers never got appreciated.

"Poor flowers."

I thought to myself. What a ridiculous thing to think but it was nice to still feel something after all the horror I had been through the last few weeks. After securing the front door and making sure the hallway was clear, I went up to the master bath and began to run some hot water. I turned to Taylor, mussed his matted hair and said,

"I know someone who's taking a bath!"

Within seconds of taking his hot bath and cuddling up on the huge king size bed, Taylor was fast asleep. I, on the other hand, lay there with my eyes wide open, watching the mid-morning sun shine through the window. I dozed in and out of sleep a few times but I just wasn't able to relax. Rufio was curled up at the foot of the bed next to Taylor's feet and he too was wide awake. I just lay there thinking of all the things that the world would never see again. Even something as simple as going to the Movie Theater and catching a Saturday afternoon flick was long gone. The simple pleasures I had taken for granted so many times would never happen again. How would the three of us survive this topsy turvy world we had found ourselves in? I was lying there listing all the things I would never see again in this fucked up world when suddenly Rufio snapped his head quickly toward the door. He bared his teeth and began to emit a quite but menacing throaty growl. My heart sank because I knew this could only mean one thing... trouble in paradise! I left Taylor sleeping soundly on the bed and grabbed the shotgun. The door had an electronic key card lock on it, so I had to prop it open against my better judgment or it would have locked behind me with no way back in. I was thinking that I would have given anything for a sharp axe or better yet a samurai sword as I made my way down the dark hall that led to the door to the other penthouse suite. If I had realized one thing during my short stint as a zombie holocaust survivor it was that guns were not the ideal weapons. They may dispatch your enemy, but for every zombie you kill with a firearm, you attract a dozen more.

Quick and quiet was the way to go and if I was going to run into something stinking and rotten I wanted to take it out quietly. I made a motion for Rufio to stay and protect Taylor and he obeyed.

I couldn't have asked for a smarter dog in such a horrible situation. The hallway was like a 'T' with the other suite at the end of one hall and another branching off and leading to the elevator. There were not many places for something to be hiding on this floor. I slowly crept up to the door to the other suite and put my ear to it. I didn't hear a peep. I was about to grab the knob to see if it was opened, when suddenly I heard a sound come from the elevator shaft. It became obvious that whatever Rufio was growling at, was on another floor. Slowly and quietly I made my way to the elevator doors. I placed my ear to them and listened hard. I could barely hear it but there it was, as clear as day. It was the sound of something shuffling around with an occasional banging sound mixed in. I had heard the familiar sound of a meandering zombie bumping its way along with no regard to anything around it. The problem was I could not tell from the sound whether it was one or two or a dozen of them, but the sound seemed to be coming from the floor below me. I suddenly thought about the balloon and the fact that it was still intact and tethered to the balcony of our room in case we had to make a quick getaway and with that comforting thought, I decided to check out the sound. Since I wasn't about to take the elevator, I went for the staircase door. After examining it to make sure it was not going to lock behind me, I started down the stairs. I was about half way down the first flight of stairs when I was able to confirm the fact that the sound was indeed coming from the floor below. As I turned and started down the second flight that led to the landing, I could see that the stairwell door to the 29th floor was standing open. It had been blocked by a garbage can, probably during some sort of evacuation from the hotel when the trouble began, but it was becoming obvious that not everyone evacuated. I couldn't help but hope that the sound I was hearing was being made by some survivors and not by another stencher, but that was only wishful thinking. As I made my way into the hall of the 29th floor, the smell hit me like a shovel in the face. It was the unmistakable stench of dead rotting flesh. I squatted down holding tight to my shotgun ready for anything. At this point I was determined not to be surprised by anything and ready for everything. I was taking inventory of all of the exits from the floor. There was the stair well I had come from, plus four elevators and as I made my way down the 'L' shaped hall and turned left, I could see one more stairwell door at the other end. If something bad happened I wanted to have a quick route out of there. Not hearing anything for a while, I made my way back to the elevators and one by one pushed the button. I wanted to know whether the elevator cars were empty or full of some unwelcome surprises. I felt a little stupid when nothing happened due to the fact the electricity had been out for months.

The hotel had to have emergency generators, but at this point who would have been there to turn them on? One of the elevators was stuck on the 29th floor and the door seemed to be slightly ajar. I tried to peek in, but it was too dark inside to see anything. I quickly knew it was not the source of the putrid smell as my nose was up against the crack while trying to peek inside. My heart was in my throat as I thought I caught a glimpse of something in the corner of my eye. I quickly turned to see that nothing was there, but I couldn't be too careful. Knowing now that I didn't need to worry too much about someone or something sneaking up on me through the elevators as they were out of commission, I started back toward where the smell seemed to be coming from. I stopped and listened again hoping to hear the sound that had lured me down there in the first place, but all was quiet. Toward the end of the second hallway, I saw a maid's cart sitting next to the open door to one of the rooms. Suddenly I heard the sound again and this time it was louder. It was definitely coming from the open room where the cart was. Deep down inside I couldn't help but hope it was a survivor that had found sanctuary in the hotel like us, but with the smell that was emanating from the room that wasn't very likely.

As I inched closer to the open door, I remembered the reaction from Taylor's little zombie sister when she seemed to smell the tumor in my brain and lost interest in eating it. I thought there might be a chance that I had some all-around zombie repellent going on, but the dead children at the balloon fair didn't seem to be dissuaded by it, so I had to be careful. I finally reached the cart that was still full of room service supplies, but they had obviously been there a while. I put the cart between myself and the doorway and pushed it as I went into the room, keeping it between me and any potential surprises. As I made my way inside, I heard the noise again. I quickly looked over to see what was causing it. The window had been left opened, someone probably jumped out of it, and the wind gusts were blowing the curtain which was knocking things one by one off of the desk. I could also see a telephone receiver that was dangling from its cord off the edge of the desk, knocking against it with every gust of wind. I was almost relieved until the next gust of wind brought with it yet another putrefying whiff of death. There it was... the source of the horrid stink. The wind was blowing through the window across what was by far the most horrifying sight I had seen in days. There on the hotel bed were the remains of what had been two people at one time. That was before they had been ripped apart by some fucking cannibalistic putrid shit-bag of a zombie. The man's head was dangling off the edge of the bed held there only by what was left of his spinal column, which was still attached to his ripped open torso. An army of maggots and flies had made their nest in his ribcage which still housed the remnants of a lung, a shriveled heart and some remains of a small intestine. It was all, however, dried up and mangled almost beyond recognition and lying in what had been a pool of blood but was now a brown crusty mass soaked into the once expensive Egyptian cotton sheets. One arm was nothing but bone from the shoulder to the wrist and his rotting lets and naked groin section was covered by the crusty bloody sheet. What was left of the girl that was with him, be it his girlfriend, wife or some cheap hooker, was also naked. Her body had been mostly devoured, with the remnants of one dried up shriveled rotten breast still attacked to a thin dried beef-jerky looking layer of flesh that covered her ribs. The lower half of her naked body was hanging off the bed to one side and what had been the soft fleshy parts of her lower body had been torn away and eaten by God knows what. I did know what... but I was trying to pretend I didn't. Her head was still lying on the pillow, dried and shriveled with eyeballs missing and lower jaw ripped off. I was truly glad Taylor had not been with me and seen this.

Suddenly I had a horrible feeling. Taylor was back in the room alone with only Rufio to protect him, and he was not much protection to be sure. I hurriedly turned back toward the door only to hear a loud moan and feel a talon-like claw smash into the side of my head. Before I knew what had happened I found myself on the floor with what looked like the remains of a bellboy on top of me, trying to rip out my throat. Just when I thought I was about to push him off, I heard another moan and glancing sideways at the door, I saw the walking corpse of a maid, probably the one who owned the cart in the hall, ambling into the room. I couldn't believe it. I thought I had been so careful... how could they have taken me by surprise so easily? I had the shotgun in my hands and was trying to fight it away from the bellboy, who had a hold of its barrel with both hands. That was actually a stroke of luck as it was much better to have him holding the barrel than ripping out my throat. His gnarly fingers had several months' worth of fingernail growth on them, which they say keeps happening even after death, which he could have used to easily scoop out my Adams apple like a melon ball. No matter how hard I tried to get the barrel of my shotgun pointed at his head, I just couldn't. He was pushing down with all his 'dead' weight, no pun intended and I had to wrench my head back and forth to avoid the horrid puss riddled mess that was dripping for his mouth and eye sockets, one of which was empty, so it wouldn't land in my eyes and mouth. Lying on my back on the blood soaked carpet; I could see the upside-down legs of the ever approaching zombie maid coming from the doorway.

Although I wasn't able to aim the shotgun I could easily aim it at the maids gaping maw that was drooping slack to one side. I knew I had a better chance of getting out from under the bellboy if the fucking maid wasn't around, so I guessed at the aim and pointed the barrel of the shotgun at what I was hoping was her head and pulled the trigger. With an ear-splitting BANG her head exploded all over the wall behind her. The aim was perfect and better yet, the kick of the shotgun threw the zombie bellboy back and forced him to release his grip. Taking full advantage of the moment, I sprang to my feet and planted the butt of the shotgun into the bellboy's mouth, ripping his jaw out of socket and knocking out most of his surviving teeth. Now if he did get to me, he would have to gum me to death. The bellboy awkwardly found his feet and started toward me again. Noticing the open window behind him and seeing a great opportunity to save some ammo, I did one of those spin kicks I had seen in those old Chinese kung-fu movies and kicked the rotting son of a bitch right in the chest, sending him backward toward the window. It was surreal like something out of an action movie. He suddenly got a strange look on his face, almost as if somehow in his rotten zombie brain he knew he was about to plunge 29 stories to his second death as he flew backward through the window. It was almost like slow motion as it happened. I even ran to the window to watch him fall as a result of some demented desire to make sure the fucker was gone. Even if a zombie could survive a 29 story drop, he would be in no shape to fuck with anyone after he landed. It must have been a combination of the putrid mess around me and the smell of the collection of rot, but I suddenly doubled over and vomited up the raw spam I had eaten directly out of the can earlier that morning.

After cleaning myself up in the bathroom, I headed back up the stairwell to the penthouse. When I got to the door, it was still ajar and everything seemed fine. Taylor was fast asleep on the bed, safe and sound when I entered the room, but the sound of my approaching footsteps stirred him awake.

"Dad, where did you go?"

The young boy asked me in his sleepy haze. He called me dad. I didn't know quite how to react but I felt my heart warm and a lump appear in my throat.

"I just went to check out a noise that got Rufio all worked up."

I answered as I sat next to the sleepy boy and stroked his hair.

"What was it?" he asked as he yawned.

I thought for a moment about what I had been through the last 20 minutes of my morning. It had all become the 'norm' in this fucked up world we found ourselves in. I didn't know how to answer the boys question at first but then it came to me... I knew exactly what to say to him.

"It was nothing, pal."

I smiled at his youthful sleepy expression, complete with mussed up hair...

"Nothing at all."

I knew in the days to come he was going to see more than his share of death and horror, so I opted to spare him this one little bit.

Day 95------ He had fallen out of a window of the apartment complex and landed three stories below. It was a fall that would have killed him if I were alive. In the process his messed up arm was ripped off and left dangling from the window frame, so he had been wandering around minus an arm for almost a week now. The girl he had bitten did turn but like most girls through his life she never gave him the time of day, so he moved on not knowing where the hell he was going, but going none the less. He had wondered around Central Park with a group of creepers in hopes of finding more food but things had gotten really bad. Survivors were so scarce now that all of them were slowing down and mostly meandering in circles going nowhere. He had tried gnawing on the odd piece of corpse he would find lying around now and then but it just wasn't the same. It didn't taste right. All cold and dead like himself. It wasn't a substitute for warm bloody flesh, flesh which was now so hard to find. He was dragging myself down a side street, literally. At this point one of his legs had gotten ripped up when he stepped in a broken sewer grate and mangled the tendons, so his foot was just dragging along. But it was while dragging himself along that he saw something moving inside of a convenience store. It was a young boy a couple years younger than him and he was rummaging around in the store for supplies. He was being quiet, making his way closer so the boy didn't hear him, but he was almost as interested to see where the boy had come from as he was to eat his brains. The boy grabbed some supplies and scurried down to the end of the street that came to a junction. It was there at that junction that he noticed the building he had been drawn to. It was the place his father had taken him so many years before. He couldn't remember the name and his brain was in no shape to read the sign but he recognized its beauty. It was one of the nicest hotels in the City. The words 'Rita Car' kept flashing in his rotten brain. He couldn't make out the name but he knew it was the place. He suddenly noticed that there was group of other creepers that had also seen the boy. They began to ramble faster toward the boy, when he noticed they were there. The boy dropped the bags with the supplies he had collected and began to run toward the hotel. He had to follow him. He felt like it was somehow his destiny.

F or an entire week life was heaven. I had locked all the doors to the hotel and blacked out all the windows in the lobby except for the ones just around the front doors and Taylor and I had enjoyed an entire week of lounging safely in the luxury of the hotel.

Between the rooftop swimming pool and the video game room Taylor thought he had died and gone to heaven, never knowing about the dead maid and bellboy. I had found a working generator in the basement of the hotel and turned it on a few hours a day to give us the creature comforts of electricity. At night we used our flashlights to get around as I didn't want the electricity on to light up the building like a Christmas tree and give away our position to either the zombies or the wrong kind of survivors. I spent most of my time reading in the cigar bar but limited myself to only one Cohiba a day since I knew nobody would be rolling any new ones and I wanted them to last. I kept a close watch on his scratch and it seemed to be healing perfectly with no sign of zombie infection. Soon after my run in with the dead hotel staff, I had done a sweep of the entire place, floor by floor and found it to be completely secured, but I knew we couldn't stay there forever.

Our balloon had long since deflated and was folded up nicely and stuffed into the gondola and stored on the balcony of the penthouse. It was seven o-clock in the evening of our sixth day there and I was about to turn off the generators so there would be no light illuminating from the hotel once dusk came. The last thing I wanted was to attract attention, but I was too late. Suddenly I heard pounding on the front doors of the hotel lobby. Someone was screaming to let them in and that someone was obviously human. I motioned for Taylor to stay put and I grabbed the shotgun and took a peak outside to see what was going on. It was a young man in his twenties and he was bloody. From his looks he looked like he had tangled with some stenchers. I crouched unseen by the door where I could look out a slit in the plastic that was covering the windows. I could see the young man but he could not see me. He looked as though he had been badly beaten but he didn't seem to have any serious bites or injuries on him. I was torn as to what to do. I had enjoyed almost a week of uneventful normalcy and this was like a rude awakening back into the cruel world that I was really in, but I had no idea what horror was about to come crashing into mine and Taylor's lives. My fingers were literally grasping the door handle and my thumb was about to push down on the lever to open the locked door when suddenly from around the corner of the building across the street came a hoard of the rotting things. They were lumbering toward the young man but were as slow as usual. I knew, however it would only be a matter of seconds until they had him. I really wasn't sure what to do. Risk our safety to save the guy or pretend he was not there and remain hidden from the mob of drooling monsters.

Time was running out so I turned to yell at Taylor to go back up to the room but before I knew what was happening, the boy flew past me and pushed the door handle, opening it. It all happened so fast it was hard to absorb the order in which things happened. The moment the door flew open, the young man tried to make a beeline for the safety of the hotel lobby, but by this time the large crowd of living dead had almost caught up to him. As he threw himself through the door one of the zombies, a very decayed but very quick older man, with half of his face missing and only one large building eyeball that was dripping with putrid green pus, grabbed the young man's foot and was keeping him from getting inside safely. The young man was kicking and screaming as the zombie tried to pull his leg close to take a bite. I pulled and tugged on the young man's arm to try and get him through the door, but it was useless. By that time several other zombies had grabbed a hold and it looked as though his death was inevitable… until suddenly with a ferocity I would have never expected from the docile little mutt, Rufio bolted right into the horde of zombies and buried his teeth deep into the lead zombies throat, ripping out a fist size wad of putrid rotting flesh that smelled like week old fish guts. The ghoul with the pussy swollen eyeball suddenly released his grip and pushed back against the other zombies that were grabbing and clawing from behind. Rufio's heroic bite allowed a moment where the ghoul released his grip and the young man was able to throw himself into the hotel lobby. Taylor thrust the shotgun into my arms and I grabbed it and began dispatching zombies right and left, unloading at least fourteen shells into the rotting putrid hoard. As zombies were exploding all over the marble tile just outside the hotel lobby, Taylor grabbed Rufio by the tail and with a jerking motion, that had to hurt the poor mutt, he pulled him into the lobby with us and slammed the doors closed.

My heart was pounding in my chest as I sat with my back against the thick glass door, looking up at the chandelier hanging from the lobby ceiling. It was blurry and my head felt like it was splitting with a sharp pain. I had to wonder if all this excitement was going to be the death of me. Causing my aneurism to bust like an over inflated balloon.

"Jesus H, Christ."

The young man whimpered between breaths.

"I thought I was dead for sure… or sort of dead… you know dead then back up just to walk around dead some more."

I slid down the glass until I was lying flat on my back, still out of breath and still admiring the sparkling diamond chandelier hanging thirty feet above me.

"I don't know who you are," I said to the kid. "But you better fucking be worth it. You almost got us all killed, not to mention now we've got an audience outside the door where before the fucking stenchers didn't know we were here."

"I know man, I'm sorry, but I didn't know what else to do. I've been barricaded in a nearby Seven-Eleven for weeks now and when I saw your balloon land on top of the hotel I knew it meant other living breathing people had to be here."

I quickly perked up and got to my knees.

"You mean you came here from a seven eleven and you didn't bring any supplies?"

I suddenly had the feeling that this kid's stupidity outweighed his usefulness completely.

Suddenly a frustrated angry look swept over the kid's face. I followed his eyes through the door, past the crowd of what was left of the stenchers that had followed him, to the street outside the hotel. There laying on the curb, where he had dropped them, were two big black duffle bags full of what I knew were probably the supplies this kid had tried to drag to the hotel with him.

"Oh, sorry I assumed you were stupid."

I rolled my eyes and shrugged, feeling like a bit of an ass.

"Those two duffle bags are packed with all the shit I could carry from the store. It's probably enough for the three of us to eat for a few weeks. I had to drop them when I got overwhelmed by those things out there."

The kids name was Mac and it seems he had been working as an usher in a large New York movie theater when the evacuation call came. He said he had barricaded himself in the theater with a few friends as trying to get back home to the mid-west was impossible. But it wasn't long before they were overrun by the living dead and his friends were either killed or recruited into the horde of walking dead.

"We really need to come up with a plan to get out there and get those supplies."

I knew such a plan was important if we were going to have enough supplies, but I knew we weren't going to go through the front, so I began to barricade the lobby doors with everything I could move in front of them. A couch, tables, chairs even a grand piano that Mac and I were able to roll into place and push on its side. Now that the hoard of the dead knew we were there, we would never be completely safe. It seemed our luxury stay at the Ritz was shorter lived than I had hoped. The week Taylor and I had spent in the safety of the hotel had put a huge dent in the supplies we could find there. Being a hotel there was a lot of food stocked up but the unfortunate part is that a huge amount of it had been refrigerated and was long since rotten. We had been living off of canned corn and veggies and other non-perishables we could find. All the bread and other non-refrigerants were nothing but piles of mold and rot.

Since fancy hotels usually only serve fresh food to their customers the food supply was scarce. What a pity you can't get spam in a five star hotel.

Mac joined Taylor and I in the penthouse suite. Yes he could have had any number of rooms in the hotel, but we agreed that the best plan was to stick together. Plus, being in the midst of a zombie plague somehow took the luxury out of the whole hotel experience.

Mac and I had sat up most of the night coming up with an elaborate plan to get outside and grab the supplies. Mac even thought he might know a place to get a fan large enough to get the balloon back up and running, but like most plans made by mice and men, ours were ours were shot in the wee hours of the morning. We were all awakened by the sound of the fire alarm, which I had set to go off in the event that the front doors were breached… and it was. Taylor grabbed Rufio, I grabbed the backpack and guns and the three of us ran to the stairwell. Since I had turned off the generator the night before there was no electricity to run the elevators, so we had to hoof it down the stairs and make the 30 floor descent, I had become very accustomed to this during our week of luxurious hotel life. When we got down to the third floor, we exited the stairwell and went to the cigar bar which had a balcony that overlooked the lobby. Sure enough the glass in one of the picture windows had given way and the putrid living dead were climbing over each other and pouring into the lobby. Lucky for us they had not seen us yet and I knew it would take them a long while to meander their way to the stairwell and up to the third floor, but time was still precious and we had to make our escape. The one consolation was the fact that the more of them that poured into the hotel would mean there would be less on the street and we could make our way out through the basement, around the building and hopefully retrieve the duffle bags without being spotted. Since Mac's close call gaining entrance to the hotel, I had estimated that since then about a hundred stenchers had accumulated at the front of the hotel. As far as I could see it would only be a matter of time before most of those had worked their way crawling and scratching their way over each other, through the broken window and into the lobby. If we timed it right we might just be able to use this breach to our advantage. I was thanking my lucky stars that days before, I had had the forethought to survey the basement and secure an escape route through the service entrance, which at the time, was clear of walking corpses. I could only hope it still was. I placed my finger to my lips and motioned for Taylor and Mac to quietly make their way back to the stairwell door. I grabbed a few boxes of cigars and stuffed them into my backpack and followed them into the stairwell. It was already past dawn so there was no problem seeing in the hotel, but the stairwell and the basement were both dark and dreary, so I broke out the flashlight.

Behind us, I could hear the walking dead crashing their way through the lobby. They were, no doubt, rambling through everything and breaking anything they ran into. I had a feeling they not only knew we were there, but that we were escaping and they probably had some sense of urgency to catch up to us. My mind was running a mile a minute hashing over what we were going to do once we got the supplies and got the hell out of there. The night before while Mac and I were making our big plan, he had told me about a car dealership not far away where he thought we might be able to get some wheels. He had planned to go there and grab a car but hadn't been able to yet. It was a good plan. We could take a road trip south and see if there were any other survivors. I sure as hell didn't want to stick around the New York area and it was becoming clear that being in the city was a very bad idea. We could hear the zombies filling up the lobby behind us and making their way in our direction. I should have known they had a second sense about them when it came to sniffing out fresh meat. We had cleared the stairs and made our way into the dark barking basement when suddenly Mac stopped dead in his tracks.

"Oh shit!" he gasped.

I looked up ahead of him and there, standing between us and the exit on the other end of the basement car park was a dead girl. She looked like she was about 18 years old and she had on a ragged but distinctive purple movie theater usher's vest with a tattered bow tie hanging to one side of her blood soaked collar.

"Do you know her?" I asked.

"Yeah, she was my girlfriend, before she became… well… one of those."

Mac answered. I gently pushed him aside and was going to take care of the problem so he wouldn't have to, but he insisted that it was his job. Back in the lobby the day before he had grabbed an ornate silver candle stick holder that was about a foot and a half long. It was menacing and he had taken it to use as a weapon but hadn't had the opportunity yet. He gripped it tightly and reluctantly started toward the snarling young girl, when all of the sudden she bolted toward him. The look on her face was almost as if she recognized him and he had done something to really piss her off. Bloody hands jutting out in front of her like gnarly eagle talons, she came at him with all her might. Mac closed his eyes and swung with all his strength and the heavy silver candle holder met the girl square in the temple, exploding her head like an over ripe watermelon. Her limp lifeless body collapsed onto the cement basement floor and twitched like a frog in a pot of boiling water.

"Take that you BITCH!"

I put my hand on his shoulder…

"I know it must be horrible to have to kill your girlfriend, but…"

"Hell no!"

Mac surprised me with his nonchalant attitude to what he had just had to do.

"The bitch fucked my best friend the night before all this shit happened. I've wanted to do this a long time now."

Mac nodded to punctuate his statement, wiped his candle holder on the dead girl's jeans and started toward the exit.

By the time we got outside there was a large group of walking dead that had followed us from the hotel lobby into the basement car park. We blocked the outside door so they could not follow us out and snuck around the hotel to the front, near where Mac had dropped the supplies.

"The car dealership is two blocks that way."

Mac pointed up a street that looked deserted but if I had learned one thing it was not to take anything for granted. Quickly and quietly we side-stepped across the street. We were careful to keep the front of the hotel in view as we made our way to the two duffle bags. They were lying on the curb and were splattered with blood and all manner of gooey zombie grey matter. We shifted stuff around so everything was being carried evenly, leaving Taylor to carry Rufio. Letting the dog run free wasn't the best idea since we didn't want to attract attention. I could see the 'Maverick Chevrolet' sign up ahead and at this point it was a welcome sight. Just getting in a car and moving in the opposite direction of town was exciting. We had quietly covered about one of the two and a half block to the dealership when suddenly Rufio began to bark madly. He squirmed so much that Taylor had no choice but to let him go.

"RUFIO!"

I half whispered and half yelled. We were so close yet so far away and the last thing I wanted to do was go hunting for a hard headed dog.

"You and Taylor go get the car and I'll get Rufio and meet you at the dealership."

Mac insisted. But at this point I was desperate to secure our transportation out of this hell-hole so bad I didn't argue at all. Rufio disappeared down a narrow alley between two buildings and Mac scrambled after him. I didn't want to lose the little buddy that had been through so much with me, but I also didn't want Mac to die trying to find him… but I had my job to do so I did it. I gave Taylor the backpack and the pistol and I carried both duffels and my shotgun. We made our way to the Chevrolet dealership as quickly as we could, but the moment I stepped into the parking lot, my heart almost stopped. The building was sealed up tight. Not only was it pad-locked but all the glass windows that allowed passersby to view the cars were covered with sliding metal shudders.

"Jezuz Freaking Christ!"

I rolled my eyes and cussed under my breath. I honestly wanted to scream but I knew that was not the thing to do, so I motioned for Taylor to follow me and I crept up to the front of the building and sat the duffle bags by the door.

"Do we have to go inside?"

Taylor asked as he gestured towards the lot full of brand new cars.

"Unfortunately yes, pal." I said with a frustrated tone.

"I never was a car thief, so I don't have the first clue how to hot wire a car. I'm afraid going inside and getting the keys is our only option. Taylor squinched his lips and nodded. He knew what we had to do and he was ready for anything. The boy and I quietly made our way around the building. It seemed to be sealed up with shutters all around until we got to the back. The back of the building was a single cinder block wall with a door right in the middle. There wasn't a window to be seen so there was no need for shutters. I grabbed a hold of the knob and tried to turn it. Sure enough it was locked, but it was the kind of door that could easily be broken into. I looked around to see if any stenchers were within earshot. Not seeing any, I took the butt of my shotgun and slammed it down on the doorknob. Once, twice, three times was a charm. On the third blow, the knob broke and the door opened slightly. It seemed our hope of getting the hell out of 'Dodge' in our 'Chevrolet' was going to be possible.

Day 101-He was by nature a quiet corpse. He couldn't moan and He didn't know how other creepers did it. He was dead and he didn't breathe but he guessed some of the others had a way of inflating and deflating their dead dried up lungs, but for him it was a plus. He had followed the boy until he escaped into the hotel with the help of another man and a boy. The other creepers seemed to be very stupid compared to him, or maybe somehow his brain wasn't quite as decayed as theirs. The creepers spent all night pushing up against the glass window of the hotel's front façade pressing and smearing their bloody hands and bodily fluid all over the glass, but he was the one that had the brain power to pick up a large rock and smash the front window so they could all get inside. The man and the boy were on the balcony above them and none of the other creepers could figure out how to get to them. He saw the man disappear with another young boy and a dog, into the stairwell. For some reason He had the feeling they would go down into the parking lot instead of up into the hotel, so that's where he went, and all the other creepers followed him down there. By this time he was tired of chasing the boy, but he was determined to catch him and eat his warm bloody brains.

Mac was out of breath, leaning on a filthy dumpster trying to figure out which direction Rufio had gone in. It wasn't his fucking dog and why was he risking his life to find it… was the one thought that was dominating his mind. He examined his candle holder and wondered if it would have been smarter to bring the pistol. Thinking of the noise it would make made him suddenly satisfied with his choice of weapons. He looked around and noticed that the alley he had gone down had led him back toward the hotel. He was about to say fuck the dog and give up when he looked down and saw some blood. It was a trail that led around the corner of the building he was behind.

"Rufio… here boy."

He whispered hoping that the dog would show up so he could get the hell out of there.

"Are you hurt, boy?"

Mac slowly and cautiously followed the blood trail around the corner. Up ahead he could see Rufio's tail sticking out behind a pile of cardboard boxes much to his delight it was wagging.

"Jezuz pal, you had me worried to death."

Mac walked up to the dog and looked behind the boxes. What he saw next made him want to puke. There on the ground was a dead boy. His body was torn open and bloody and Rufio was licking blood from the boy's face.

"Rufio cut that out and let's go… that's disgusting. You're going to become a zombie dog or something… you little mut!"

Mac reached down and picked Rufio up. The little beagle was light but still he didn't really want to carry him, but he knew he had to if he wanted to get back quickly. Just as he picked Rufio up, Mac noticed something. The dead boy's blood was fresh. It wasn't dried up and the boy wasn't decomposed. It only meant one thing and it wasn't good. It meant he was a fresh kill and whoever or whatever killed him was probably not far away.

Back at the dealership, Taylor and I had gone into the dark building. It was completely empty except for a few dead bodies lying around, but the good news was they weren't walking around trying to eat anyone. It seemed that the keys to the cars had been kept in a safe in the office, or at least that's what I was guessing. I looked around and found the keys to a lime green Chevrolet Spark which was perfect because it was small and compact and would zip through wrecked cars on the highway nicely. I loaded the supplies into the car and waited for Mac, who was taking much too long.

In the alley where the dead boy was lying, Mac had been cautiously surveying the area to make sure no walking corpses were lingering around, especially since he was much closer to the hotel than he wanted to be. He was turning to leave when he heard something move in a pile of boxes in the alley. The place looked like a shanty made by some homeless guy or something because there were several large boxes placed together to form a make-shift shelter of some sort and something was moving inside. He knew he had been gone way too long and wasn't eager to rouse the attention of any nearby stenchers but his curiosity was getting the best of him so he held tightly to Rufio and squatted down to look inside the cardboard shanty. There in the dark corner of the large cardboard refrigerator box was what appeared to be a frightened little girl huddled up in the far corner.

"Hey there,"

Mac said with a tender voice.

"Don't be afraid, I won't hurt you. Come with me and we'll get you somewhere safe."

He put Rufio down and began to climb part of the way into the box. He could hear a sound coming from the girl that distinctively sounded like she was crying. He figured the boy must have been her brother and when he got attacked she hid in the box. Despite the shadowy interior of the box, he could see that the girl was alive and not one of the walking dead, but she was not quick to trust him.

"Come on little girl, I want to help you but you have to trust me so we can get somewhere safe."

Mac was trying to coax the girl out of the box when he suddenly heard a very familiar and unwelcomed moaning sound. It was faint but it was thick with the voices of more than one stencher. He knew he had been discovered. Mac reached into the far corner of the shadowy box and grabbed the crying girl and ran for his life, retracing the direction he had come in. The mob of stenchers had just rounded the corner and they seemed to be led by a one armed male zombie just a bit older than Mac and in some strange way the look on his face made Mac feel like he was coming specifically after him.

At this point I was very worried. Mac had been gone almost 45 minutes and in zombie apocalypse, terms that was an eternity. I was literally sitting in the car waiting with Taylor in the back seat, ready to start up the car the moment he arrived. I had actually given myself about 15 more minutes to wait before I gave him up for dead and got the hell out of there. I know it sounds pretty harsh, but we just couldn't wait any longer than that. Suddenly I heard Rufio's distinct bark and saw Mac come running out of the alley with a small girl in his arms. Behind him about twenty yards was a hoard of living dead that were moving unusually fast and at the front was another boy about Mac's age. He looked so familiar at first and then I realized something horrible. My heart sank and I suddenly felt like I was going to throw up. The young one armed zombie leading the group was my son Brandon. He had been about 5 when I had been put into cryo and when my wife and I divorced she moved to New York with him and I never saw him again.

Through the decaying flesh and dried up features I could barely make out the boy I once knew that had grown into a man, but the one thing that convinced me that it was him was the shark tooth necklace that was a souvenir I had obtained on one of my many salt water fishing trips I had taken in my early years of marriage. I had given it to him when he was five so he would always feel that I was close to him even after the divorce. It had the initial 'B' carved into the enamel of the tooth and even though all the dried blood I was sure it was the same one. Mac was running for his life and Brandon and his hoard of the living dead were not far behind. I wanted to call out to Brandon to make him stop, but I knew that it would be futile. He was one of them and there was nothing I could do about it. What a hell of a way to be reunited with someone you love from your past. He was a zombie.... one of the worst kinds. He was a zombie that I loved and knew I was going to have to destroy. Mac made it to the car and put the small girl in the back seat. She was about the same age Brandon had been the last time I had seen him. I took my shotgun and began to dispatch every zombie I could, without shooting Brandon. I took out an old woman to his right, whose scalp had been peeled back from her skull and then I blew the head off a younger housewife to his left who was definitely a fresh kill and looked almost normal except for the gaping hole in her chest where her lungs had been torn out.

I shot zombie after zombie as the group got closer, but I left Brandon intact, still leading the charge. Mac opened the driver's door, grabbed the shotgun from me and pushed me into the car.

"Get the hell out of here, I'll hold them off."

He said in some stupid effort to be brave. But at this point the zombies were on us. They had reached the car and were already grabbing at him. Brandon jumped on Mac's back, throwing his one arm around Mac's neck and spun him around pulling him into the crowd of living dead. He began to shoot into the crowd, dispatching zombies' right and left but Brandon was on him and there was no getting him off.

"GET THE FUCK OUT OF HERE!"

He yelled as Brandon took a huge bite out of his shoulder. The car was already idling so I shoved it into gear and sped off, only to slam on the breaks about 15 feet away from the hoard. I grabbed the pistol from the front seat and with a not in my stomach and a shaky hand, I aimed it right at Brandon's head and pulled the trigger. His head exploded in a spray of blood and brain matter and he collapsed to the ground taking Mac with him. The other zombies piled up on Mac like an overzealous high school football tackle. I sped away leaving the gore behind me as my eyes welled up with tears. I had just killed my son and I had watched a kid I barely knew give his life to save Taylor, me, my dog and some little girl none of us even knew. As I drove off, teary eyed I just convinced myself it was just another day in a world full of shit. In an apocalyptic world where everything had gone wrong.... very wrong and to make things ever worse, I glanced in the rear-view mirror to check on Taylor and the little crying girl and there on her arm, something Mac had obviously not noticed, was a bloody red swollen bite.

By the time I got to the interstate, Taylor had gotten the girl's arm wrapped up and disinfected with the first aid stuff that I had stuck in my back pack. I wasn't at all confident that it would make any difference. I could only hope the poor child's fate was not going to be the same as everyone else around us. During the 30 minute drive to the interstate, Taylor had gotten the child to talk a bit and as I listened to their conversation my heart sank. The tidbits of information I was gleaning from the child's account of what had happened to her and her family only made me feel even more hopeless. Based on what the girl was telling Taylor, her father and brother and she had driven up from Florida to search for her mother who had come to New York for a business trip. As she put it,

"The dead people were trying to hurt us, so we left to go to York and find my mommy."

Hearing her say those words to Taylor made my stomach churn. I had sort of decided in my head that I was going to travel south and see if I could find some semblance of normal civilization. I was hoping the infection had not spread that far, but now my plans were completely screwed. I had already started south on the interstate which was so littered with abandon vehicles and rotting corpses that knowing my chances were slim or none to find civilization in the south; it was obvious I had to make another plan. I was racking my brain trying to think of a place that might have the best chance of no infection and short of making a road trip to the west coast I couldn't think of anything that seemed feasible. Where in the hell could I possible find uninfected survivors? If the infection had spread as far as California, there would be no way the three of us would survive a road trip across the zombie infested wasteland, and for what? Just to get to L.A. and find out it's a cesspool of living dead? NO FUCKING WAY!

There had to be another plan… but what was it? Suddenly my thoughts want back to the moment I pulled Rufio out of his cry chamber. I remember thinking to myself there was a possibility that there could be other rooms full of chambers with people who were still in stasis. Maybe that was the answer. To go back to where it had all started and clean the place up and turn it into a safe haven. Wake up the survivors and start our lives over in the seclusion of Eternal Slumber's fortified laboratories. It had taken me forever to get to New York what with a plane crash and slow ass hot air balloon, but in reality Eternal Slumber was only a couple hundred miles away. I could drive there in a couple of hours but not on the tank of gas the Spark currently had. Most dealerships put as little gas in the tank as possible and that was the case with this car for sure. I was definitely going to have to find a station somewhere and try to scrounge up some fuel if I was going to make the trip back north.

The arrow on the fuel gauge was pointing at 'E' and the last thing I wanted to do was to get stranded. I had changed highways and was going north back in the direction of Eternal Slumber's headquarters. The road was not as littered with wrecked cars as it was winding north through the mountainous terrain of Upstate New York where there were many more forestry areas and for some reason people evacuating the city didn't choose to come this way. I was about three hours out of the city and Taylor and the little girl, whose name I found out was Becky, were both asleep in the back seat while Rufio snored in the passenger's seat next to me. Up ahead I could see one of those all-purpose trucker heaven truck stops. The huge red sign that stuck out above the pine trees read 'Trucky's Bar, Grill and all-purpose Truck Stop' it was a mouthful but it was also a very welcome sight. I knew I would find trouble there, but I also knew it would be the only fuel I would find for miles. I shook Taylor awake and quietly handed him the pistol.

"Stay here and keep watch. Don't wake up Becky unless you have to. I will be right back."

I had pulled up next to the pumps in hopes of finding a way to unlock them, but I had a backup plan and that was to try to siphon gas from one of the vehicles that was parked around the lot if the pumps were inaccessible. As I slowly made my way into the truck stop, clever in hand, I could see that it had been ransacked. There were caps and 'T' shirts and other souvenirs littering the floor, but not much edible foodstuff seemed to be left on the shelves. I heard something at the register and turned to see an elderly man lying across the counter. His body had been ravaged by the living dead and he had been lying there decaying for months. I walked over to the register to see if there was a way to turn on the pumps when suddenly the corpse moved. 'Jesus, it's still alive!' I said to myself out of shock. Its jaw and one hand were really all that could move, but it was still animated and dangerous if I were to get too close.

The gas pumps were the old kind that weren't all computerized or I would have been shit-out-of-luck. There on the wall beside the cash register was a key that had the words 'gas pumps' written on the plastic keychain. I was in luck. With the debris and over turned display racks blocking the isle leading to the back of the counter I really couldn't get back to where the key was. I was going to have to reach across the register, dangerously close to the writhing corpse. I began to reach over the counter and was just about to grab the key when I heard gun shots. Taylor was yelling for me from the parking lot where the pumps were. I glanced up and could see him aiming the gun out the car window, but I couldn't see what he was aiming at. I quickly grabbed the key but as I did the old corpse lunged at my arm, clamping its jaws tightly onto my shirt sleeve. I was lucky as hell as it didn't even get close to the flesh of my arm, but still I almost shit my pants when it happened. I had the key but now putrid grandpa had a hold of my sleeve and was trying to grab me with his bony hand. I ripped my sleeve pulling it out of his mouth and I came down hard in the middle of his skull, with my clever, splitting its skull two. I knew Taylor would not have shot the gun if we weren't in for some trouble and I really didn't have time for dead grandpa's crap.

When I ran outside I could see what Taylor was shooting at. Down the road, the direction we had come from was a group of zombies that were huffing it toward us at a very fast pace. I ran over to the pumps and with a shaky hand unlocked the pump and shoved the nozzle into the opening to the gas tank. I held my breath for a moment as I could only hope that the gas reservoir under my feet was not completely empty. The chances of it still having gas in it were slim but I pulled the handle on the pump down and squeezed the trigger. To my surprise and amazement gas started to flow.

"Hurry up… hurry up… HURRY THE FUCK UP!"

I was mumbling under my breath which was not making the gas pump any faster. Five gallons…. Six Gallons… I watched the gauge spin counting the gallons and glanced down the road at the approaching dead. They were coming fast, faster than the freaking gas was pumping. At fifteen gallons the zombies were at the edge of the Truck Stop parking lot. I had to pull the nozzle out and secure the lid to the tank. Suddenly with the nozzle still in my hand I got a wonderful idea. I pulled back on the trigger, used the little trigger lock to keep it flowing and threw the spewing nozzle on the ground. I got into the car and started it up and waited.

"What are you doing?"

Taylor asked me as he grimaced at the sight of the gasoline gushing onto the ground.

"We're going to BBQ us some zombies."

I took the pistol from him and rolled up the windows and locked the doors. The gasoline was covering the ground all around the car. Sitting there with the engine running was actually quite dangerous but at this point I didn't care. I was willing to risk it for the sake of taking out a couple dozen zombies. Suddenly the zombies were all over us. They were scratching at the windows and rocking the little Spark, smearing their putrid rotting goo all over the nice new paintjob. I waited till all of them were surrounding the car, then I quickly pulled away, running over several of them, popping a couple of skulls under the tires like squeezing an over ripe TIC. As I pulled away, most of the zombies just stood there in the puddle of gasoline with expressions that looked like they were trying to figure out where I was going. Before they could gather their wits and start to follow again, I aimed the pistol at the ground where they were standing and squeezed off a shot. Suddenly the group of about two dozen or more zombies went up in flames like the 4th of July. I know it's a bit sick but my heart leapt with joy as I sped off leaving the burning zombie bonfire in my rearview mirror. Minutes later as the glowing flames disappeared over the horizon behind us, there was a sudden flash of light. It was the entire truck stop exploding, leaving a mushroom cloud of smoke rising into the evening sky.

The sun had set and the darkness up ahead was a frightful sight, knowing what was lurking around in it. The little Spark moving down the road at 70 miles an hour was all that protected us from the things that really did go bump in the night. I had just passed the municipal airport sign and saw the burned out car where I had met Taylors sister just weeks before and I knew I would be back at Eternal Slumber's headquarters within ten minutes. What would I find there? Were there really other people still sleeping in cryo stasis and if so would they be angry at me for waking them up in this horrible new world? Was I doing it just for me, because I needed to have normal people around me to make life a bit more palatable? I was really starting to second guess what I was planning to do. I looked over at Taylor, who had crawled up into the front seat with Rufio. He had his sleepy head propped up against the window and was fast asleep. I knew my brain could explode any minute and I would be gone. Hell I was pretty damn surprised it hadn't happened yet, with all the stress I had been though the last few weeks. If I were to die, where would that leave Taylor? Can you imagine a boy and his dog alone in this place?

Even the girl probably wasn't long for this world, with that bite on her arm, and if Rufio's aneurism took him then Taylor would be completely alone. He would not only be alone but he'd be alone with a potential five year old zombie waiting to happen. I knew it was the right thing to do. Waking any other potential survivors would at least leave someone with Taylor in the event that my brain gave out. I was already on borrowed time and only God knew when I'd kick the bucket. I passed the old woman's house with the cats. God I didn't miss that place, but seeing it made me know that Eternal Slumber was just up the road and no sooner had I thought the thought and there it was. The building that I had fought so hard to get out of, the place where I had to fight the keys away from Phil, my first real zombie threat. I thought back to all that had happened since I had woken up. Over the weeks my emaciated body had gotten strong and some fat had even accumulated and padded my once skin and bone physique. I didn't know what to expect when I got there, but I was ready for anything.

As I pulled up into the parking lot everything was dark. The building had absolutely no signs of life but I was hoping that meant no one or nothing had disturbed it since I left weeks before. Becky was still asleep so I carried her inside leaving Taylor to carry just the backpack and cleaver. I had the pistol with me just in case. The girl seemed to be fine. Her bite didn't look infected and she didn't have a fever. I would have thought if she was going to become one of them, she would be showing signs by now. The building was dark except for the flashlight I had gotten from one of Mac's duffle bags. I knew I had to do a thorough search of the building but it really could wait till morning, so I placed the sleeping girl on one of the cushy couches in the lobby and we settled down there for the remainder of the night. I however didn't sleep a wink, but Taylor and the girl did.

The moment the sun was up and the first rays of light shone through the front windows, I decided to leave Taylor and Becky sleeping and take a look around. The first bit of business was to find and identify the electrical source if there was one. I flipped a switch in the hall and the lights flickered to life, so I knew there had to be some elaborate generator system, but where was it? Just past the café was a pair of official looking doors that had a sliding bolt lock on them. It was locked from the outside and I was surprised that I had not noticed them before. They had one of those 'No Unauthorized Personnel' signs on them so I investigated. Just past the doors was a staircase that led down into a basement. I remembered Dr. Benson's recorded diary and his mention of Mrs. Morehead being locked up in the basement morgue, so I proceeded with caution and prepared myself mentally for any sudden surprises. At the bottom of the stairs was a long hallway with some doors that led off to the left. There it was… the sign I was hoping to find. It read 'Generator Room'. I opened the doors and cautiously went inside. I left the hallway door opened so I could make a speedy exit if something unexpected reared its ugly head.

The walls to the generator room were covered with buttons and monitors and off in one corner of the room were two huge generators, but neither of them was on. I flipped the light switch and the lights came on but the generators still stood there silent. I was puzzled as to how this building could have electricity when the generators were not activated. I looked around some more and noticed what looked like about ten huge battery looking things lined up against the opposite wall. They were all wired up to cables that ran along the side and disappeared into the ceiling. Then it dawned on me. I wasn't familiar with electrical storage technology or devices like the ones I was seeing, but I realized the only way this place was able to function was if it had a permanent supply of electricity and the only answer had to be solar energy. I could only guess that there must have been a network of solar panels on the roof of the building and what I was seeing in front of me were the storage units that collected and stored it. That was very good news as far as I was concerned. This meant we could clean out the premises and take up residence here and have an endless supply of power with generators as a plus to back up the system if something went wrong. Halle-fucking-luiah my plan was sounding better and better. I smiled at the thought of securing the outer gates to protect us and cultivating the land and planting gardens for food… hell the possibilities were limitless. Suddenly my daydreaming was rudely interrupted by a putrid smell. I thought I heard a soft moan as well so I ran to the hall and stuck my head out. There was nothing there. I glanced at the stairwell and then back down toward the other end of the hall where I had not been and I could see nothing. I let out a sigh, because I had been holding my breath subconsciously out of fright. I chalked it up to my imagination and decided to go down the hall and explore further. There was what looked like an employee break room across the generator room and another door at the end of the hall. That's where I was heading. I got to the end of the hall and saw two double doors with a plaque on one of them that read 'MORGUE'. The door on the right was ajar and there was something smeared on the edge, like someone with a greasy hand had pushed the door open. I was about to open the door when something on the floor caught my eye. I reached down and picked it up and examined it closely. It was a hospital wrist band that looked like it had been bitten off. My heart almost stopped when I read the name on the tag, MOREHEAD.

Suddenly there was a scream. It was the scream of a little girl and it came from above in the direction of the lobby. The realization that I had not been imagining things, hit me like a brick. I had heard the moan and smelled the distinctive aroma of death and I knew exactly what it had to be. I cocked the pistol and ran as fast as I could back to the stairwell busting through the doors and back into the lobby. There she was, the bitch who started all this crap and she had Taylor pinned to the ground.

"Bill, help me!"

He yelled when he saw me emerge from the basement. The putrid naked old woman had the boys arms pinned to the floor and her gaping maw was snapping at him with the ferocity of a wild dog. She was a horrid sight with her sagging rotting breasts flailing around like potatoes in a pair of pantyhose. Her jaw full of jagged teeth had the skin ripped away and head full of long white hair was matted with four month old dried blood. Luckily Taylor had the strength presence of mind to place his foot against her chest keeping her snapping mouth just out of reach of his tender neck. It seemed she had knocked the gun out of his hand leaving him helpless to do anything. The rotting putrid bitch hadn't seen me yet, so I ran up behind her and planted the pistol handle into the side of her head with enough force to knock her off the boy. As she tumbled to the ground, Taylor rolled to one side and grabbed the pistol and before I could get off a shot, he unloaded the cylinder into the old woman's chest, but it had little effect. With unbelievable speed the old woman jumped to her feet and came at me, but I was ready. I lifted the barrel of my pistol and planted it into her gaping mouth and pulled the trigger. The force of the blast took the back of her head right off, sending dried blood and brain matter across the lobby leaving her headless body standing there like some horrible emaciated mannequin, but before she could collapse onto the ground, Taylor flew by me, screaming and tackled her headless body to the ground.

"You stupid old bitch!"

He yelled as he pounded his fists into the dead woman's chest with tears running down his face.

"DIE, YOU STIPID SMELLY UGLY BITCH!"

I dropped the gun and grabbed the boy. He was crying hysterically, out of his mind with rage. I could only guess he had finally snapped from the trauma of the moment. As long as I had known him, he was calm and collected in every situation, but he had finally had enough. I hugged him tight and let him cry into my chest. My knees buckled and we both collapsed on the ground. We both cried and then to make things even more dramatic, Becky ran up and hugged us both and we all just sat there on the ground and had the first good cry any of us had had since all this had started. I held the two kids in my arms for what seemed like hours, until finally the tears were gone and we all had gathered our wits about us. I called Rufio over to us and gave him a big hug and told the kids it was all going to be alright. The worst was over for the moment and we were safe. At least I hoped we were… I hated that I could not promise them that, but for the moment we all believed it… we had to believe it… or all would be lost.

I stood in the front door of the building, the sun on my face, smoking my last Cohiba. It wasn't a pretty sight. The front gate to the complex was teaming with the living dead. I recognized a few from the truck stop. They were charred and burned. I knew they had followed the car down the road until they found us. If that wasn't bad enough, they brought friends with them. There were probably a hundred or more. I never bothered to count them. The level of decomposition was horrible. Some of them could barely move but some of them looked like fresh kills. It just goes to show you that while I was out there, hoping to find survivors, they were there. Out there wanting to be found, but I failed. I just didn't know where to look. Things have been quiet, giving me time to sit down and write this journal of what's been going on in my new life and the rest of the world since I woke up. I don't know if anyone will ever read this but it's therapeutic just to write this shit down.

It is June 10th 2016 and it's been well over six months since Taylor, Becky and I came back to the complex. Not long after dispatching that Morehead bitch, I found the room, the room with all the intact cryo chambers in it. I knew some of them would be pissed off at me for waking them up in such a world, and some were, but they seemed to get over it after a while. Once I was able to actually sit down and have a conversation with Becky I found out the 'bite' on her arm was actually a cut and it had been caused by her brother that died. It wasn't infected and she's as healthy as an ox, which is nice to know since Mac gave up his life to save her. Rufio and Taylor are good and as inseparable as a boy and his dog can be. The area between the building and the fence is plenty enough room for them to run and play and for us to plant some small gardens where we're growing vegetables and some fruit trees. Things have been good and the 'sensational seven' so I call them, are just happy to be alive. Pretty much all of us with the exception of Taylor and Becky are living on borrowed time and we know it but that just gives us a reason to cherish each day we're given. We had to make some room in our yard for a couple of graves. Two out of the nine I revived, that didn't last long after resuscitation. Their bodies were just too riddled with cancer to be able to last long. They at least had a few good weeks out of the cryo chamber before they gave up the ghost. The seven that survived, plus Taylor, Becky and I make up ten in all. We may be all that's left alive in this world full of the walking dead. We're all very different but we have no choice but to put our prejudices aside and get along. The two gay guys, Matt Shafer and Brian Keitherson both had rich families that froze them back in the late 80's when they found out they had HIV. One is a hairdresser and the other is an interior decorator. Very cliché I know, but their skills certainly come in handy. The place looks much better since Brian has been awake and my hair has never looked better. Kathy Riggs, who is actually pretty damn hot, had a rich husband 20 years ago when she was put under. Seems she had breast cancer and decided to be frozen since it was too far along to be cured. She is an entertainer, a ventriloquist to be exact, so she gives us all a good laugh with a make-shift dummy she fashioned out of some old cushions and a mop head. John Watts, whom I've become really good friends with, is a doctor of all things. He was frozen just days after me it seems, with a diagnosis of incurable prostate cancer. He's been great trying to keep everyone healthy and he's one of the smartest guys I've ever known. The only asshole in the group is old Bob Blomendal. He was some big-wig movie producer back in the day and every day he makes me more and more sorry I ever woke him up. Oh well shit happens, right? The last two of the seven are Deborah Lance and Max Sullivan. She's a sweet housewife whose rich husband put her in cryo about ten years ago due to her lymphoma. She seems as healthy as can be and she has one of those "little firecracker" personalities. Maxwell is a sweet kid. He's 15 years old, or was when he was put to sleep a few years back. It seems he was diagnosed with leukemia and didn't have very long to live. Well that's the one thing we all have in common and that is why we are all misfits destine to run out of time, but hey, none of us are promised a tomorrow so we've all pretty much decided to live like there isn't going to be one. The one thing that has been on my mind though is that as crazy as my story is, there are others…. there have to be others out there who have a story to tell, of how they survived and are hopefully still surviving this sick fucked up world.

More later… there has to be more…

REANIMATED DIARY

May 15, 2015

I've decided to start writing things down every time I get the chance. It's not easy to stop moving and take a breath without getting your head ripped off. I can barely gather my thoughts with the constant banging coming from downstairs. Those fucking things just won't stop! I've managed to barricade myself in the upstairs apartment of some convenience store. I'm trying to get out of the city but it's tough with all those things out there roaming around. This place is safe, at least for the night, as I've been able to tightly secure it by blocking the only door in. As luck would have it, there is a window with a fire escape that leads to a fenced-in alley that is clear. Hopefully, I can get out that way in the morning, but there's no going out the way I came in because they know I'm here.

If you had told me three weeks ago that I would be here right now in this place, shitting my pants because flesh eating cannibals were trying to smash in the door, I would have told you to go see a shrink. I guess this is what I get for being such a selfish ass. I should have paid more attention weeks ago when they were talking about the virus. Some virus that originated in some medical facility in upper state New York that was let out when some infected patients escaped. I never would have believed it could spread so fast, like wild fire.

Like the prick that I am, I had been so focused on ME, not giving a shit about what was going on in the world outside my condo, that it finally came back and bit me on the ass… my name is Vance Singleton. Three weeks ago I was a successful businessman, living in my Manhattan penthouse condo looking down my nose at the rest of the world, but today I'm hunted prey running for my fucking life. I will NEVER…. EVER…. Forget the date May 10th 2015. If I live another day, or 50 more years, that day is a day I won't be able to forget. It's the day my life changed forever….

I stopped writing last night because something happened and I didn't have it in me to continue, so I'll pick up where I left off in a minute. But first, as I wrote last night, I heard something on the fire escape. You know the one that was supposed to be my safe exit. It was one of those things. I guess it was my light. I keep forgetting those fuckers are smarter than I give them credit for. Anyway, seems the bastard pulled himself up the ladder and made his way to my window. The only weapons I have with me at the moment are a baseball bat, a large butcher knife and my .22 caliber pistol. I wasn't about to fire that thing and let every pus bag on the block know where I am, so I dispatched that fucker with a well-placed blade through the center of his skull. It's unsettling how simple it's become to end someone's life. Killing has become a hell of a lot easier the last few days, but I'm not sure I'd even call this killing! How do you kill something that's already dead? I haven't been able to do much looting yet, but I hope to find some better weapons once I'm out of the downtown area.

Anyway, I wanted to finish what I was saying about May 10th. It was about 5:30pm on a Monday. I had been listening to the news on the television for days, you know in one ear and out the other. They had been talking about some virus that had been spreading through the state. Something about a cryogenics lab up north that had been using some bogus chemical in their freezing process that caused adverse effects on their patients, causing them to become hostile and dangerous.... Well they got out somehow, and it was spreading like wild fire. It sounded like some science fiction bullshit to me, but now I am sorry I hadn't given it more credence, but I guess that's just me. I still shit my pants when I think about what I was forced to do, but I guess you never know what you have in you until the time comes. It was approaching dusk and I was on my balcony, of all places, doing some writing on my computer and smoking a cigar. I remember so vividly how I sat there, trying to decide whether I wanted to make a cup of coffee or not (sometimes I'm just too damned lazy to use that fucking cappuccino machine) but when I finally decided to do it, I suddenly heard a loud thump on my front door.

I looked out of the peephole in the door but didn't see anything but shadows. I could only hear moans and then a scream come from down the hall. I hooked the chain-lock and made sure the door was bolted and, believe it or not, I started back to the kitchen. Looking back now, I realize I was in some state of denial. I knew deep down inside that the world was falling apart outside those doors, but I was determined to go on with business as usual. You know…. Ignore it until it went away. I spent my life doing that sort of thing when I was faced with something I didn't want to deal with. That's when it happened. I turned to go back to the balcony, walking through my overpriced condo full of overpriced furniture, when suddenly there was an ear-splitting crash and the door burst open.

I quickly spun round to face the door and there to my horror stood Mr. Garza the doorman. He looked horrible with his blood-soaked uniform and his gaping hollow abdomen. He looked like a fish that had just been gutted. Behind him was a group of six or seven building residents. Most of them I either had known or had seen in the elevator, but they were all bloody and mangled, and were nothing like they had been the last time I saw them. Mrs. Bennet had one of her eyeballs dangling on what was left of her bloody cheek and the lower jaw of Mr. Jenkins, my neighbor, looked as though it had been ripped from his face completely, leaving his tongue twisting and writhing like an oversized purple slug. It was a horrible sight and all I could think to do was run back to the balcony.

As I made my way through the den, I almost stumbled over my roll top desk and that's when I remembered my pistol. I hurriedly opened the secret drawer in the bottom of the desk and grabbed my .22 pistol and the small box of shells. I didn't dare look back but I could hear Mr. Garza and the others lumbering through the living room behind me and stumbling over the furniture. I ran the last ten feet to the balcony and started to slide the French doors shut, but Mr. Garza and Mr. Jenkins were too fast for me. They were right behind me and made it onto the balcony, squeezing through the door just as I pushed it shut.

Mr. Jenkins tripped on the metal track of the sliding door, and fell on the tiled balcony floor, but Mr. Garza was quickly up in my face. I took my gun and placed it under his chin and pulled the trigger. CLICK! It wasn't loaded! SHIT... I knew I had to think fast, so I dropped the gun and grabbed him by the throat and pushed him over the balcony railing, sending him to what I hoped was another death 21 floors below. Now I had to deal with Mr. Jenkins, who was fumbling to his feet. As I grabbed the top of his head, I noticed that a crowd of those horrid things had already gathered in my den and were already banging on the French doors to the balcony. I shoved my fist into the gaping hole that was Mr. Jenkin's mouth and used his head like a boxing glove, (avoiding the teeth) smashing it against the outer brick walls of the balcony. It was actually that fake "brickette" shit they installed for aesthetics but it was hard and it did the trick. The pummeling of Mr. Jenkins head didn't kill him, but it left a huge bloodstain on the fake bricks and dazed him enough that I was able to pull him over to the rail and send him over the side as well. Two down... ten to go.... OH SHIT... make that twenty!

The crowd of zombies in my den was growing by the second. It was as if every dead pus bag in the building knew there was fresh meat on the balcony in 21-05. I was thanking my lucky stars that when the contractor was doing the renovations to my condo a year before, I had him install those fancy French doors with extra thick safety glass. I had lived in another condo years before where there had been some break-ins when the intruders had gained access through the residents' balconies, so I was thinking about the crime rate in New York when I had them installed. Little did I know it would be blood-thirsty zombies that would eventually make them pay for themselves. When the contractor installed them originally, I had found it odd that they came with two locks, one on the inside and one on the outside, so you could lock intruders out no matter which side of the glass you were on. Odd? HELL NO! Now I was singing their praises!

I sat there in shock for an hour, shaking like a whipped puppy, watching my dead neighbors smear blood, pus and fecal matter all over my French doors, but the glass was holding and they couldn't get though. As I stood there looking 21 stories down at the slow but certain demise of the city I had called home for over 20 years, I knew I was trapped and it would take a miracle to find a way off of this prison balcony. A gun, an empty coffee cup, and my laptop were the only things I had on the balcony with me. Well, that and some large potted plants, but they were pretty much useless. I had left my cell phone on the table next to the couch so I had no way of trying to call for help. I had no way of knowing how far this virus (as they were calling it on the news) had spread. Was there even anyone out there to help? The wireless Internet was still working, so I used my laptop to try and message someone... anyone. I tried Skype and Oovoo and every other messaging program I had to try to contact someone, but there wasn't anyone out there. I even logged onto Facebook and tried to contact one of my two friends on my list but nobody was online. Go Figure! It was just me, my balcony and a 21-storey drop straight down. I knew I was in for one hell of a night.

It seemed like it took for fucking ever but the morning finally came, May 16th 5.00am and the sun was peeking over the horizon. Between my dead neighbors pounding on my balcony doors and the distant screams and explosions through the city, I had gotten a grand total of maybe 20 minutes of sleep. I would have given my left arm and both testicles for a rope, but that just wasn't going to happen, so I had to start being creative and come up with a way to get off that balcony without falling 21 floors to my death. I could see Mr. Garza and Mr. Jenkins down below. They were both writhing on the parking lot asphalt below. Every bone in their bodies was probably broken but they were both still alive. They looked like little ants with broken legs wiggling around on the ground.

I did some investigating and noticed that the barrier between units on the balcony had ornate rod iron fixtures that ran down the length of the outer wall of the building, making it possible to climb down to the units below. Now all I had to do was conjure up the guts to climb out over my balcony rail and make my way down. Suddenly, I heard a loud thud, followed by a faint CRACKING sound. I looked at the rabid corpses in my den (now there had to be at least 50 of them) and one of them, a man I didn't recognize from my building, had grabbed a tiffany lamp my ex-wife had gotten me for one of our anniversaries and he was using it to try to smash through the safety glass.... and it seemed to be working. I don't know how many pounds of pressure the glass was designed to take before it gave way, but I am guessing 50 zombies and a tiffany lamp was pushing the limits, so I started taking some deep breaths because I knew within a few minutes I would have to grow a pair and take the proverbial "plunge".

I had just leaned out and grabbed a hold of the rod iron fixture when I heard the sound of shattering glass behind me. I jumped over the railing just as the balcony filled with putrid corpses that were rambling like crazy to get at me. They were fighting each other to get as close as possible, even pushing each other over the rail like wild animals in a feeding frenzy. I was able to get a foothold on the balcony rail under me and to hold on for dear life as they reached out with their mangled tattered claws, trying to grab me, but I was just out of their reach. It must have been adrenaline that kept me going as I climbed down from one fixture to the next but I didn't dare look down because I knew I would freeze in terror.

To be on the safe side, I climbed down three floors to a unit under mine, which I knew to be empty. I just happened to know the people who owned it and knew that they had been away on a holiday to Europe for at least a month. I climbed onto their balcony and busted into the empty condo. That's where I got the baseball bat and the butcher knife from their kitchen. Too bad the liberal bastards were anti firearms, because it would have been just too perfect to happen across another good weapon, but no dice. Anyway, that was then and this is now....

May 17th 2015

7:45 am: I actually slept in a drainage pipe last night. It ran under the highway and seemed safe, but I didn't get much sleep. I could hear the moans and shuffling feet of those bastards all night. A couple of them got way too close for comfort but the upside of it all was that when the sun came up I could see that there was a small strip mall nearby that happened to have a pawn shop next to a 7-Eleven. Whoopee fucking do! The things that excite you in times like this.

8:00 am: The pawn shop was a washout. The place was locked up as tight as a drum and the glass windows were barred, so getting in would have meant a shit-load of noise and I just can't afford that. Most pawn shops have tons of guns but I can't take the chance to find out. As I was sneaking up to the 7-Eleven, I noticed a small group of corpses lumbering a ways up the street. They had no idea I was there but they made me nervous as hell. I traded out the duffle bag I'd been toting around with me for a backpack. The 7-Eleven had a nice display of them on the back wall. Everything from the kind designed to carry your laptop, to the small schoolgirl version with Hello Kitty on them. I opted for a large manly one that would carry a ton of shit.

I was forced to pick the lock to the front door (a skill I had learned in my college days) so I knew that the place most likely hadn't been looted much, if at all. I was pleasantly surprised to find it hadn't been, and there was an abundance of food. Some of the bread products were still edible and the power was still on, so the refrigerated items were still okay for the most part. I stuffed as many canned goods as I could in my pack, along with a couple of packages of hot dogs that I knew I would eat before they spoiled. I knew it was only a matter of time before the power grids were off and civilization would dissolve into oblivion eventually, so I was going to take full advantage of what I could scrounge at the moment. I had never seen a 7-Eleven quite as large as this one, and it sort of looked like it had been converted from something else, as it didn't have the same layout as most 7-Elevens I had been in. Anyway, I am going to hang here a while and open a can of spam. I love that stuff.

8:45am: I was right. This particular 7-Eleven has a huge walk-in freezer in the back, just next to an exit that leads to the alley (which was unlocked, so my lock picking was a waste of time). I noticed there were signs of a struggle back here and evidence that this place had been overrun by the dead at some point, and then I made the most gruesome discovery I have ever seen in my life. When I opened the freezer, I found what I could only guess as having been a family of four trying to barricade themselves from a group of the living dead. They are dead and I mean really dead, not the 'die and then start twitching around eventually coming back to life' sort of dead. They have been here for a long time, as they are frozen solid and caked over with frost like some morbid family of snowmen. I'm not making a sick joke; I'm just trying to describe it. It's a shame because from what I can see none of them were bitten, they just went into the freezer to wait it out, not taking into account that those fuckers take their sweet time when it comes to leaving. I learned a long time ago you don't try to "wait them out" because it's not going to happen. They only leave when they think there isn't any food left. I stuffed a few pizza pockets and frozen burritos into my pack and left.

Who cares what time it is..... I don't know why I am writing this shit down. I guess it's a way of keeping me sane. I don't know and I doubt anyone will ever read it, but fuck it. It makes me focus on something besides surviving. It's been exactly a week since I did a Bruce Willis off the balcony of my condo and I've probably traveled a grand total of 20 miles. I am on the outskirts of the city but things are not much better. I'm still ducking and weaving from car to car in parking lots and scurrying through alleys like a sewer rat. This just isn't any kind of life. But I guess it beats the hell out of the alternative.

3:20pm: I have managed to get out of the city by way of the highway. It's littered with abandoned cars, some of which still have the owners decaying inside. I saw a few that had turned after being attacked and bitten, but were trapped inside their vehicles. It's creepy and a bit sad that they are trapped there for eternity, but I'll be dammed if I'm gonna be the one to teach them how to use the fucking door handle. At the moment, I'm sitting in the cab of a semi-truck abandoned on the highway. It's one of those sleeper cabs and I'm very tempted to stay here tonight, but it's just too early. If I knew how to drive one and it wasn't such a diesel hog I would try using it to go north.... Go where? I don't know but I think north is a good bet. It's going to get cold, but that just might be a big plus. Up the road a couple of miles I can see what looks like a farmhouse. Earlier, back down the highway a bit, I found a gun shop. I abandoned my trusty .22 that I've been afraid to even use, for a .44 mag. I just figure it's better to blow their heads off than just make a hole in it. I loaded my pack down the rest of the way with ammo and grabbed some binoculars. I would have done a bit more window-shopping but that particular strip mall was teaming with those things.

5:00pm: It took me what seemed like forever to get to the farmhouse. Upon approaching the house, the first thing I noticed was the classic 1967 VW bug in a garage off the barn. I had one like it back in college and it given the great gas mileage and mobility, it would be a great way to make my way up north. The moment I walked up on the porch I knew I wasn't alone. I pulled the .44 mag out of my belt and squeezed it tightly in my fist. The front door was ajar and the immediate area was empty. The place smelled of rot and there was a sound, like someone moving around down the hall, that I could faintly make out. I whispered loudly to see if anyone "living" was there, but the minute my voice echoed down the hall the banging started…

7:35pm: The banging has been going on almost nonstop for two hours. I decided to stay the night here in the farmhouse but I am going to have to deal with the fucker in the back room. Earlier I went out and checked on the VW. It seems in good shape. I found the keys on the dresser in the bedroom and was able to start the engine; however, it was only for a few seconds. Can't make any loud noises or you end up with an instant fan club. I traded my kitchen butcher knife for a machete I found while rummaging around in the barn. I found a pitchfork as well, and figured it would be the perfect weapon to use against whomever or whatever is in that back bedroom. I got down on my knees in the hall and looked under the door, and as far as I can tell there is only one of those things in the room. I only saw one shadow and one set of feet from under the door…. I'm going to go deal with it…. be back later…

8:30pm: OH MY GOD…. OH MY GOD…. OH MY FUCKING GOD!!!! I can barely write… my hands are still shaking. I can't believe what I found in the back bedroom of this FUCKING house. What kind of sick fucks lived here? I still have the taste of my own vomit in my throat from where I lost it back in the bedroom. When I pushed the door opened, the smell almost knocked me over. If I have pieced correctly what happened here, I would have to gather that the people who lived here had two twin boys around the age of seven or eight. I can only guess that one of them turned and then bit the other one, because what I found when I entered that room were two twin boys handcuffed to opposite ends of a large wooden bed frame. One of them was significantly more decomposed than the other and they had obviously been feeding on each other. Both boys were turned and both undead and they had probably been locked in the room and left there for a week or two. The room was wall-to-wall blood and pus and god-only-knows what other bodily fluids those boys had smeared around, but how could parents leave two boys behind like that. If they turned into bloodthirsty zombies while their parents were around they should have put them out of their misery. God... I am so sick to my stomach and having to lop off those boys' heads didn't help.... I'm going to try, and I stress TRY,... to get some sleep.

May 18ᵗʰ 2015

12:50pm: The VW ran like a charm, getting me to highway 87 and all the way to Kingston. The highway was littered with hundreds of vehicles but the bug was able to maneuver in and out of the abandoned traffic. It probably took twice the time it would have on a normal non-zombie apocalypse day, but, hey, I'm here. As I write this, I am sitting at a roadside park three miles outside of Kingston. I found a map in the glove box of the bug and, having looked it over, I have come up with a plan. I plan to make my way north east up to Ticonderoga and find some sort of lakeside boathouse on Lake Champlain so I can make my way up to Canada in a boat, which should be much less problematic. I am sure I can probably find lakeside fueling facilities up and down the shores of the lake and who knows.... I may even end up with the dream boat I've always wanted.... Hang on... I hear something moving over by the bathrooms. I'm going to check it out!

1:20pm: The Bitch almost bit me. Shit, I need to be more careful. I should really stop going an investigating every fucking sound I hear. I guess I just have this burning desire to actually find a survivor somewhere. I heard a can banging around in the woman's restroom so I went inside. The woman inside the restroom had once been someone's dear old granny. Sweet old cookie baking demeanor aside, she was now a withered old hag with about a month's worth of ROT that made her look more like a wild-eyed ghoul. Those things can hear pretty dam well because the moment I entered the restroom, the bitch came flying out of a stall and tried to rip out my throat. The machete I picked up back at the farm came in really handy. I'm zero for on the head count. Okay, time to take a piss and move on.

5:55pm: I got into Ticonderoga about 30 minutes ago. The bug's engine was acting up so I pulled into a Motel 6 parking lot. I'm sitting here in the motel office, where it seems safe for now. Maybe I can stay the night here and get an early start. Power is still on and the place is empty. It's got one of those manager apartments that opens into the office area. I just checked around a bit and there is even frozen food in the fridge. I better take advantage of these sorts of little finds while they exist. The power grid won't stay on forever.... But that makes me wonder if it's still on because someone is maintaining it or if it simply hasn't broken down yet.

8:30pm: I woke to the sound of a loud THUD. I guess I had dozed off for a few hours on the couch, but now things are getting bad. THEY are out there. In the last couple of hours they have swarmed the place. I don't think they particularly know I'm here, but something has drawn them here. DAMN! I just heard a gunshot. As I'm sitting here writing this, I heard a gunshot and it's very nearby... sounded like it may have come from one of the rooms here in the motel. I can't help but guess that's what's brought them here. SHIT! There went another gunshot! I better go investigate. I'll write more later....

12:45am: I woke to the sound of another gun shot. My earlier investigation went nowhere, since I was unable to leave the office safely so I decided to draw the blinds on the office windows and get some sleep. Whoever is shooting has drawn a big crowd, but they seem to all be focused on direction of the gunshots and don't seem to know I'm here. Which is certainly good news for me. This motel is the type that has two floors with outside walkways running in front of the rooms and a central outside staircase, so there is no way to get to the survivor without going out into that crowd of pus bags and since they all seem to be congregating at the other end of the motel, I can only guess they are in one of the farthest rooms. I picked up the phone at the desk and it seemed to still be working but since I didn't know what room the survivor is in, I couldn't call them from the office. I sure did want to give them a piece of my mind and tell them to stop shooting their fucking gun! With their goddamned gun going off, things are only going to get worse.... Wait... it's the phone.... It's ringing and it's flashing the room number 207. I'm going to answer it and see who this idiot is.

2:00am: Her name is Andria. It seems she hiding in this Motel 6 for three days. The gunshot started when one of the zombies that has been stalking her for days made its way to the door of her room. The problem is that 1 zombie + 1 gunshot = 100 more zombies. She said she dispatched her original pursuer, but now she has a steady flow of corpses showing up at her motel room door, not to mention the fucking parking lot. I told her barricade the door and try to get some sleep and that I would come up with a plan and get her and I out of here safely. I'm supposed to call her back at 6.00am....time to make a plan!

May 19th 2015

6:45am: I'm sitting here looking at the leather binding of my diary thinking to myself that there will possibly never be another book bound anywhere on the planet. Never another story written, or another play produced, never another movie made, or another can of Coca-Cola canned. The world is falling apart and there's not a damned thing I can do about it. Andria is DEAD... or sort of dead.... however that works. A scream woke me up at 5.00am. I tried to call her room to see if she was okay and there was no answer. Through the window I could see the corpses swarming into her room, through the busted in door. I never even got to meet her. She was just a scared voice on the other end of a motel telephone... but still a real live living person. Would I ever meet another one?

8:00am: According to my map, the shore of Lake Champlain is about a mile from the highway. My bug is worthless but I think I can hoof it since it's mostly forest between here and there. The corpses had filled the parking lot. Even more of them showed up after they got into Andria's room. It's amazing how a fresh kill brings them out of the woodworks. I noticed how they reacted to the sound of the phone ringing in her room so I came up with a plan to leave the office without them seeing me. I looked at the motel layout and found the number to the room at the farthest end of the building, room 215 and dialed the room….I let it ring off the hook. The zombies could hear the phone from outside and eventually they made their way up the stairs and congregated at the door of that room. If there was anyone hiding in there, they are shit out of luck. But I had to do what I had to do. Hell, I got away without a scratch… I just hope it wasn't at someone else's expense.

10:30am: I never thought I would be saying "thank God for drug dealers" but today was my lucky day. Between the motel and the woods were a couple of streets I had to go through that looked like the "shady" part of town. You know the kind of place I wouldn't be caught dead in on a normal day. The street I went down had a few sleazy nightclubs located on it, and they must have been the kind of places that attracted the lowlifes and dirt bags in town because I found a black sedan crashed into the front of a strip club. In the sedan was a bag or what I can only guess is crystal meth (plastic bags of some sort of crystallized shit but I wouldn't know for sure cause I've never touched the shit) and a 9 mm pistol with a silencer. I couldn't have come across a genie and wished for a better weapon than this. The only down side is that there is only one extra clip of ammo besides the one in the pistol. I'm guessing 30 rounds all together. I'm not normally a gun-guy so I'm just guessing here.

I got to try out the silencer on my way through the woods when I had to go through the campground from hell. I could see the lake from the campground but between it and me was a small army of walking corpses. From where I was hiding, it looked like a Cub Scout leader and three of his scouts. I wonder if there is a merit badge for killing walking dead pus bags? Anyway, the three young teenaged zombies and their leader looked like they had been turned early on, probably when all this started. They were pretty ripe and I didn't want to get any closer than I had to. I used my silenced 9mm and shot them all in the head from 30 feet away. God, I love this gun. I need to find more ammo for it.

11:15am: Walking down a narrow portion of the lake, where the current was pretty strong, I saw a heavyset naked man without a head, floating down river. I can only guess he had been one of those things and someone dispatched him by separating him from his head. It was disgusting but by far not the most gruesome sight I've seen thus far. There is a boathouse gas station and restaurant just up ahead. I am hoping I can find a boat there that I can use to continue up river.

May 21st, 2015

When will I learn not to underestimate those pus bags? The last two days have been hell. I haven't updated this diary because I was overwhelmed by a group of those bastards and I dropped my backpack and wasn't able to get to it for two days. When I was making my way up the riverbank, I ended up finding what looked like the perfect boathouse complete with a few motor boats and some larger ones. The minute I started toward the marina, an army of those fuckers came at me. They saw me before I saw them. It turned out that the fat man floating in the river wasn't dead…. Or completely dead…. Oh fuck, you know what I mean. His head must have been under water making it look like he was headless and, at some point, I don't know when, he got out of the water and started following me. I saw him first. I was squatting in the bushes checking out the marina when I heard a snapping twig behind me. I turned and it was him. I recognized that bloated naked body immediately… shiny rubbery skin blown up like some morbid balloon animal. Slashed purple lacerations all over his torso and legs and, now that I could see his face, I almost wanted to puke at the sight of his puffed up lips and swollen eyelids. I have no idea how he could see me as his eyes were swollen so tightly shut. I wasn't going to fuck around with him so I dispatched him quickly with my machete….in case you are wondering… now…. he really is headless!

Seeing the fat man urged me to make a run for the marina and that's when the army of darkness decided I was their new meal. There was an alley between an old fish and tackle shop and the Marina and that is where the horde (at least 20 of them) came from. When I first saw them, they were literally about ten feet away from me, so priority one was to get across the parking lot alive, so when I stumbled and dropped my backpack, there was no stopping to pick it up. I didn't make it to the marina but I was able to zigzag my way across the street to the garage of a gas station and that's where I was for two days.

There was junk food in a vending machine and bottled water in the refrigerators that were still working, THANK GOD! So not having my backpack wasn't that big of an issue at the moment, but I knew I needed to get it back. The garage was connected to a small convenience store area but there was a separate office in the back that I was locked out of, but I was completely fine with that, since I could hear something moving around behind the door. I'd be lying if I said I wasn't curious, because I couldn't help but think there was a small chance that the sound was coming from some poor fool who was hiding and still very much alive. I knew the chances of that were small but I guess I was always looking for a reason to hope.

I waited a few minutes quietly to see if there was any rhythm to the sound behind the door. You know, a phone receiver dangling from the cord or an oscillating fan left on.... That sort of thing, but the noise was clearly someone or something moving around in the office and my gut was telling me to leave it be. My curiosity got the best of me and I pressed my ear against the door to try to hear telltale sounds of some undead pus bag lumbering around in the office. Sure enough, when I stopped and listened closely, I could hear a wheezing gurgling sound accompanied by an occasional moan. I decided to leave it alone.

The marina was pretty close but it could have been a hundred miles away for the good it did me. I laid there listening to the groaning coming from the office and thinking about how the hell to distract those pus bags outside long enough to get my pack and high tail it to the marina. Then I got what I still think was a brilliant idea. I had been in that fucking gas station garage for 48 hours and why I didn't think of if it before.... I could have kicked myself! The front door to the convenient store portion of the gas station had one of those cheesy motion sensor noisemakers that went off when a customer came in the door. You know, sort of the modern version of those old timey tinkle bell that were hit by the door when it opened and closed, alerting the shop owner of a new customer. Well the modern motion sensor doorbell came in a variety of noises. There was everything from croaking frogs to birds chirping to cats meowing and even barking dogs…. Oh, and I think you could even get a cow mooing. Anyway, I hadn't checked to see if this one worked as I was not about to make any more noise than I had to, but I carefully ripped the thing off the wall and, thank god, it had its own battery pack.

I took the sensor and duct taped it between two tennis balls (the convenience store happened to have a sporting goods shelf, thank god) to give it a bit of cushion when it landed in the field on the other side of the store. My plan was to throw the sensor out there and hope one of those fuckers shambled near enough to make it chirp. When one of them hears the chirp, and more are drawn over, the more there are, the more it will chirp, and the more it chirps, the more will be drawn over. I went to the side of the garage that was opposite my pack and the marina and opened a window. There in a grassy filed were about three of those fuckers meandering around. It was perfect. I threw the "noise bomb" over to where the three pus bags were. The thing hit one of them in the face and landed at another ones foot. It let out a loud chirp the moment it hit the ground. The sound could not have been more perfect. It was a barking dog, but it had that "little yappy dog" sound to it and it was earsplitting. It must have annoyed the shop assistant to death before the end of the world happened.

The three zombies were instantly agitated. They looked around to find the souse of the noise but in the semi-tall grass they could not find it, but every time they moved it yapped. It worked like a charm. The more they moved the more it yapped and the more it yapped the more of them came to investigate. It would go on like this until the battery ran out. Within 15 minutes every pus bag that had been mulling around in the parking lot, between me and my back pack had gone to the back of the building for some "yapping dog." Only to find disappointment, I might add.

After loading up a sack with some fresh supplies, when the coast was clear, I opened the door to the shop, ran out across the parking lot, grabbed my pack and got my ass to the marina as fast as my legs would take me. That's where I am now and I'm feeling the love! *NOTE TO READER… when you're putting together your zombie survival kit, add a few of those annoying yappy door ringers. They come in REAL FUCKING handy!

May 24th 2015

There was nothing but death and decay in the marina, but I'm happy to report that none of them were up walking around. They were just poor bastards that had become various sundry meals for the pus bags. I am guessing someone had dispatched them all because they all had various head traumas that kept them from "coming back", I'm guessing. I dragged the corpses into a broom closet and sealed them up in there and spent the night in the marina. There were plenty of petrol cans and fuel to fill them with so I loaded up. I had been right when I thought I had seen a houseboat from down the river. When I got to the marina there it was in all its glory. I am in it now. It's a 2001 Fantasy 17x82 and it is loaded. It's got to be brand new. It probably belonged to some gazilionaire who had way to much fucking money to know what to do with… Anyway I don't think he'll mind my using it. My plan now is to get some much needed rest… the real kind that allows you to get a good night's sleep without having to worry about having your brains ripped out in your sleep. It's been nine days now since my escape from the balcony and I've been surviving, but that's all, just SURVIVING! Its damned lonely and I would love to actually find some other survivors, so that's what I plan to do. I am going to use the petrol I've stocked up and go up the river keeping my eyes out for survivors. The houseboat has a radio in it, but so far nothing.

May 25th 2015

I had anchored the boat out in the middle of the river. I can only guess I was near a sandbar or something because I awakened to a sound. Thank god I didn't move much, and only cracked an eyelid, because when I did, that's when I saw it… or her… or whatever! I laid there motionless. My mind brought me back to a podcast I had listened to online. This zombie movie enthusiast and his pal had an online show where they would talk about and review zombie movies. I had always been a fan, well, until now that is. It's a bit different when it's real. Anyway, in their podcast they always had listener questions they would talk about and one guy had written in and asked the question "Will zombies attack you if you're sleeping and not making noise?" I was thinking what a good question that was, back when I heard it, and the show host and his pal were talking about how noise attracts them usually so it might be possible to survive if you are asleep. Well, I had been and there it was and it hadn't even noticed me yet.

I was lying on the couch, asleep under a blanket, because it had been cold the night before. Somehow, this teen girl zombie had found her way into my houseboat. She was wet so I can only guess she had come up from under the water and pulled herself onto the deck at the stern the boat. At first, all I could do was thank my lucky stars I hadn't been snoring. I had slept with my machete so I was prepared for anything, but still it freaked the hell out of me that one of those fuckers could find me on the safety of a boat in the middle of the fucking river, talk about a false sense of security. I learned a huge lesson there. NOTE TO SELF… be sure to lock the fucking door to the aft deck from now on!

I am guessing the girl was about 15 years old. She was very messed up, with all the flesh ripped away from her left arm and a huge portion of her face gone. Her clothes were ripped to shreds and her ribcage was exposed on her right side. She had probably been a beautiful girl when she was alive, but now… she wasn't a pretty sight at all. She was just roaming around the galley, almost as if she were looking for something. I can only guess she could sense my living, breathing flesh, but didn't know how to pinpoint it with no sounds for reference.

I slowly pulled the cover off of me and I think she must have heard it, because at that very moment she turned to face me, and instantly her blank slack expression turned to disdain. She had found her prey and she was going to go after it with everything she had. As she lunged at me, I flew up from the couch and planted the machete into her neck. Her arms flailed around in a vain attempt to grab me, but I used the blade to push her back through the sliding glass doors to the deck and pushed her against the rail. With the machete blade through her neck, I angled the sharp side up and with an upward thrust, took off her head, sending her backward into the water where she had come from. Will the drama never end? I guess there is no rest for a zombie holocaust survivor.

I've read in zombie fiction novels and seen in some movies where they speculate about how zombies can survive under water. Given the fact that they are not able to, nor have any need to breathe, they are able to simply meander around on the bottom of any body of water, only at the mercy of the creatures down there that eventually nibble away at their rotting flesh. I would imagine they could stay animated down there for a long time, especially if the water at the bottom is particularly cold. Since I don't think they swim per se, I can only guess my visitor had walked up on a sand bar and it was shallow enough for her to pull herself up. The boat is equipped with a depth finder and, boy, am I ever going to start using the dam thing!

May 26th 2015

After dispatching the zombie teen, things were pretty quiet yesterday. The houseboat was a real find and it certainly gave me a sense of security. I've been making good time up the river and there should be a small town coming up, at least as far as the map indicates. Wait, I'll be right back....

I was right, I heard some gunshots and there is a town coming up portside. There are some survivors or at least I think there may be. Just offshore is a small shopping complex with some tall buildings that form what looks like a "town square". Just above the bank and trust there is a big sign hanging out of a window on what looks like the 4th floor. It says "Help". Since zombies don't shoot guns and the shots seemed to come from that direction I can only guess someone is alive... I mean REALLY alive. I want to get to them quickly. I don't want another situation like the one back at the motel. Plus, I really could use some company. It's just too fucking lonely and I'm afraid I'm going to lose my mind....

11:33pm: Well I'm still alive and I feel like it's just barely. I got shot in the arm... it just grazed the flesh but still WHAT THE FUCK! After anchoring my boat *(I named her Maxine after my mother)* I went ashore and made a beeline for a small motorcycle shop next to a Sears and Roebucks on the town square. It was closer to my position than the bank was. The cycle shop had a small generator shed just off of one side so I darted in there for cover. I had a good view of the bank, which was just on the other side of the square. I could see a woman at the window and she had what looked like a small caliber rifle in her hands. I tried to wave her down and get her attention and that's when I heard the shot. A bullet whizzed by me, stinging my right arm as it took a chunk of flesh with it. She saw me alright, and she thought I was one of them. Since when do zombies wave at you and try to get your attention? "Stupid bitch"

After tending my flesh wound, I grabbed my binoculars and scoped out the building adjacent to the bank. It seemed to be some sort of apartment building with one of those security doors with a list of tenants and their call buttons. It was securely shut, but there was a small band of pus bags banging on the door. I knew the only way I would get the small band of dead-heads away from the door was with a noisy distraction, just like the one I had come up with back at the garage. I looked through my pack to see what I had that would make some noise. Nothing! Only some food and my gun and a small glass of coke I had found in the boathouse fridge. When I found it, I remember stuffing it in my bag, thinking since it was one of the old fashioned glass bottles I might be able to break it and use it to smack one of those fuckers upside of the head if I found myself in a pinch for a weapon at some point. That's when I got the idea. I took off my watch, guzzled the coke *(I couldn't bear to waste it)* then I set the alarm on my watch to go off in one minute. I always hated that fucking watch because when I used the alarm, it was always so loud it got the attention of anyone within earshot. It went off one time when I was in a church at a funeral. Everyone in the place turned and looked at me with disdain. How embarrassing was that? It's ironic how what once embarrassed the hell out of me was now going to probably save my life. I fastened the watchband around the empty bottle and threw it in the direction of a large parking area on the far side of the square.

I waited for it… then there it was! SMASH! The bottle shattered in the parking lot, getting the attention of most of the pus bags gathered at the apartment complex door. First, only about five of the twenty or so zombies started to meander toward the sound of the breaking glass. The others just seemed to ignore it, but then the annoying chirping sound of the alarm went off. Suddenly, the remaining twenty or so zombie heads turned toward the sound and within seconds they were all wandering over toward the broken bottle. The moment their backs were to me, I made my move. I darted across the grass and ducked behind a statue of some old geezer with a sword in his hand… probably the founding father or something. Lucky for me, the woman in the window was watching the entire thing, so she knew I was coming.

When I got to the door of the apartment complex, I ran my finger down all the buttons and there was a faint voice on the intercom. "I'm in apartment 4-A" the woman's voice spoke and the door buzzed open. I was thinking that I had gotten pretty good at fooling those pus bags, but when I pulled the door opened, I glanced over at the crowd of zombies and about three of them had looked back at my direction and had seen me entering the building. I guess they heard the voice over the com. DAMN!

The door locked behind me and I was in the building safe and sound, but I had four floors to climb and I didn't know what to expect between me and the woman's apartment. Holding my machete tightly in my hand, I made my way to the second floor. Three more of those fuckers were wandering around in the hallway. Jesus, I almost puked. One was a woman and she was stumbling along the hallway holding onto the arm of a small dangling body. Let's just way it was the size of a baby doll… but it wasn't a doll. She/it was coming towards me and hadn't seen me yet, so I stayed in the stairwell until she came close enough then I lunged out at her and with one powerful swoop, I sent her to the great beyond to be with her baby. I found if I told myself things like this, I could live with all the violence and dismemberment much easier. "Keeping the sanity… keeping the sanity"… that was the mantra I kept repeating in my head as I chopped my way though the other two creepers and made my way to the fourth floor.

Her name was Clair and she was a 30-year-old housewife, who had been keeping herself and her 10-year-old son, Charlie, alive for days in some random apartment they had barricaded themselves in. Neither of them was hurt or bitten and the food I had tucked away in my pack *(which I shared with them)* made them act like it was Christmas morning.

My watch alarm was one of those digital ones that didn't stop unless you turned it off or the battery ran out, so it was still in full force when we got down stairs. The three zombies that had seen me enter the building were waiting at the door for us, but the other 22 or so were still trying to figure out what that annoying chirping sound in the parking lot was. It would only be a matter of time before they figured out it wasn't dinner, so I told Clair and Charlie to stick close to me while we made a run for the houseboat.

I smashed out the small glass window in the apartment complex door and dispatched the three pus bags with my silencer, which was a bit stupid now that I think about it in retrospect, because my smashing the glass out alerted most of the zombies in the parking lot, but we had a big enough head start that it really didn't matter. Having a safe house that moved around was in our favor too, because we didn't have to worry too much about them following us back there. Charlie twisted his ankle just as we got to the statue, so I grabbed him up "piggy back" style and we high tailed it to the boat. Pretty uneventful I might add, which was a welcome plus in our favor. They are asleep now and I'm sitting here writing by lamplight and we're safely anchored… in deep water I might add.

May 29th 2015

8:47am: I haven't written in a few days but that's because there hasn't been much to write about. We've just been slowly making our way up river. I've seen a few vessels floating in the river, most of them stuck on sand bars or run ashore. One of them had a living dead crew. It was a yacht with about six bodies that I could count but none of them actually alive, that I could tell. The thought of scavenging on the yacht crossed my mind…. but only for a moment. I quickly decided it just wasn't worth the risk.

My boat is equipped with three separate cabins, so I have my own space and Clair and Charlie share theirs. Things have been pretty quiet, well up until this morning. I awoke to the sound of Clair banging on my door. It seems she had been playing with the radio and found a distress call amongst the static. The message seemed to be coming from Plattsburgh, which according to my map is only about 10 miles upriver. We are have been making pretty good time and we're nearing the Canadian border just beyond Plattsburgh. I'm thinking if I am able to contact the folks on the other end, I should try to help them if at all possible.

1:11pm: I sat on that damned radio for three hours this morning but nothing. Clair took it upon herself to do a bit of an inventory and found that we are running lower on food and ammo than I thought we were. I have a tendency to procrastinate and put things off. I guess somewhere deep down in my mind I think the ammo fairy is going to magically replenish the supplies. It's really because subconsciously I don't want to venture out into the "forbidden zone" as I think of it, which has become anywhere outside the safety of this houseboat.... I know you can't live forever.... But hell, you can sure as fuck try!

8:42pm: Jezuz freakin H. Christ! I knew we shouldn't have fucking done it.... but Clair was insistent that we go, and that she go with me. It had "bad idea" written all over it, but we went and we left Charlie in the boat.

About three miles out of Plattsburgh, on highway 87, there was one of those big super Wal-Mart stores. You could see it from the river, on the opposite side of the highway, just across a huge cemetery that ran from the shoreline to the highway. There wasn't a pus bag to be seen from where we were, so I thought we could get there and back quickly enough for Charlie to really be in any danger. I really couldn't believe my eyes... we got across the cemetery with no problem. Nobody was popping out of any graves like those old Return of the Living Dead movies, but the minute we stepped foot on the Wal-Mart parking lot, about 12 of those fuckers started climbing out of some of the cars that had been abandoned in the lot. We thought leaving Charlie in the boat, with the door locked would be okay for that short of time, but that proved to be wishful thinking.

We got through the parking lot, but it took the last of my silencer rounds to do it. In the store it was chaos. There were about 15 of those fuckers but they seemed to all be going about their own business, almost like they were shopping. I had seen movies where the living dead, or zombies if you will, had a tendency to go back to what was familiar to them in life and these pus bags in the store were doing just that. Clair and I had to sneak around but we were able to get past most of them without being spotted as long as we kept down the noise. We grabbed two of those "green bags" you know the ones you use over and over again instead of plastic... well they hold a lot when they have to. Anyway we loaded them down with canned goods and ammo and I even found a nice pistol for Clair and a shotgun in the firearms section along with enough ammo to choke an elephant.

Things were going fine until we started back out. I guess the little bit of racket we were making didn't go completely unnoticed, because as we started down the large center aisle of the store, we had a crowd following us, which forced us to go to a different door than the one we had come through and guess what.... THE FUCKER WAS LOCKED! The 15 or so pus bags were all coming up the aisle toward us, but getting to the other side, where our unlocked escape route was, wasn't going to be possible, so I quietly motioned for Claire to jump behind the one hour photo counter we were could hide while I came up with a plan.

The fuckers were not in much of a hurry, which proved to be in our favor. I looked around and found a plastic bottle of that solution they use in the print machines and my heart jumped with joy when I read the words "extremely flammable" on the side. I quickly ripped a strand of cloth from my shirt, shoved the end of it in the open end of the bottle and loosely fastened the cap, leaving a bit of the chemical-soaked cloth sticking out. It was a gallon jug and made the perfect Molotov cocktail from HELL! Thank God, the zombies were all in a group, making their way up the aisle and they were still far enough away that we could light them up and make a run for it.

I was a bit apprehensive when I lit the end of the cloth since I didn't know if it was the liquid that was flammable or the fumes…. Or both! Anyway, I lit the cloth and with all my might hurled the jug of liquid death at the group of approaching corpses. It was like slow motion as the jug flew through the air and caught the store manager (or his walking corpse rather) square in the stomach. It almost looked as though he made an attempt to catch it but the moment it hit him, he disappeared in a red ball of fire about 10 feet in diameter. Clair and I bolted for the unlocked door with our bags and left the writhing mass of putrid, sick-sweet smelling, barbequed death behind us. I was feeling the love and damned proud of myself until we got about halfway across the cemetery. That's when we both heard Charlie's ear-shattering scream. If only we hadn't had to stop and BBQ those motherfuckers.

Charlie is bitten! While, we were gone one of those scuba-diving bastards slithered its way out of the water and up on the deck at the back of the boat and broke into the cabin. Charlie (bless his heart) managed to fight the thing off and kick its head in, during the attack, but not without getting a nice big bloody chunk taken out of his left leg. The ironic thing is that it was the corpse of some dead boy scout, probably close to Charlie's age, that got him. I had to wonder if the little fucker followed me all the way from that "boy scout jamboree" I had back at Ticonderoga, just before I found the houseboat. I know these bastards can be relentless, but that's a bit crazy if you ask me. Anyway it really doesn't matter. The kid's living on borrowed time and I know what needs to be done, but I'm not going to be the one to do it…. at least not yet.

May 31st 2015

9:30am: The last couple of days have been crazy sick. Dealing with Charlie has not been easy for Clair and I've been trying to be there for her, but it's tough. This is the first time I've actually seen the process up close and personal. The first couple of hours after he was bitten, Charlie seemed fine. I actually thought maybe by some miracle he was immune, but after about 12 hours the signs were more than evident. The fever is the first real sign. It just burns you up. It almost hurt to touch the boy's skin once the fever had a hold of him.

It's hard to watch but once the fever takes hold it literally boils the brain and the victim is pretty much gone. Still technically alive, but gone, nonetheless. Once the fever hit Charlie, it took another six or so, hours for the life to drain out of him. You can tell when that happens because he slowly cools down and eventually becomes cold as ice and his last breath slips away like an escaping dove. I won't go into gory details, as it's pretty much straightforward. Clair held little Charlie in her arms until the life finally left him, then I told her to go into the other room and I held his head in my lap and waited. I didn't want her around when he "awakened".

I learned a valuable lesson from the experience, because I held Charlie in my arms until I could feel his body twitch. It took about two hours from the time the life left him. Once he began to twitch and his milky lifeless eyes opened, I hugged him tight and quietly snapped his little neck, severing the spinal cord for sure. His body went limp. It was over... I laid him on the floor and was preparing to find something to cover him with, when suddenly he began to writhe again. His body twitched as if it had no sort of organized motor function at all. It was obvious that he was trying to get up, but his body didn't seem to respond to what his reanimated brain was trying to tell it... That's when it hit me. There is a reason you have to destroy the brain. You can't just destroy its connection to the body. The dead boy was alive with no way to move. He was a zombie quadriplegic for lack of a better term.

The sight of the boy writhing on the floor made me throw up. Clair was pounding on the door begging to come in, but I wasn't about to let her see him like this. I quickly grabbed a large beach towel from the wardrobe and wrapped the kid up in it. Then with a deep breath, an uncontrollable flow of tears running down my face and one heavy STOMP, I put an end to his agony. Then, just when I thought it couldn't get any worse, there came a gunshot from the other room. I guess she couldn't take it, knowing her boy was gone and she was now all alone in a world gone to hell. Clair had found peace from a single bullet under the chin. As quickly as they had come into my life, they left it. Will I ever get used to this fucked up world I was now a part of? At this point, I'm not sure surviving is enough.

3:45pm: When I ended my last update earlier this morning, I promised myself I was not going to write this shit down anymore. But since then, I've come to realize that it's actually therapeutic. It's like somehow writing it down distances it from my own personal reality. Almost like I'm ready a story someone else experienced. I know, "Denial ain't just a river in Egypt"! But hey, if it helps, it helps!

As luck would have it, there was a tiny island in the middle of the river. It was about the size of the foundation of a large house and was the perfect place to put Charlie and Clair to rest. It would have been easy to just toss them over, what with all the other dead bodies floating around, but I had to give them the dignity of an honorable burial. It was kind of nice; instead of having their own personal grave plots, they have their own personal island to rest at peace on. The makeshift funeral was safe enough to do there, but I still didn't waste any time lingering around. I have no idea what tomorrow will bring, but I hope it's something a bit more encouraging than the last few days. I'm signing out for now.

June 2nd 2015

10:10pm: I never actually believed in God. I always looked at him as a convenient fairy tale for impoverished lower income types, or people with an undeveloped grasp on common sense, but now I have to wonder. I'll start by saying it seems I have a new friend. I woke up from a cat nap this evening to the sound of a squeaky high-pitched voice, saying what I could only make out to be "Help me, Popeye, help me!" At first I thought I was dreaming about Olive Oyl, that skinny ditzy broad in the cartoons, but sure enough when I got up to investigate, I heard it again.

I literally searched for the source of the illusive voice for half an hour when I finally pinpointed where it had to be coming from…. It was above me. As I climbed the ladder leading to the roof of the boathouse, I heard the voice again, even clearer and it said the oddest thing. "Something evil this way comes". The light of dusk made it hard to see anything on the roof of the boat, but as I ascended to the top, I heard a nearby flutter of wings. I had mounted a small flashlight to my silencer and swung over in the direction of the sound. My jaw literally fell open in absolute disbelief. There perched on the two-foot railing that ran along the top edge of the roof was the most beautiful McCaw I had ever seen in my life. Obviously, someone's pet that had escaped the surrounding nightmare and made it to the safety of my little boat. He was a welcome and very colorful sight.

Surprisingly, the bird came to me and perched himself on my shoulder.... Well... with the help of a small fish cracker I dug out of a box in my stash. As welcome a sight as the little fucker was, I started to get worried after an hour or so because he just wouldn't shut up. The last thing a guy needs in a post-apocalyptic zombie landscape is a chatty little sidekick that's attracting attention everywhere we go.

I remembered seeing a falconer documentary on the Discovery channel back when. The Falconers always had those cool little hoods that they would slide over the bird's head to keep him calm and quiet... so I gave it a try. I took one of those small purple velvet sacks you get with a bottle of Crown Royale and I cut a small hole for his beak and slipped it over his head. Instant peace and quiet! Now if he's quiet through the night.... This will be a match made in heaven, if not, I'll be eating the closest thing to chicken that I've eaten in weeks for lunch tomorrow.

June 2nd 2015

Several more days without incident, I could get used to this. Sam and I have been getting along wonderfully. I named him Sam after "Toucan Sam", who used to delight me with his fruit loops cereal every morning as a child. I know Sam is a McCaw and not a Toucan, but who the hell cares, right? Anyway, he is almost as good as a watchdog when it comes to the creepers.

I dropped anchor yesterday near one of those riverside strip malls to get some much needed supplies. It's got a convenient dock that runs quite a length of the river. Sam's been nice and quiet the entire day except twice when he did his little "Something wicked this way comes" routine. When I looked out at the docks, sure enough there were two creepers shambling up the dock a bit too close to the boat for comfort.

Sam's intuition is either a really cool coincidence or he's one really intelligent bird. Anyway, they are out there and I'm in here and I'm too tired to give a damn at the moment and since they don't know I'm here, I'll take care of them in the morning when I leave for the strip mall. I plan to get an early start tomorrow and see what's worth taking. I'm not anticipating anything crazy but who knows what can happen.

June 3rd 2015

Its 11pm, I'm safe and sound but I have no idea where Sam is. This really hasn't been my day. Let me explain. This morning, I quickly dispatched the pus bags on the dock and made my way into the riverside shopping center. I know I keep calling it a shopping center and a strip mall, but it's one of those places that is like a line of shops facing the river. Not an enclosed building, which is a plus in my book. The place had been badly ransacked and there wasn't much left. It made me think for a minute about how things are only going to get worse. I'm less than a month into this situation and supplies are random at best, but soon whatever is left will either have been picked over to extinction or inedible from rot and decay. I better start learning how to hunt rats and squirrels.

Now that there is another mouth to feed, I've been trying to think about him as well. I was lucky to find a pet store in the complex that was next to untouched. There was every type of bird treat you could imagine, so I loaded my pack down with a couple of bags. Got some new trainers to make sure I can outrun any of those fuckers out there. The fresher they are the faster they are but still they are walking dead and I have not met one yet that I couldn't outrun, but better safe than sorry.

There was one of those shops that sells pseudo military outfitting, so I found some black cargo pants, some long sleeve black pullover's and a couple of those fishing vests with all the pockets. If I'm going to be a survivor, I'm going to dress the part. I have been doing a lot of thinking about weapons and their effectiveness. This little strip mall by the river was heaven for melee weapons. The more I have been in the position to choose between a gun and a silent melee weapon, I have always chosen the latter, so I figured I better load down on stuff that will come in handy and will be easy to tote around with me.

In the strip mall was one of those fantasy shops where all the geeks play War Hammer and shit.... Well you could not have paid me to go in a place like that except on this particular trip something caught my eye. Mounted on the wall behind the cashier was what looked like a replica of Conan's broad sword. When I read the plaque, it actually said on there that is was a scaled down authentic copy of Arnold Schwarzenegger's sword from the 1984 movie 'Conan the Barbarian'.

The fucker was about three feet long, sharp as a razor, and would do a hell of a lot of damage if stuck in the middle of a mob of those pus bags. Needless to say, I tucked it in my belt like a medieval knight. I was glancing in the cash register when I heard the unmistakable sound of a gun clicking. You know the sound it makes when it's out of ammo but someone is pulling the trigger. As I spun around, I was thinking how I had scanned the shop and in my mind deemed it clear of pus bags, but I guess I was wrong.

I turned and looked at the door to the back room and there in the doorway, with a revolver in her hand, what I presume had once been the young girl who ran the shop. Now, I've been on the run every bit of 22 days and this girl has been dead every bit of that if not more. Her skull was covered with dried blood and what was left of the flesh on her skull and face was dried up and pulled tight like an ill-fitting mask. Her eyes, one bulbous and dripping pus, were glazed over with a thick film of white cataracts and where her nose had been, was nothing more than a gaping hole, caked with dried blood.

I only knew she had once been a teenage girl because of the clothes she had on and the finger of her right hand was pulling the trigger of a revolver, over and over again. It must have been some post death response to something she had been forced to do in her last moments of life. She let out a soft moan, thank God! It could have just as easily been one of those blood curdling ones that alerts every dead fuck in a hundred yard vicinity. Her slim legged Levis were rolled up and soaked with blood and her sketchers had seen better days. She wore a tight brown T-shirt with a cartoon monkey on the front that covered what had once been a perky set of tits. She was probably 17 years old and this had probably been her summer job. All I could think was 'poor fucking kid'.

She shambled slowly toward me and appeared to be having a struggle just standing upright. I guessed she was one of the early converts to the zombie nation and probably recruited soon after the entire plague began to spread. She was no match for me and when I pulled the sword from my belt and pointed it at her face, her trigger finger began to click faster. She was agitated and wanted me dead like her. It's weird the shit your brain says to you when you don't' expect it. As her hinge-like jaw wagged up and down, I imagined her saying, "Come, join the zombie nation." And with that disturbing bit of commentary running through my brain, I swung the sword up in the air and came down hard, planting it in hers. Conan would have been proud. Rest in Peace lil sister!

With my new toy wiped down and tucked in my belt, I was wondering what Arnold Schwarzenegger was doing at that precise moment. Had he joined the ranks of the living dead or was he the leader of some anti-zombie survival group in California somewhere? God, I'd love to join that group! I know, sounds stupid, but I actually think ridiculous random thoughts like that help keep me human. Anyway, I moved along making my way down the strip mall. The occasional creeper would pop up and I'd pop down out of sight until the coast was clear. I was keeping my eye out for anything. The population of creepers was surprisingly small, but I didn't want to get too careless.

I found one of the circle K convenience stores and ducked inside for food. The electric was still working and the place had quite a few items left that were salvageable. I loaded my provisions backpack down with Red Bull, water, Coke and my favorite frozen burritos. The last batch I had gotten was long gone and I knew I wouldn't be running into many more of these gems, so I took them all. Canned tuna, canned meat, and boxed stuff like Mac and cheese I knew would last forever, so I made them second priority, but I loaded the sack down till I could barely carry it.

It was getting late and I knew I needed to head back to the boat, but I wanted to try to find one more melee weapon, something lighter than the sword but every bit as effective. I quietly snuck out of the shop and was making my way across a small alley, when I saw them. There across the way was an Ace Hardware store right next to a sporting goods shop. That's when the idea came to me.

I had been thinking of my sister and her kid, who lived in Colorado. She was the only real family I had left and last Christmas I had gone to visit them for the holidays. I remembered this zombie game her boy Brandon was playing and he had tried to get me to play it too. Not really my thing, but it was an interesting game. I can't remember the name, but it was about this guy who was trapped in a mall full of zombies and in the game he could build all sorts of weapons. Some were ridiculous like exploding wheel chairs and such, but one of the weapons his character built was something that would come in very handy in real life and there in front of me were the two stores where I would find just the elements I would need to make one.

I snuck into the Ace Hardware and grabbed a box of nails and a hammer. There were a few corpses littering the place, but none of them were up walking around. So making good time, I rushed into the sports shop and grabbed two heavy-duty wooden bats. That's when my inner 'cave man' took over and I ended up walking out of the store with two "nail-head" bats, one in each hand. I have to admit I was feeling pretty bad ass as if I could take on the world, but little did I know the shit was about to hit the fan.

"Help me Popeye, help me!" I heard Sam's squawky voice coming from above me. I ducked down as I looked up. My first reaction was that his loud obnoxious parrot voice was going to attract every creeper in the vicinity. Then I had a horrible thought. Why the fuck was he so far from the boat? Why would he have followed me to the strip mall? Something had to be wrong. I was loaded down pretty heavily with all the loot I had pillaged. Two backpacks full to the brim and a nail-head bat in each hand. But I ran as fast as I could back to the marina, where the boat was tied up.

I took out about five pus bags on the way, taking off their heads with my new melee weapons. The sword was awesome, but I didn't have time to admire its handiwork completely. Sam flew above me, eventually perching himself on a tall signboard just at the entrance to the docks. That's when I stopped and saw why he had come to find me…. Smart bird! The boat was swarming with those maggot filled motherfuckers. They were everywhere. I had only been gone a little over two hours, but they had somehow found their way on and now there had to be 75 to 100 of them. No fucking way was I going to get my boat back.

They started to notice me and turn to my direction. I could tell by the bloody smudges that some of them had gained access by way of the dock, but I could also tell that many of them had actually come from the water itself. I reached into my weapons pack to get a cocktail I had thought to stick in there a few days back, but two of those motherfuckers were on me in seconds. They had managed to get in front of the mob that was now tripping over itself trying to get off the boat and over to me. I stuck one of them in the face with 'Conan' and took the other one's jaw off with my nail-head. Once they were down, I had just enough time to light the cocktail and throw it though the glass doors of the houseboat. It was like a box full of barbequed zombies. The smell made me retch, but they were done and they weren't going to get me.

So back to square one; I lost the boat and what few supplies I had left on it, but I had my life and my feathery little pal if I can find him again. He was spooked by the flaming houseboat, but I'm sure he'll turn up sooner or later. I'm sure not going to cry over a burned houseboat. As a matter of fact, I was getting a bit seasick. Maybe it's time to find a zombie-stomping 4-wheel drive and take to the roads for a while, besides the border of Canada isn't all that far away.

June 7th 2015

The world just keeps getting sicker and sicker. But wait, before I get ahead of myself, let me fill in some blanks. After my boat bit the big one,

I hoofed it out of town as "stealthily" as I could. I kept catching glimpses of Sam flying up ahead. Not only had we reconnected, but it was almost like the crazy bird was leading me to something. Well, he did! About a mile out of town, I ran into an abandoned army roadblock and that is where I commandeered the perfect vehicle. It's a hard top army jeep, and someone was nice enough to leave some MREs in the back seat. They are a nice addition to my food stash. Anyway, things were pretty quiet as I made my way up highway 87 toward the Canadian border until I met THEM. Just when things seem to be going your way and you start thinking maybe there is a God, you meet someone who proves that reality is most likely the opposite. Out of all the survivors on the planet I could have run into, I had to run into Zachariah Stutsman, ordained Amish pastor and his family, or what was left of them.

I had made a comfy little perch for Sam, in the back of the jeep and was making my way north, when I saw what looked like a small farm about 100 meters off the main highway. With smoke coming out of the chimney of a small smokehouse next to the main farmhouse with lights on in the windows, I figured it must be occupied by actual "breathers", so I stopped to check it out. It was after nightfall and I'll admit that the idea of finding actual survivors and maybe having a warm bed to sleep in was a comforting thought. Zachariah (I'll call him Zach for short) was a slim wiry man dressed in shabby black Amish garb, complete with cracker hat and he had a daughter by the name of Emma. She was a haggard 15-year-old that looked like she might as well be 40. They welcomed me into their house but from the moment my foot passed the threshold I knew something wasn't right.

Things started off very friendly with Emma fetching me a glass of iced tea and some cookies at her father's command, and I do mean COMMAND. He wasn't a very pleasant man barking orders at his already haggard exhausted daughter. It almost made me feel guilty to drink the tea, but it was the way she carefully slid the door to the dining room open and squeezed through the crack as she came and went. It was almost as if there was something in there she didn't want me to see. After fetching the tea for me, her father patted his lap and insisted the girl sit on it while we chatted. The fact that the world had gone to hell seemed to be a non-issue to the man as he began to spout all his religious rhetoric as he fished to find out if I was a holy man or not. You know, a "believer" or a "heathen". I am heathen through and through by his standards, I'm sure, but I kept my beliefs (or lack thereof) to myself and dodged most of his pointed questions.

The look on his daughters face was something between terror and extreme sadness, as she sat on her daddy's lap and I couldn't help but notice how he slid his hand up and down the girl's thigh while he talked, and how uncomfortable it made her. Now my moral compass is nowhere near always pointing "north" but I can spot an unholy "holy man" when I see one and Zach was making me as uncomfortable as he was making the girl. The preacher talked on and on about his former family and how they had gone to be with God, as he caressed the girl's thigh. Then I noticed that his other hand, that started off on the girl's waist, was now moving up and his fingers were rubbing the girl's dress just at the bottom of what was her blossoming breast. At that point I was sorry I had stopped but something in the girl's eyes were pleading with me not to leave and I had a good idea why. It was very obvious that this "daddy's girl" was way in over her head and she was helpless. Zach asked me why I hadn't touched my tea yet and I replied that the cookies were so good I wanted to eat them first and wash them down with the tea, but as I reached for the last cookie on the platter, I noticed a small slip of paper tucked under it.

I palmed the slip of paper as I ate the last cookie and when Zach wasn't looking, I glanced at it and read what it said. "Tea is drugged, pretend to sleep". It was then that I knew old Zach was up to something, so I placed my hand over my concealed 9mm silencer that was under my vest and I acted like I was getting sleepy. As Zach talked about anything and everything, I pretended to get sleepier and sleepier and finally I laid my head back and acted like I was losing consciousness. The moment my eyes closed, Zach went ballistic, ranting about how he had seen the girl "eyeballing me" and how he was going to teach her a lesson. He grabbed her by the hair and dragged her into the bedroom, all the while thinking I was out cold.

The moment the door slammed behind them, I jumped up, pulled out my 9mm and went to the door to hear what was going on inside. That is when I heard that all too familiar sound coming from the same dining room Emma had tried to keep me from getting a glimpse of. As I walked toward the dining room, I caught a whiff of the stench of death. I slowly slid open the dining room doors and almost gagged when the full-blown smell hit me like a brick in the face. All I can guess is that it was the rest of Zachariah's family. There was a woman, two young boys and a male teen all tied to the chairs and writhing to get out. They all had what looked like three-inch sections of wooden broom handle, held in place with heavy twine and lodged in their mouth's to keep them from biting. From what I could guess, they had to have been dead for more than a month.

I remember thinking to myself how things couldn't possibly get sicker than this, when suddenly they did... and how! Suddenly, I was startled out of the funk I was in by a blood-curdling scream. It was Emma and it was coming from the bedroom. With my 9mm in hand, I ran to the room and broke down the door and to add to the horror that I had already been introduced to, there was Zachariah on top of his daughter trying to rape her. This is where everything sort of gets blurry. I don't know what came over me. I can only guess that killing has become so easy that I didn't even flinch, when I put my 9mm to the preacher's head and pulled the trigger. The sick Amish preacher fuck was DEAD and I had no idea how his daughter was going to react, but to my surprise she thanked me with a hug as she cried into my chest.

I took the sobbing girl to my jeep, put here safely inside and went back into the house to take care of some unfinished business. After putting a slug in the collective heads of Zachariah Stutsman's dead rotting family, I started back to the jeep, but was stopped dead in my tracks by an aroma that I had not smelled in longer than I could remember. It was the smell of meat smoking in a smoke house and, for a moment, every other thought in my head disappeared. The thought of cured smoked meat made my mouth water. I glanced over to see that the girl was okay and, seeing she was, I slowly crept up to the smokehouse, which was a good 50 yards away. I know what you're thinking.... After going through what I had just been through, how could I be thinking about smoked hams and pork loins, but after eating canned food and non-perishable packaged shit for a month, the thought of loading down on cured meat was very inviting. I took a quick look around to make sure no walkers were sneaking up on me and I went for the smoke house door.

The smell was fragrant and strong but it had a strange sweetness to it that I had not smelled before. With the thought of hams, sausages and other smoky delights, I literally licked my lips as I spun the wooden lock from horizontal to vertical and slowly pulled open the door. The thought of the yummy delights in the smoke house belonging to crazy Zachariah put me off a bit, but I also wasn't about to look a gift horse in the mouth when it came to food, he was a farmer for God's sake and, when it came to the Amish, they had a rep for being experts of living off the land. In the world I'm now living in, things around you are constantly what you can call "sick" but sometimes they can go from sick to sicker and that's exactly what happened the moment I opened the door to the smoke house. I have made my own stomach churn enough just rehashing the last three days events so I will not go into great detail about what I saw in the smoke house, but let's just say it wasn't pork that the good preacher Zachariah had been smoking in that wooden shack for the last few weeks. It seems he and his family had been living off of the flesh of other humans…. Not unlike their rotting zombie neighbors…. More later!

June 17th 2015

7:45 am: It's been ten days since my last update. The first five days of that, Emma was in a catatonic state, almost completely unable to communicate. I really think Sam my little feathery friend has had a lot to do with helping the girl come out of her shell. Yesterday, she came out of her shell for the first time and started telling me a bit about what happened to her family. It seems her father had gotten a correspondence from his older elderly aunt (most likely not by phone, being Amish) shortly after the zombie shit had hit the fan. Apparently, she and her elderly husband lived somewhere south, near Albany or Troy. She seems to think that it wasn't far from the medical facility where all this started. Her story, if I understood her correctly, is that her mother and father had gotten the message that something horrible had happened to her uncle. He had been attacked in his yard by some crazed lunatics and got killed. Then it seems the lunatics were trying to get into the old lady's house. Emma's father was trying to make his way down there with his wife, in nothing more than a horse drawn buggy, when they too were attacked. Emma's mother had been bitten in the attack, but they were able to turn and make it home without any further injury.

Ah, the seed of destruction. That single bite was the undoing of the Stutsman family. The way Emma's story goes, the mother got deathly sick and 'turned' and ended up biting the older brother, who in turn ended up joining the ranks of the undead and biting both of his brothers, before good old Zachariah could subdue them all. According to her, the family members in the living room had been there for well over a month and a half, keeping in mind that this part of the state had been overrun well before New York was affected. Emma said a couple of weeks into the horror, her father started acting weird.... "crazy like" in her words. It was then that he and his daughter had run out of food and he started to lure the odd straggling survivor that came upon his farm, into the house, and they inadvertently ended up in the smoke house. She admitted to me that she had resorted to cannibalism out of sheer terror of what her father would do to her if she didn't obey him. It was about that time that the poor girl was forced to take over her mother's "wifely" duties, if you know what I mean. She said that by the time I had stumbled upon the farm, her father had been out of his mind for weeks. Well, I can't say it makes me feel better for blowing his brains out, but in this sick new world... shit happens and then you move on!

I'd like to meet the fuckers in that medical facility that started all this shit. I'd love to put a slug in their brain pans... but I'm sure they're long since stumbling around slobbering and eating each other's brains. I have tried to get something on the jeep's radio, but with no luck at all. At the moment we're camped out in a small church about a mile from the Canadian border. It's several stories tall and we're right up at the top, barricaded in so we can get a decent night's sleep. Sam has been very quiet lately, which I'm taking as a good sign. Usually when he goes into his "something wicked" routine, it means there actually is something wicked lurking around. I'm not a religious man, as you know, but I have to say that being in this church does give me some strange feeling of comfort. It's not like I think the "Good Lord" is going to come down off of his thrown and save us if we get overrun by walkers, but, hey, any little bit of peace of mind I can get is welcome.

4:20pm: Okay, so the church idea wasn't a very good one. Emma and I are still in the upper floor of the church, but they have somehow gotten in. I can hear them banging on the door in the hallway, trying to get in. I don't know if they can smell us or hear us or what happened, but they know we're here and it's not good. Emma is sitting in the corner and Sam is perched on her knee. She's petting his feathers with a blank stare in her eyes. It's like she is unaffected by what is going on, she kind of fades in and out of this state of catatonic bliss, like she's in another place or something. I guess it's just a defense mechanism, but I can't blame her, she's been though more than any 15-year-old girl should ever have to. Well, there is no way those fuckers are getting through the door, but still their banging and moaning is driving me insane. I've got to try to figure out a way out of this mess. Hopefully, I'll still be alive later to share more…. We'll see!

June 29th 2015

Well, this diary started with me, but it's not going to end with me. Last night, Emma and I got out of the church… she is safe and sound. I told her about my diary and I asked her to continue on with it if anything happens to me, and something has. The reality of what it all means probably hasn't hit me yet but during our escape from the church I got bitten. Some old bitchy hag of a zombie took a chunk right out of my fucking arm. Getting out of the church wasn't easy and we had a hoard of those fuckers waiting for us on the ground.

To get out of there, I had to do an Errol Flynn out of the window of the top floor with some curtains I ripped in strands and tied together. I hit the ground first, with Emma close behind me. With my nail bat, I was able to hold off the dozen or so zombies that were there to meet us on the ground and that's where old "Nellie Nibbles" met me on the ground and took a chunk out of me. It took me completely by surprise. She had her gnarly yellow rotting teeth around my forearm and was biting down before I knew what was happening.

The Nail Bat is great for clearing out a small crowd, but it can slow you down sometimes, when the nails get stuck in the skull of one of those fuckers and you have to pry the bat out of their head before you can continue cleaning house. That's actually what happened. I had hit this gigantic rotting man square in the skull, he looked like a football coach or something, and the nails on the bat got stuck in the bone. I had his head pinned to the ground with my foot and was trying to pry the bat loose when old Nellie got me. I have to give the bitch some credit though. For a rotten old hag, she was pretty damned fast. I almost want to laugh. If you're reading this diary, and have followed me this far in my journey to survive, don't be sad. I have to admit that from that day I was dangling off my 21st story balcony, I never would have dreamed I'd get this far.

I am taking the whole thing much better than Emma. I can't blame her. She can't help but think about the fact that after I "turn" and she has to dispatch me, she is going to be alone. I'm not a praying man, but if I were, I would pray that we find at least one other survivor before I turn. I've been teaching her how to use the gun and the other weapons. She's not a very strong girl, but I have a feeling she will rise to the occasion. Anyway, to finish my story, we got out of the church and fought our way through a small sea of zombies, and finally got to the jeep and were able to get the hell out of there. We finally crossed the border and now we're camping in a clearing in some woods just off the beaten path of a road side parking area about 30 miles north of the Canadian border, which we had no problem crossing. The customs officers were no problem at all, especially the one I had to shoot in the head.... Just a little zombie humor, anyway, I'll write more, later if I haven't turned yet.

June 30th 2015

6:33am: Well I'm feeling a like shit, but I'm far from being a zombie yet. I have a nagging low grade fever and I'm feeling a bit achy in my muscles. I'm finding it a bit strange the things that are going through my head. I never thought about the dilemma I would have once I ever got bitten, but I've been thinking about it all morning. The decision I am faced with is rather or not I want to just turn and be one of those things or if I want to be killed once I turn. Now you have to realize I've never had a suicidal bone in my body and frankly the thought of blowing my brains out or having someone else do it, really scares the hell out of me. Part of me just wants to turn and slink off into the darkness, but I don't want to hurt anyone else, namely Emma. She is such a good kid and she has been through so much. We'll be breaking camp soon and hitting the road.

10:10am: Okay, I'm still here and I'm not going to dwell on the negative. I still feel like shit and I can feel it slowly getting worse, but I have some time before I become a piece of walking beef jerky. We stopped for gas at one of those large roadside trucker stations. There were only three walkers there and together we dispatched them quickly. One of them was probably the most disgusting thing I have yet to see. He looked like a college kid, probably a jock. He had what was left of a football jersey on and his entire chest cavity had been ripped open and he was basically hollow. Missing lower jaw and eyes, he was just meandering around, following whatever sounds he could decipher. Seeing him really did make me think twice about becoming one. I would hate to end up like him and putting him out of his misery really felt like we were doing him a favor.

When we finished off the others, I let Emma do most of the work, as she needs to get used to feeling comfortable taking those bastards out without feeling regret or guilt. We gassed up the jeep and filled the three gas cans we salvaged along the way, so we should be good for a while. I don't want Emma to have to make this kind of stop again for a while. I'm hoping long after I've gone my separate way.

1:15pm: We had a blowout. We were winding our way through an interstate pile-up and I'm sure we must have driven over something sharp that eventually took out our left front tire. Emma is changing it after I explained to her what to do. I'm just too weak to do it myself. The pounding in my head is almost unbearable and my muscles are so tight and sore that getting up and walking around is a major task. I can still write though, so I decided to enter at least one more entry. Sam is still with us and he seems to be doing okay. He certainly keeps Emma happy. She just loves the bird. She's teaching him Bible verses and he can actually say the beginning of the Lord's Prayer. He gets a bit stuck on "Hallowed be thy name". She seems to be doing okay with the changing of the tire and she is in okay spirits, except I know she is worried about me.

The tire blew right under a huge billboard sign that advertises some sort of theme park about 50 miles away. We both decided that getting there would be a good goal for us, probably lots of food and maybe even somewhere to hold up for a day or two... for her to hold up. I really don't think I'm going to be around that long....

2:30pm: It's time... my body is on fire and I can barely move. I'm in the jeep and we're parked in the parking lot of the theme park. I don't know what it's called... honestly I can barely see. I see the huge sign at the entrance to the park, but I can't make out what it says. Emma is outside at the back of the jeep, crying. I had to beg her to use the silencer and put me out of my misery once I turn. I don't want to live as one of those things... if that's even what they do.... Live. I can feel it.... burning me... killing me on the inside. I thought somehow I could fight it... but I can't... its taking me... and... I... can't... do... anything... GRRRAWWWH

July 1st 2015

9:47am: My name is Emma Stutsman.... I told Vance that there would probably never be anyone to read this, but he kept writing in it religiously. I'm not sure what to write, but I promised him that I would continue his diary if something happened to him. It was very important to him and I made a promise, so I'm going to keep it no matter what. Vance is gone. He's not 'dead' as far as those things are concerned. I told him I would use the gun and end his misery, but I couldn't bring myself to do it. He turned while he was sitting in the jeep and thank God his seatbelt was fastened. After he became one of those things, he lunged for me, but he couldn't reach me for the seatbelt. Three different times I pointed the 9mm at his head but my hand was shaking so badly and my guts were turning flips and I just couldn't do it. Finally, after an hour or so of him writhing around in the jeep, fighting the confinement of the seatbelt, I took the sword, held it to his chest to pin him back and I unbuckled the seatbelt and ran for my life to hide.

Now he's gone... and I'm not sure where. I hid in a ticket gantry, so that I could see him but he couldn't see me. He finally left the jeep and wandered off somewhere. He must be the most handsome zombie I've ever seen, since he's not all torn to shreds and never will be since they don't really rip apart and eat their own. I just hope his soul is in a happy place. I always imagined that these walking corpses are just husks that are animated by some scientific chemical imbalance or something. I choose to believe that the actual person, or their soul as we call it, has gone to be with God.

Enough about that, I guess I should write about what's gone on since Vance's last and final entry. He left me quite a bit of food, weapons and ammo and most importantly he showed me how to drive the jeep. He even let me get in some practice yesterday while we were coming here to the theme park. I don't feel pretty confident driving it but I guess I don't have much of a choice. I did decide to stick around here at the park awhile. The parking lot is pretty empty and the jeep is parked in a safe place between some abandoned rigs. I have done a bit of exploring around the outer grounds, but I have not ventured into the actual park grounds.

The entrance to the park, where the ticket booths are, is probably three hundred meters away. There are a few roamers hanging around there and I'm sure there are more inside, but this place is huge and I am sure there are some valuable things to find here, namely more food and supplies. This is my first time to see a theme park up close, so I am a bit excited to see what's in there. It's too bad I had to wait till the world has fallen apart but better late than never. My father didn't believe in places like this. He said it was where the Devil's minions abound, but he pretty much ended up being the devil himself, so I don't put much stock in his opinion. I plan to have something to eat and then venture into the park. It's called the WONDERLAND Family Fun Park.

3:30pm: There is a huge fence that surrounds the entire park… and this place is HUGE. It has five different kinds of rollercoasters, dozens of kiddy rides, everything I ever imagined a place like this to have and even though the electricity is still working, there is no way to ride any of them. In certain places, the outer gates are swarming with those undead things, but inside the parks fences there are only a few here and there. Even if they banned together and attacked at once they would probably be manageable… Oh dear, I'm starting to sound like Vance. That reminds me; I thought I saw him today. I was rummaging around inside of one of the theme park's restaurants, and I looked out the window and could see a section of fence. I could have sworn I saw Vance, or what is left of him, just meandering around out there, trying to find a way in. I probably should have put him out of his misery after he turned, but I just couldn't do it. Please forgive me, Vance…. I'm weak!

6:26pm: The sun is going down and I thought I saw something strange just before I left the park to come back to the jeep. It looked like a young boy. Not a zombie boy, just a regular boy. I say young, but I mean early teens, maybe even twelve, but he saw me too, I think. I am not sure it wasn't just my eyes playing tricks, but it makes me wonder if maybe there are other survivors in this park somewhere. It's huge enough for whole church congregation to hide without being seen. It's funny that I used that reference. I used to secretly hate going to church with my mother and father but now I would give anything to be in the same room with all those people…. Alive that is. I miss my family… even my father. I know he did so many horrible things to me, but he wasn't in his right mind. Before all this stuff happened, he was very strict but he was a kind loving man. He loved my brothers and I, and he treated us right. I guess the horror of this new world we live in and his losing my mother, just caused his mind to snap.

I think I'll fix something to eat now and try to get some rest. I need to feed Sam as well. I just let him fly around as he pleases. I don't really think those things out there care much for fresh fowl carcass, so he doesn't have much to worry about. I have started getting the hang of keeping this diary. At first it was a bit strange, but I sort of like it. It keeps me from feeling too alone. I'll write more in the morning… maybe after I go check out the park again and see if there really is a little boy living out there somewhere.

July 3rd 2015:

I woke up yesterday to a horrible sound and my jeep rocking back and forth. It seems even thought I tried to hide the jeep between two large trucks, those 'things' still found me. I'm safe inside, but I'm trapped in here with nothing to do but write in this diary. I have to admit it helps me keep my mind off of those things… sort of. I packed both backpacks with all the supplies I had and was prepared to make a run for it the first chance I got, but before I could I found myself surrounded. It's horrible… stuck in here for hours, having to do my unspeakable into a large cup that happened to have been left in the jeep by Vance. I can't even open the window to get rid of the contents. I was thinking that I could probably start up the jeep and drive away, even though those creatures are blocking both the front and back, but when I went to start the engine, it wouldn't start. I think I may have done something Vance warned me about…. I think I may have flooded it. At the moment, I'm lying in the back floorboard and waiting, hoping that if they can't see me, they will eventually leave, but that hasn't happened yet.

It's driving me crazy… those smelly, gruesome zombies, smearing their decaying bodily fluids on the windshield and windows. I don' know how I'm going to get out of this. OH MY GOSH! I just looked down at the date on this diary and realized something… today, July 3rd, is my 16th birthday. With all the horrible stuff that has been going on the last couple of months, I hadn't even realized that my birthday was coming up. I can't believe it's today… I wonder if I am going to see 17. How ironic is this?

This is the beginning of my Rumspringa. I know you're thinking what on Earth is that… let me explain. When an Amish child turns 16, they are able to go into the world and make their way, experiencing all the things the world has to offer, without being held to the rules and regulations of the Amish church. Well now's my big chance and what a world to be sent off into. Wait! That windshield is break…

July 5th 2015:

7:30am: That shit is all kinds of fucked up! I just checked out the prior entries into this diary. Those poor bastards... That Vance guy didn't ask me to carry on with it, but I'm pretty sure he would have wanted me to, so here goes. I'm not used to this sort of shit. Writing down my thoughts and stuff, but I'll give it my best shot. I really think that poor girl would have wanted us to carry on, giving future survivors of this God awful shit-storm some way of knowing what it was like while it was happening. I'm not sure why, but maybe to make them appreciate not having to go through it? I'm personally pretty confident that someday these fucking zombies will all rot all up and blow away like dust in the wind and things will evolve again into a thriving society, but, hell, who knows. Maybe I've just watched too much sci-fi shit in my youth. Guess I should introduce myself... Craig Slaminsky here. Everyone just calls me SLAM! I picked that nickname up when I was the leader of one of the biggest biker gangs in North America, before all this shit hit the fan. I'm pretty sure I've survived only because I've always been a natural born 'skull cracker'.

We've been holed up in this theme park for about a month now. It's pretty much home for the eight of us. The park itself is fenced in and there are only a few of those shit bags in the park, so we move around pretty freely. We saw the girl and her friend Vance drive up. Little Billy (Billy the kid we call him), was out rummaging for food when he caught a glance of the girl. We were actually debating whether or not to go outside the gate and get her, but I guess we debated a little too long.... Me and Jake finally went out there yesterday and that's when we found her. All chewed up and still in the back seat of her jeep. She had turned... but she was pretty docile. The other shit bags had already wondered off enough that we could get her out of the jeep and bring it inside the fence. I hated to do it but I had to plug her in the head and put her out. Okay, I'm stopping here for now... Got some trouble at the East gate. Later!

12:45pm: Well, two of those shit-bags found their way through the East gate. Lucky for us it was only two. If a whole mob of those fuckers had found that weak place in the fence we'd be in for a world of hurt. The new weapons that Vance guy made work great. I particularly like the Conan sword. Works for me!

The eight of us have been here, living together, like I said, coming up on a month. Billy the kid was here when we got here. He was some poor little tyke that lost his parents here at the park when everything went wrong. Let me quickly rattle off the others who are here with me. Well, there's me, Slam, and Billy and Jake, he's some queer theme park performer that was left over from the staff here, but he's cool for a fag.

There's Beth and Tina, a couple of college girls who were backpacking their way into Canada from the US when all this happened. They're both pretty fucking hot if you ask me, but they're not really into burly biker types. Karl and Maxine are a married couple in their late 50s, sort of the mom and dad of the bunch. They've been great for little Billy…. And then there is Wayne the 'weasel' as I like to call him. He's one of those asshole bossy types. He was… or still is… the manager of the theme park, so we are a bit indebted to him for letting us be here, but I've had to hold back from wringing the guy's neck a few times. He's an okay guy, just bossy as hell. And I ain't nobody's bitch! Get what I'm saying?

I think that girl and her friend Vance brought some sort of parrot with them, because suddenly this colorful bird appeared and is flying all over the park. We catch a few words here and there but can't really make out what he's saying. I only think he came with them because he appeared when they did. Weird, if you ask me.

3:15pm: Billy showed up with that bird. I finally figured out what he was saying. "Popeye help me" that's one weird thing for a fucking bird to say, but it gave us all a good laugh, so he's welcome as far as I'm concerned. I don't know how that kid caught the bird but they are best pals now. He needs something to keep him occupied. I'm always afraid the kid's going to go wondering off somewhere he's not supposed to be… you get me? I don't want to have to be the one to… you know, if he were to turn….. Anyway, I've got shit to do. More later!

10:30pm: I was out walking the perimeter when I found the kid crying. He's been tough as nails this whole time I've known him. Running off alone, scouting the park bringing back useful stuff. Maxine is always yelling at him and telling him to stop running off alone, but he's a firecracker. We all worry for the kid, but since none of us are his real parents he only listens to us to a point. I think he's got a death wish deep down inside. He doesn't seem to be afraid of anything. Tonight, I can only guess, it all sort of came to a head… the reality of his parents being dead or undead as it were. I know they are still out there… he pointed them out to me once. He catches a glimpse of them from time to time, lumbering around among the other shit-bags. The kid and I have bonded quite a bit, but he still doesn't open up to me about what's going on inside his little 11-year-old head. I try not to influence him too much…. The last thing he needs it so grow up like me… a middle aged biker with a bad attitude, but on second thought, it's a new world out there. Maybe if he did end up like me that might be the very thing that saves his life one day. Okay, time for this grizzly to hibernate. I'm supposed to go out on a supply run with the weasel tomorrow, so I'm up at the butt crack of dawn…. Later!

July 6th 2015:

July 6th 2015:

12:45pm: Well Wayne and I ventured into a portion of the park we hadn't been in before. You see this theme park is divided into five sections. In its glory days when families came here to enjoy the fun and fantasy of it all, there were five separate wonderlands they could enjoy. But now they are more like five levels of hell, well make that four, because the jungle safari section where we hold up is completely cleared out, and each section is fenced off from the others. There is an underground network of tunnels full of offices and break rooms and changing and shower facilities where all the costumed character workers used to prep. With the network of tunnels, they could go to and from any section of the park without being seen by the general public. Well, what was once a series of convenient access tunnels is now a dangerous unexplored potential death trap. So that's where the weasel and I went this morning.

We didn't get far, but we did get into corridors 'A' and 'B', which were where most of the offices for the park management were located. We were hoping to find a cafeteria or something like that, where we could stock up on food and supplies. I don't know about the rest of the world out there and whether they still have power, but the park has had a steady flow of electricity up until a few days ago. It started as short flickers and then a couple of blackouts yesterday, which lasted about five minutes each. I am sure it's just a matter of time before the grid all over North America is completely out. There are generator rooms in each section of the park, but we haven't even tried to get any of them started. It's just a task none of us have felt up to volunteering for, since we hadn't had the need.

With all the gift shops in our section of the park alone, we have been well stocked on batteries, but they won't last forever. This morning we took plenty of 'em to help us with our exploring, in case we lost the lights again while we were underground. Corridors 'C' through 'E' go a few floors deeper and branch out to the farthest sections of the park. We've pretty much decided we're going to save those for later. No need to press our luck now, since we have no idea what to expect in there.

6:15pm: SHIT! I lost Wayne somewhere in corridor 'A'. We were exploring when we heard a sound, like a whimpering of a dog or a child or something. The sound seemed to have an innocence about it but at the same time was creepy as hell. It sounded like a small child calling out, but around here you never know if it's going to be an actual child or the horrid remnants of what was once a child.

I was going to come up with a plan of attack to go and investigate, but the fucker just took off after it and now I don't know where he is. I spent an hour calling his name in hushed tones, so as to not attract anyone or anything that wasn't him, but he hasn't responded. Corridor 'A' is the longest corridor of them all. Imagine the corridors under this place like a wagon wheel. Corridors B through E are like the spokes of the wheel. They all intersect in the middle, but corridor A is like the wheel itself. It makes a huge circle around the park and intersects with every corridor. This makes looking for the bastard almost impossible.

We'll literally have to scour every damned inch of the underground just to find him and I just don't think I'm going to do that. Hell, I didn't even like the guy! Anyway, back to the tree house. We're all sleeping in it and we're gonna see what we come up with in the morning.

July 7th 2015

It's 7:40am and I'm doing a quick entry to this diary while I wait for Carl. He and Maxine were arguing about his involvement in searching for the Weasel. Anyway, while I was waiting I wanted to explain something. I mentioned a tree house last night. Well, I failed to explain to whomever eventually finds this and reads it, that we're all safe and sound for one really good reason. We live in a tree house. This park has its "jungle" section and in the jungle is what they call "Tarzan's Jungle Tree House" It's a huge manmade tree with lots of elaborate little rooms and walkways and rope ladders, built right into it. It's the perfect fucking place to live if you want to stay away from dead people who can't climb trees. The only way into the tree house is through a five person cable and pulley operated elevator. It's built to look like it's all made of logs and bits of rope from a wrecked ship, but it's actually made of metal, fiberglass, and steel cables. It also runs on a counter-weight system, so no batteries required. Since we have control of its movement up and down, we can secure it at night so nothing or no one can sneak in. All the rooms are very elaborate, with their "Tarzan of the Jungle" motif, but everything is fake you know, molded fiberglass furniture, nailed down props and plastic leaves, but each room has its own hammock and that rocks. Okay, Carl is coming, so I guess he won the argument. We're gonna go find the Weasel, I guess. LATER!

1:00pm: SHIT... THERE'S SOMETHING DOWN THERE! I'm guessing it's what's left of someone's kid, but it seemed more like a rabid blood-covered chimp or something. It jumped on Carl and almost ate his face. He's okay physically, but I don't know if his heart can handle another heart-thumper like that. We got down to the middle of the "wagon wheel" where all the corridors come together. I swear.... I know why the weasel went after that thing.... it makes a sound just like a child whimpering, like some poor lost toddler crying for its mother. The kind of sound that moves you, while at the same time, sends chills down your spine.

We found Wayne, by the way. Or part of him. It was only a section of his left arm, which I was able to identify because his watch was still attached to it. I'd love to believe he's still down there and only hurt with part of his arm missing.... But reality is that he's one of those fucking things now. I wouldn't wish that on anyone, but I have to admit it couldn't have happened to a nicer guy! My gut tells me he's still down there, wondering around dead, bumping into walls in the dark, just waiting for something warm and bloody to dig into. Well that ain't gonna be me.

4:45pm: The others are having a "meeting" to try to decide what to do next. Like it or not, Wayne was sort of our 'go-to-guy' for anything we needed to know about this park. Not having him around is going to make life a bit more difficult.... I'll be back when I have some news.

July 8th 2015:

7:13am: So it looks like Me, Jake and Karl are going in. I've traded the notebook in for a hand held digital recorder. Jake noticed that I had taken over this diary that belonged to that girl Emma (I think was her name). Anyway Jake liked the idea of keeping a diary so he gave me this digital recorder he found in one of the offices he was rummaging around in. It's got fresh batteries and 500 TB memory card. It's plenty of room to record a million diaries for a million lifetimes.

Anyway, enough of that shit, I'm actually going to carry this thing with me as we go back into the tunnels. Sort of document a play by play as things unfold. Our goal being to find the Weasel if he's still around there, but mostly to find out what's down there and put it out of our misery. We will never be safe until we clear this place out completely... can't have any rabid rug-rats wandering around down there.

8:15am: We've been down here about ten minutes. I just remembered to turn this fucking thing on. It's really bad down here. If them zombies don't kill ya, the smell sure as hell will.

Okay, I'm whispering because I don't want Karl and Jake to hear what I'm saying. This is a really shit idea. We found Wayne's arm for fuck's sake. The thought of him possibly still being alive and uninfected are a big fucking ZERO in my book.

"Hey turn that thing off! They're going to hear us!"

Back later, CLICK!

8:45am: The stench is almost unbearable, but we really haven't seen anything yet. The occasional moan from somewhere in the distance is all we're able to make out. With the lights out, this maze of hallways down here is a brain fuck. We have already been through the series of "wagon wheel" shaped hallways, though they actually empty out into what looks like a sub-basement full of pipes and electrical conduits. A place obviously not meant for the general public, but for maintenance men.

"I saw something up ahead... c-mon."

That was Jake... He's leading the way. You would think being the 'big biker' that they would insist on ME going first, well, they didn't and I'm just fine with that. Karl is old but he's a bit of a bad ass. He sure has bigger balls than I do. Guess I'm going to follow them. I'm signing out for now... save some battery juice. CLICK!

9:05 am: SHIT! I don't know where they went. I was right behind them and they turned a corner and there was this horrible scream. I don't think it was either of them, but now I can't find them. I'm hiding in an electrical room. It's so dark down here I can barely see anything. I keep hearing this moaning growling sound. It's like nothing I've ever heard. I thought those things just died and came back... whatever is down here sounds like it's some sort of zombie mutant or something.

"Ahhhhrrrg .... HELP! .... it's got me... get it off of me..... it's just a ki........."

Oh God, did you hear that? It sounded like Karl. Wait.... Oh God... I can see something moving round in the shadows. I'm looking through the door that is just barely cracked open. The only light is coming from

Karl's MAG LIGHT that is lying on the floor shining upward. There is something there. It's moving in and out of the beam, but keeping mostly to the shadows. I can't really make it out, but it's got Karl and I can see that it's… oh God…. It's dismembering him. SHIT… I can't watch…. CLICK!

It's a kid…. It's a fucked up zombie kid with the strength of some sort of mutant monster. It's eating Karl. Ripping him to shreds and eating him. Oh God… it's looking over here. SHIT! IT SEES ME! … NO…. NO… NO… CLICK!

February 20th 2016:

CLICK! Hello…. Does this thing work?

BITS AND PIECES
ANTHOLOGY

Becky and the Biker

By Keith Carpenter

The sound of a child crying, that's what it was. The soft whimper of a small child taking in gulps of air between sniffling moans. It is so typical of any unhappy six year old, but Becky wasn't unhappy. She wasn't throwing some God awful tantrum so her mother would buy her a new toy, or trying to get one over on her older brother. She was afraid... frightened for her very life and she was there all alone, as the sound of her crying echoed down the long darkened museum corridors.

As far as sounds go, especially the ones that assault your senses, the sound of a crying child can be annoying as hell, but the sound that accompanied Becky's cries was even more unnerving. It was the relentless pounding and nail scratching that was coming from the other side of the bathroom door next to where Becky was sitting, on the smooth tile floor. The sound of the banging was Becky's third grade teacher Miss Cardwell. She was locked in the bathroom banging and scratching at the door because every fiber of her being wanted to get out, but Becky wasn't going to open the door. It had been locked with the key that was in Becky's hand with her chubby little fingers clenched tightly around it. Becky had been instructed that she was no to open the door no matter what she heard and Miss Cardwell was the one who had instructed her so. It was just after midnight and Becky was a scared little girl. She had good reason to be. She was six years old and she had been away from her mother and father for just under a week, which is how long it had been since the 'incident' happened.

***

Nobody really had an explanation, but a week earlier, while Becky and her class of first graders were on their annual field trip to the Museum of Natural History, something extremely unnatural happened. A small group of people burst into the museum and began to kill everyone in sight. They were crazed and violent and they all looked to be some sort of band of accident victims with their horrid wounds and mangled limbs, but they didn't seem to be slowed down by the violence that they, themselves were subjected to, because they were violent and rabid like wild animals.

Miss Cardwell had tried to protect her kids but many of them had succumbed to the insanity that seemed to be spreading like wildfire, before Miss 'C' could get them to safety. The teacher, perplexed and confused, grabbed the hands of a few of her kids and ran outside to find shelter from the madness, but it was even more horrible out there in the streets, so she led the kids back into the museum and found a small room behind one of the exhibits where she hid with five of her students until help could arrive. Somehow, between 7:45am, when the kids had loaded the bus in anticipation of a wonderful and fun field trip, and 12 noon, the world had gone crazy.

Miss Cardwell sat in the small utility room nursing the bite wounds of two of her kids, hoping that help would come, but it never did. Eventually, Jared and Tammy succumbed to their bite wounds and died, but to Miss Cardwell's horror, they didn't stay dead. After coming back to life, Jared and Tammy attacked the other students before Miss Cardwell knew what was happening and the vicious cycle started. For three days Miss Cardwell and Becky survived in the utility room living off what had been packed in the five kids' lunch boxes. Eventually, Johnny and Maxwell, Becky's two remaining classmates, succumbed to the bites they had received from Tammy and they too came back as retched little cannibals, but Miss Cardwell, who was a beefy woman, was able to pummel the living dead children into submission, eventually decorating the inside of the small room with six-year-old brain matter, but not without being bitten on the shoulder before it was all said and done.

Somehow Becky was able to get through watching her classmates turn into living dead monsters without a scratch, but that was because being the youngest, Miss Cardwell had favored her and pushed her behind herself shielding her with her body when the other dead children were attacking. But now it was inevitable. Miss Cardwell had been bitten and she had seen firsthand what happened to victims of the bites from those crazed lunatics that had uprooted the world as they had known. Knowing the inevitability of the situation, Miss Cardwell took Becky by the hand and ventured from the safety of the utility room. She knew she needed to find another survivor who would be willing to take care of Becky and protect her from the savage place the world had become.

The woman and the small girl were making their way down the dark corridor that led to the west wing of the museum. It was in that section where the exhibits for the medieval kingdoms and the pre-historic people were showcased. Miss Cardwell led Becky quietly down the corridor. They were making their way past the exhibit labeled "Dungeons of the Dark Ages", as quietly as they could, when they heard a crash just down the hall from them. Miss Cardwell could see bits and pieces of armor skidding across the highly polished granite floor just up the hallway ahead. There was a whiff of that putrid smell of fresh decomposition and something moaned in the shadows where the bits of armor had come from. She knew something was in there and she had a good idea what it was. It had knocked a display piece over and the chances of it having been done by an intelligent living breathing human being were slim at best, besides they had been there several days and the stench of a human who hadn't had a chance to shower didn't compare to the stench of one that had started to decompose.

Miss Cardwell, Erma was her first name, but the kids didn't even know that, grabbed Becky and ducked behind a 15th century Iron Maiden that stood amongst the dungeon exhibit pieces. She gently placed her hand over Becky's mouth so any quiet 'little girl' whimpers she might expel would be too soft for the zombie to hear.

"Shhh, Becky, you have to be absolutely quiet."

Erma whispered in Becky's little ear as a tear ran down Becky's cheek. They both stood there as still as the statues around them looking down the hallway in anticipation of what they were going to see. Erma's shoulder was throbbing and she was feeling feverish. She felt like she could have passed out but she knew she had to stay well to take care of Becky. The sun had gone down and the building had been working on emergency power for at least two days. There were only a few emergency lights that lit each hallway and the closest one to them was down the hall, just past whomever or whatever had knocked the suit of armor over. Erma knew it because she could now see the light casting a shadow of the zombie on the corridor wall as it slowly lumbered toward them.

"Becky you stay right here. I'll be right back."

Erma left the little girl standing next to the cold iron lady. Being an ancient torture device made it a bit strange, but just the presence of it made Becky feel a bit more secure. Erma Cardwell slowly snuck down the corridor toward the approaching zombie. She hadn't seen it yet, but from the shadow it was casting, she could tell it was another living dead ghoul just by the way it lumbered and lurched down the hallway. Erma crept up behind the figure of a 15th century executioner and quietly wrapped her hands around the handle of its 6-foot long executioner's axe. It was only a replica of what one would have looked like in the 15th century, but it was real enough. Forged sharpened steel mounted to a 6-foot long oak handle. She wasn't sure how heavy it was going to be, but she had no choice but to find out.

"Miss Cardwell, I have to go to the bathroom."

Becky whispered to the teacher, who was trying to quietly sneak up on the approaching zombie.

"Shhhh…. Not now, Becky. Stay there and be quiet!"

Erma had turned back to look at Becky, who was hugging the Iron Lady. With a frustrated look on her face, she turned back to continue her sneak attack and there in front of her were the grotesque mangled remnants of what had once been the museum security guard. Fredrick Swanson was the name engraved on the blood spattered name tag and for some odd reason that was the one thing she noticed before feeling the ghouls cold clammy hands wrap around her neck.

Erma Cardwell tried to struggle against the horrid smelling zombie, but even though he was almost a week dead, he was still very strong. With the dead security guard only arms-length from her, she didn't have the swinging room to really use the executioner's axe and she was finding herself quite helpless. Fighting to keep "Dead Head Fred's" gaping dripping maw away from her neck, she struggled for her life when suddenly, just as Fred's gaping putrid mouth was about to sink its gnarly grime-coated teeth into her throat, she heard a "THWAK" sound and suddenly she saw the end of a spear jutting from the middle of "Dead Head Fred's" mangled twisted face and in that very instant, she felt his claw-like fingers relax and the dead security guard fell limply to the ground.

"Ewwww, he's stinky!"

The little girl said as she stood there wrinkling her nose with her hands still clutching the end of the wooden spear she had taken from a nearby exhibit dummy.

"Did I do good?"

The shy little girl asked with a cute, somewhat cheeky smile.

"You did very well, Becky."

Erma hugged the girl and took her by the hand and headed down the hallway toward the bathroom.

***

"Get your fucking ass out of my way or I'm going to blow your fucking brains out too!"

Bear was six foot seven, had one of those ZZ Top beards that went to this belly button and he wore what had once been a white sleeveless 'T' shirt under his triple extra-large black leather vest that was stained with blood, booze and God only knows what else. It was probably brain matter, but he didn't want to think too much about that. He was the leader of a wicked biker gang that called themselves the "Rebels of Rot" or "ROR" (roar) as they liked to call themselves. They had begun to joke about how fitting their name had become in the previous week since they spent it smashing in zombie skulls and looting every department store they could break into without being overwhelmed with stenchers. Bear had even taken the head of a particularly awful looking stencher and mounted it on the front of his Harley chopper. It went well with the bikes "skull and crossbones" theme.

It was just after dark and the gang had been shooting stenchers in the parking lot of a local mall, but Shane, everyone called him 'shit for brains', kept stepping between Bear and the zombies he was aiming at. It had been more than a few times that Bear had almost blown Shane's head off along with the zombies he was dispatching and the sad thing was that Bear probably would have neither noticed nor cared much. He was known to be a heartless son of a bitch and he liked it that way. The gang had filled their evening with casual zombie target practice and had all but cleared the parking lot of zombies but the one thing they had not thought about in their fun-filled fire arm folly was the fact that their gun shots had attracted more than they bargained for.

"Hey Bear," Shane pointed up the darkened street that ran along the mall parking lot. "I think we better get out of there."

The biker gang, and there were only ten of them, had not counted on the fact that the worse weapons a person could use against the living dead, were fire-arms. They were nothing more than noise makers and, in an environment where humans were outnumbered at least ten to one, making noise and drawing attention to yourself was not a good idea. From where Bear was standing he could not see anything coming down the dark shadow-laden street, but he could certainly hear what was coming. From the dark emptiness of the eerie shadow-filled street came a chorus of wails, moans and occasional guttural bellows. From the sound of things, there had to be well over a hundred sick putrid stenchers coming toward them. Bear held up his shotgun and cocked it in the air, loading another shell in the chamber.

"If those motherfuckers want a piece of me, let them come and get it."

The gang stood their ground, not really knowing the full extent of what they were in for. Bear was thinking maybe a dozen of two of the things would come skulking from the darkness, and he was not only ready for them but he was looking forward to splattering some more zombie brains all over the pavement. Much to his horror, he was not prepared for what came limping and lumbering into the lamp light of what, just seconds before, was an empty street. The moans became overwhelming as literally hundreds of living dead lumbered toward them at a surprisingly hurried pace. Bear dropped the toothpick that had been clinched in his teeth, virtually all day, and he turned and ran for his chopper. Bear's momma hadn't raised any fools and he realized this wasn't a fight he wanted any part of.

Nine of the bikers mounted their choppers and began to frantically pump the starters in hopes of making a speedy exit, but the hoard of undead were on them before they could do anything. The first to go were Blake and Slam and their bitches Sugar and Isabel. The two women were riding double with their men so it made them a bit slower out of the shoot. The zombies had pulled them off their bikes so quickly they literally didn't know what hit them. Before Bear knew it, his four friends were sprawled out on the cold pavement with their guts laid out like spilled German sausages. Shane's bike wouldn't even start, so he left it and tried to make a run for it, but he was quickly overrun by a dead check out boy and three zombie children. Bear was able to take out a few zombies with his shotgun but there were way too many of them for it to matter.

He rode a couple of yards on his bike to get far enough away from the carnage that he could get in some shots with his 45 that he kept strapped to his thigh, but even with that advantage, he was not able to save the other members of his group. Max and Jerad, who were the only gay bikers in the group and shared a bike, made it farther than the others, but they too were overcome and ripped to shreds. Max tried to help, as Jerad was pulled from the bike and his face and arm ripped off by five mangled rotting freaks that were fighting over his flesh like dogs with a bone. It was his attempt to save Jerad that was the end of him as he fired bullet after bullet into the group, but not taking the time to aim for the head meant certain death for him, because barely scathed by his bullets, the group turned their attention to him and pulled him down, bike and all and had him torn to shreds in seconds.

"Meet me at the corner of 1st and Bounty."

Bear yelled to the last two survivors of his biker gang. They had gotten away from the hoard but there were too many undead between them to get to where Bear was, so there was no way they could follow him. They nodded in agreement letting him know they heard him over the sound of the carnage and Bear took off like a bat out of hell toward the end of the block. As he rode for his life, Bear looked back to see if his friends got away okay, but it was just in time to see three fucked up stenchers ramble in front of their bike, causing them to topple and their bike to fall over onto the pavement. Taking full advantage of the situation, every zombie within leaping distance of the toppled bike, jumped on them like a high school football tackle, and before Bear could do anything it was over. Every single member of the Rebels of Rot was dead, except for him.

"FUCK, FUCK, FUCK!" Bear yelled angrily as he watched his remaining gang members get devoured in his rearview mirror. He slammed on his breaks but it only caused his bike to fishtail and skid sideways into a cluster of metal trashcans, wrecking the handlebars to the point that the bike was no longer useful. Getting up, he brushed the garbage off, grabbed his shotgun and ran for his life. The hoard, that had never stopped coming, was gaining on him and he needed to get as much distance on them as he could.

***

So there Becky was, sitting on the smooth marble floor next to the bathroom with the relentless pounding of Miss Cardwell's fists against the inside of the door. Her tears had dried and she had cupped her hands over her ears to muffle the sound, but what she would do next, the little girl had no clue. She didn't know where to go and she didn't know if any of her family was still alive, much less how to get back to her house from the museum. She was just too young and too scared and too vulnerable. Suddenly, the pounding stopped. It had been going on relentlessly for hours but now it had stopped.

***

When Miss Cardwell had taken Becky to the bathroom after her encounter with the security zombie, she had collapsed inside and told Becky to go outside and lock the door. She tried to tell Becky in a way that a six year old could understand that she was going to die and come back as one of those things that had done so many bad things. Becky understood and agreed to do what Miss Cardwell told her. Erma explained to the girl that she needed to go back down the hall and get the big ring of keys from the belt of the security guard she had just killed. The reason she needed to lock the door was unspoken and Becky understood why.

After a short trip down the hallway to the security guard's corpse to get the keys, Becky had come back to the bathroom to find Miss Cardwell dead. She was lying on the floor and was not breathing. Not really realizing the urgency of the situation, Becky sat by her dead teacher sad and almost to the point of tears, when suddenly the woman's body began to lurch and twitch. Erma's eyes flew open and she turned to look at Becky, her eyes pale and milky with a film of death covering them. She slowly began to fumble to her knees in an attempt to get up as she gnarled her teeth and grabbed at the girl.

Becky quickly jumped up and ran out of the bathroom. She knew that the thing rising from the cold tile floor was no longer her first grade teacher. Becky slammed the outside door that led from the men's and woman's bathroom corridor to the rest of the museum. She tried to stick one of the keys in the lock but it didn't fit. Inside the bathroom corridor, she could hear her dead teacher slowly pushing the door to the lady's bathroom open. She knew it would only be seconds before she was pushing on the outside door and breaking out into the museum corridor.

The second key didn't fit... the third key didn't fit... the poor panicked six year old, was frantically trying to find the right key. She could hear the zombie Miss Cardwell shuffling down the short corridor from the lady's bathroom to the outside door. The fourth key didn't fit... the fifth key didn't fit. Now zombies for the most part don't have the brain power to know how to use a door knob, or even one of those push-down door rails, but the door that led to the bathroom corridor was one of those doors with a big metal handle that you just pulled and it closed slowly with a hydraulic fitting at the top. It had no knob or locking mechanism. To secure it close you simply had to put a key in the keyhole and secure it.

The sixth key didn't work and by now Becky could see a shadow moving through the crack at the bottom of the door. Her dead reanimated teacher would be pushing on the door literally in seconds and even in her little girl mind with her little girl logic, she was smart enough to know that if she didn't get that door locked, there was no way she would keep her teacher from getting through. FINALLY, just as there was a slight push against the other side of the door, not hard enough to open it, the seventh key slid inside the slot and Becky turned it with a 'click'. Just then there was a horrible BANG on the other side of the door and when it didn't open, the angry zombie on the other side let out a screeching wail that echoed down the hallway. Becky collapsed to the floor in a sitting position, with her back against the wall and the key tightly clinched in her hand and she began to cry.

***

Bear was out of breath. He had been running for blocks and finally he was able to stop and take a breather. It had taken him several blocks and a lot of ducking into doorways and working his way through dark shadowy alleys but he had finally ditched the hoard of stenchers that had been following him since they had gotten a taste of his biker gang. The path Bear had taken that zigzagged through downtown led him to a burned out gas station that was all but destroyed. He had dropped his shotgun and his 45 only had three rounds left in it. He knew if he ducked into the gas station he would most likely run into the kind of trouble he had previously gone looking for but now was trying to avoid.

He crept up to the door of the station and as he feared he heard the familiar grunts of a living corpse feasting on the remains of what had once been a warm blooded human, probably just moments before. A human that was doomed to eventually rise up and become just like the creature that killed them. Looking around, Bear knew he had few choices. Down the street to his right there was a large group of stenchers meandering around, just waiting for something to capture their attention so they could lumber off in pursuit of it. To his left were several burning vehicles, and they too were surrounded by too many living dead for him to take on by himself. Bear was tired and hungry and ready to find somewhere to hunker down and get some rest without having to worry about being eaten in his sleep. That's when he noticed that just down the alley in front of him; he could see a large gothic building. He wasn't familiar with the area but to him it looked like a library or a museum or something. So with three bullets in his only weapon, he snuck down the alley avoiding anything that moved.

***

Becky's stomach growled loudly. She hugged her mid-section to try and stop it in fear that the now quiet zombie on the other side of the door might get riled up again. It had been at least fifteen minutes since dead Erma had made a sound. She had probably just lost interest in the door as zombies do sometimes when something else distracts them, but Becky didn't know this and she didn't want to do anything to make her start up her pounding again. Suddenly, without warning there was a sound on the other side of the door. It was a soft whimper almost like a puppy or some small animal. In her naïve six-year-old mind, Becky wanted to believe that maybe somehow her teacher was all better. She looked up at the door and slowly started to get to her feet.

She heard the whimper again. This time it was a bit louder. Somehow in her young mind, Becky thought, "Maybe it wouldn't hurt to just open the door a little bit and see what Miss Cardwell was doing." The sound suddenly changed. It now sounded to Becky like Miss Cardwell was crying, as if she was sad that she had tried to hurt Becky. The little girl quietly slipped the key into the slot and slowly turned it. Just as the key slid the bolt in the locking mechanism to the side and it clicked into place, the door came crashing open. With a crazed look in her twisted zombie face, Erma Cardwell lunged through the door and knocked Becky to the ground.

Becky had quick enough reflexes to think to shove the huge ring of keys *(all seventy five of them hung on a four inch diameter metal ring)* into her zombie teacher's mouth. This kept the teacher from being able to bite anything, but she was still lying on top of the tiny girl pinning her to the floor. Erma clinched the key ring in her mouth and flung her head from side to side angrily. She was frustrated that she could not clamp her teeth around the little girl's throat, but she didn't have the brains to figure out what to do about it. Finally, after about five violent head jerks side to side, the key ring flew from the zombie's mouth and landed down the hallway at the feet of a big burley man who had just stepped onto the scene. He was well over six foot tall, had a black leather vest on and a beard that went down to his belly. He wasn't sure what he was seeing and as Becky was almost completely obscured from view by the large teacher's body he stood there sizing up the situation.

Finally, it dawned on Bear what he was seeing. He quickly ran up to Becky's zombie teacher, who was now trying to take a bite out of her tender six-year-old throat, and kicked her in the head as hard as he could with his big black steel-toed shit kickers. Erma Cardwell's head flew back and her jaw ripped almost completely out of its socket, spraying the wall behind her with a blood spatter even Dexter would love. Bear then used his foot to push Erma backward onto her back and he pointed the shotgun in her face and pulled the trigger. The racket from the gun was ear-splitting and rang down the museum halls like a cannon shot, but the six-year-old girl was alive and safe as she lay crying on the cold hard floor.

"Hey little lady, are you ok?"

The big burly biker picked Becky up off the floor.

"Who was that lady?"

He asked Becky as he hugged the scared child close to his big burly chest.

"She was my teacher, but one of the kids from my class bit her and her shoulder got hurt and she died."

"Well, I'm sorry I had to do that to her, but I think she was trying to hurt you."

"She was... and she told me if she fell asleep and woke up again that I needed to stay away from her."

"Is she the only one of... you know... those bad... I mean, are there any more of them around here?

The biker asked in a gentle voice that seemed odd coming from him.

"Yeah, she is the only one now. I had to stick the other bad man with a spear to make him stop hurting Miss Cardwell and he was the only other one around."

Bear put Becky down and brushed the hair away from her eyes.

"Well, you are probably the bravest little girl I think I've ever known. By the way, my name is Bear."

"You mean like a teddy bear?" Becky asked with a smile.

"Yeah... I guess it is... just like a teddy bear."

The big burly biker was having an awkward moment. He had never been so close to children because usually when parents saw him coming, they got their kids as far away as possible.

"Now let's see if we can find something to eat... this 'Bear' is HUNGRY. Do you know where the snack bar is in this place?"

Becky took the big burly biker's hand and led him down the hall in the direction of the cafeteria. She knew where it was because Miss Cardwell had purchased juice boxes for her and the other students when they first arrived at the museum a week before.

***

In the dark but safe recesses of the museum curator's office Bear slept soundly on a big cushy couch, with the sweet little six-year-old girl curled up next to him. It was the first time he had slept soundly in what seemed like forever. He would never have admitted it, but he felt safe for the first time in days. The two of them, safe and alone without a zombie in sight, slept peacefully.

A small stain of blood soaked into the couch cushion. One of them had been bitten and the other didn't have a clue. The room was dark and peaceful like a tomb. But the peace didn't last. Soon, it was replaced by something completely different.

The sound of a child eating, that's what it was, the ravenous grunts of a small deadly zombie child. She was feasting on a mountain of a man, gorging on the warm steamy intestines of the man who had saved her. His throat ripped out and his eyes opened, staring into the darkness, his face frozen in a puzzled expression of disbelief.

THE END

###

Soundproof
By Thomas M. Stoops

Mark places jars of baby food into his olive drab green Army back pack. He takes special care separating the jars of food with less noisy items, such as boxed dry goods and canned goods. This was a hard lesson learned on his first trip from the abandoned grocery store.

Closing the pack and securing the top flap with the two adjustable straps, Mark pauses to listen for any unwanted shoppers trying to enter his personal shopping center. He hoists the pack onto his back and secures the waist belt. He takes a deep breath and begins to walk toward the east wall of the grocery store.

While walking past the isles, he runs his hand over top of the fresh buzz cut he gave himself. The long light brown hair that was once worn in a ponytail came to a quick end after a deadhead got a hold of it, nearly dragging him to the ground. Fortunately, Mark was able to pull away, but loosing much of his ponytail in the process.

Upon reaching the emergency exit on the east wall of the store, Mark adjusts the sheathed machete on his right hip, shuts off the headlamp flashlight and puts it into a side pocket of his backpack. Pushing on the door's panic bar, he opens the door enough to see down the alley where delivery trucks used to travel to and from the loading docks. After his eyes adjust to the warm afternoon sun, he is able to see that section of the alley is clear. He opens the door further, poking his head out and looking in the direction to the rear of the store, all is clear. Mark steps out onto the alleyway.

Holding the side of the door, Mark guides the door shut right before his fingers get pinched so it closes with a quiet click. Turning to his left, Mark starts down the alleyway towards the rear of the grocery store.

Looking up the hillside through the eight-foot chain link fence that runs the length of the alleyway, Mark can see a guide rail at the crest of the hill where another shopping center is located. He hopes not to see a staggering deadhead appear and come tumbling down after him, drawing unwanted attention to his whereabouts.

He reaches the back of the grocery store and stops to peer around the corner to make sure he is alone. To Mark's relief, the loading docks are deserted, except for an abundance of trash all over the ground and an overturned delivery truck.

Mark quickly moves towards the chain link fence to the rear of the property where the adjacent parking lot for the apartment complex is located. He slips through a split in the fence that he had made weeks ago with bolt cutters he found in the utility room of the grocery store. He pauses to listen and survey the area for any deadheads.

While looking at the three yellow brick, four-story buildings that make up the apartment complex, Mark whispers to himself, "So far, so good. It's only a matter of time before my luck comes to an end." Just then, he hears glass break in the distance, but he can't pinpoint from which exact direction the noise came. "Time to move", he says, as he hurries toward the driveway between building two and three that leads to the street.

While running, he keeps his focus on a beat up yellow 1978 Chevy pickup truck. It is facing the street parked next to the walkway leading to the front entrance of building three. The truck bed is full of furniture, boxes, a television, but minus a camping cooler that he took on his way back from his first trip to the grocery store.

As Mark reaches the rear of the truck, he can smell what he believes to be the truck's owner. The upper half from the waist up of the poor bastard is laying just in front of the truck and the lower half was dragged down to the end of the driveway just before the street. By the contents in the bed of the truck, the unlucky fellow may have been on his final trip back to the truck to make his escape. Unfortunately, it truly was his last trip all together.

Crouching down as he reaches the front of the truck to make his usual scan of the area, it is difficult for him to see up and down the street.

The street is full of abandoned vehicles still waiting in a traffic jam to get onto the main street at the end of the block to the right.

With nothing that has grabbed his attention; Mark proceeds to walk the rest of the driveway toward the street. As he reaches the street, he can see that something was recently chewing on poor Frank at the end of the driveway.

Mark calls these pieces Frank because, on the front bumper of the yellow Chevy truck, there's an air brushed plate that reads "Frank and Tina". Mark isn't even sure if Frank is Frank at all, but it gives his mind something to think about by giving this poor bastard an identity. He imagines what type of guy Frank may have been and how close he was to getting away in his yellow escape vehicle.

As Mark starts to cross the street, he notices some movement in the corner of his right eye. A deadhead is four cars away, down on its knees with its back to Mark, making a meal of another poor unfortunate bastard. Mark freezes and holds his breath. The deadhead is oblivious to its voyeur's presence and remains focused on its dinner.

While his attention is on the dining deadhead, Mark doesn't notice another deadhead coming towards him from the left walking across the front lawn two houses away. It's not till the shambling deadhead reaches the sidewalk and kicks a glass bottle with its foot when Mark does realize there's more dining patrons in the area. With the noise from the hungry customer, the deadhead that's on his knees stops with dinner and turns to see his dessert.

Mark pulls the machete out from its sheath and begins to run to his left toward the deadhead on the sidewalk. Once within three feet of his target, Mark raises his right arm, swings, connecting with his target, cutting through its neck. The deadhead stops, and its dead head falls from its shoulders still biting at the air, hitting the ground.

The other deadhead is only twelve feet away when Mark spins around to realize he knew this walking, festering mess. This wretched creature must have met his demise while on the job. It was wearing a work shirt that had the name patch "Dave" above the right breast pocket. "Tony's Garage" was the patch above the left breast pocket. This particular garage is just a few streets up, and Dave had worked on Mark's car numerous times in the past. Mark sighs as Dave gets about four feet away and says, "Sorry Dave," and then proceeds to give him the same treatment as the other stink bag.

Dave's head falls to the ground and almost rolls onto Mark's right foot. Staring down at Dave's head as it bites at his foot, Mark gives the hungry melon a swift kick as if trying to make a goal in the World Cup. He kicked it so good that the head hits and breaks the windshield of the yellow Chevy truck.

"Shit!" he says under his breath hoping he didn't draw more attention to himself. Mark stands still, looking and listening to see if he created any more fatal attractions. After hearing a couple of moans from the direction of the apartment complex, he takes a quick look around to make sure that his chances of being followed are zero and runs back to his original route.

Mark's house is on the next street up, and he definitely doesn't want to be followed. If it wasn't for his house being so close, he wouldn't have taken the time to dispose of his unwanted friends in the first place.

Mark slows down after reaching the concealment between two of the colonial houses across the street from the apartment complex. He can see the back of his house at this point and continues walking until reaching the back corner of the house on his right.

After looking around the backyards of his once annoying neighbors, he takes a look back towards the apartment building to make sure he doesn't have any company. Confident that he's hiking alone, he begins to walk toward his house. Looking up and scanning the solar panels on the roof of his house, Mark thinks to himself of how following through with spending the money on the solar power system was an absolute excellent choice. The power grid has been off for five weeks now, but he still has lights and the ability to cook without having to use fire.

Just before jumping the waist-high divider fence separating his yard from his neighbors, Mark stops and takes one last look around. With the area still clear, he swings his right leg over following with the left and races towards his house.

Running towards his back porch, he's already pulling his keys out of his left front jeans pocket, feeling for the key with the rubber key cover. He finds the key just as he reaches the back porch, shoves it in the deadbolt, turns the key, opens the door, rushes through the threshold, and shuts the door without making a sound.

With the keys still in his right hand, Mark leans against the door with his right arm fully extended and in a slouching position staring down at the floor while catching his breath. Without raising his gaze from the floor, he turns the deadbolt knob that's at his head level. Shifting his gaze from the floor to the deadbolt that is midway down the door, he reaches down turning the knob to lock it and stoops down locking the one that is a foot up from the floor.

Taking a couple more deep breaths, Mark stands up and turns around facing the door leading into the house. Locating the key on the key ring, he unlocks the top deadbolt and proceeds to unlock the lock midway down and the one close to the floor. Opening the door, he steps into the dimly lit kitchen, shuts the door and locks it. Taking his backpack off and setting it on the floor he says to himself, "Home sweet home."

Staring down the hallway that leads to the living room, located at the opposite end of the kitchen, Mark stretches with his arms above his head. He begins to walk toward the living room and stops halfway in the hallway, where the basement door is located to his right. He reaches over with his right hand and opens the door and turns to walk down the steps.

Mark almost trips over the deadbolt locks that are sitting on the top step of the basement stairs. He plans to install these locks this evening on the basement door and the door leading into his recording studio below.

Before the zombie apocalypse brought civilization to a screeching halt, Mark was an audio recording engineer and ran an audio recording business out of his basement. Business was doing well after he acquired a series of jobs recording soundtracks for television commercials and radio commercials for local businesses. He still helped local bands with their dreams by recording their music CDs of stardom and financial success, but the commercial gigs were what paid the bills.

Mark walks down the basement stairs and at the base of the stairs he turns left facing the entrance door to the recording studio. Unlocking the door, he leans in, pressing his right ear against the door and listens before opening the door. There's a faint thump and suddenly the doorknob starts turning back and forth.

Taking a step back, Mark watches as the doorknob continues to move back and forth. After about five seconds, the knob stops moving. Another five seconds passes and Mark grabs and turns the doorknob opening the door inward slowly. After opening the door completely, five feet away is a little blonde hair boy walking away from the door.

The boy stops and turns around staring at Mark expressionless. Mark stares back at the boy, while pulling his key out of the doorknob. The little boy slowly cocks his head a little to the right still with no expression on his face, as if he was looking straight through Mark's body.

Mark tucks his keys into his right front jean pocket, taking a couple steps forward while shutting the door behind him. As soon as the door shuts, Mark says, "Hi buddy!" The boy's face lights up and he begins to laugh and squeal as he runs towards his father. Picking up the little boy Mark asks him, "How's my Nathan today?"

Nathan is a special needs child with severe delays as far as his mental capacity. The boy is five years old with the mentality of a two- to three-year-old and the vocabulary and emotional responses of an advanced one-year-old. His condition is due to a selfish and inconsiderate mother, who could not control her drug and alcohol desires during her pregnancy with Nathan.

Fortunately for Nathan, Mark was an audio engineer with his own in-house soundproof recording studio. It would have been impossible to travel with Nathan anywhere due to his inability to comprehend the life sustaining need to be quiet.

After checking on Nathan and a brief playtime, Mark leaves the studio, closing and locking the door behind him. The happy father heads back upstairs to make Nathan and himself dinner.

Mark reaches the top of the stairs and stops for a moment to listen to the eerie sound of silence. He says to himself, "I would give anything to get back the hustle and bustle sounds of life outside."

Mark turns left and walks back towards the kitchen, looking into the boarded up dining room as he passes it on his right. He picks his backpack up off of the floor and slings it over his shoulder. Turning around, he heads back down the hallway and through the boarded up living room, where the stairs leading to the second floor are located.

Stopping at the top of the stairs, he thought he heard a noise come from the front of the house. Every once in a while, a deadhead will find its way onto his front porch. He doesn't understand why, other than it may be someone he once knew and they show up out of habit, such as the mailman or an angry ex-wife. Satisfied that there is no mail delivery today or an argument to be had, he turns left to the one bedroom he set up as his kitchen.

Mark walks into his makeshift kitchen and sets his backpack down on the floor next to the neatly stacked cans along the wall to his right. Next to the cans is Nathan's bookcase that's now used to store the pots, pans, and to keep the dry goods off of the floor. In the center of the room stands the dining room table. On the table sits two hotplates, a microwave, a toaster, a griddle, a deep fryer, an indoor electric grill, a plastic gallon jug of water, newspaper and a fire extinguisher.

Mark begins to unpack his backpack and put everything in its respective places. He turns the deep fryer on while passing the table on his way to the bookcase. Putting a large box of instant potatoes on one of the shelves, Mark grabs a big mixing bowl and sets another smaller bowl inside of it. Using the bowls as a basket, he puts three spice jars, a container of salt, a partial bag of flour, two zip lock bags – one sugar, one oatmeal - into the bowls and then grabs a box of cornflakes. He spins around and places the bowls and cornflakes onto the table. He turns to the stacks of cans on the floor and picks up two cans of premium chunk chicken breast and returns to the table.

Separating all of the choice ingredients while arranging them neatly on the table, Mark reaches for the manual can opener that's lying on top of the microwave next to a framed 5x7 picture of Nathan and a stack of paper plates. He opens the cans of chicken, drains the liquid into a bucket on the floor next to the table and dumps the chicken into the large mixing bowl. He then pours some oatmeal in with the chicken and kneads the mixture together with his hands until he's satisfied with the consistency.

Setting the large bowl aside, Mark adds some flour in the smaller bowl and begins crushing cornflakes in his hands letting them fall down into the bowl. Satisfied with the amount of cornflakes, he adds spices, and mixes the concoction with his hands. Mark then forms little chicken nugget patties out of the chicken and oatmeal blend, sets them into the dry mixture flipping them repeatedly until coated and sets them into the fryer basket. After having made a dozen nuggets, Mark drops the basket into the fryer.

As the nuggets sizzle and crackle in the hot grease, Mark takes Nathan's sippy cup from the shelf and grabs the box of powdered milk. He sets the sippy cup and its cap on the table, pours some powder into the cup, adds water from the water jug that's sitting on the table, and mixes the milk with a butter knife. It's not something Mark would drink, but Nathan loves it nonetheless.

Walking back over to the bookcase, Mark puts the powdered milk back on the shelf and takes a serving tray off of the top of the bookcase. He sets the tray on the table, pulls the basket out of the fryer and turns the basket upside down dropping the nuggets onto a newspaper.

Mark sets two paper plates onto the tray and Nathan's sippy cup as well. He places six nuggets on each plate, grabs a bag of potato chips from the bookcase and sets the bag on the tray. Picking up the tray, Mark heads for the stairs.

After descending the stairs into the living room, Mark stops to look through the crack in between the boards covering the front window. There are more deadheads wondering around the street than usual and that worries him. The increased number of deadheads wondering around makes it difficult to go out and get supplies without being noticed. As soon as attention is drawn to the house, the deadheads will be all over it and that is not what Mark wants to happen.

Turning to make the rest of his way to the basement, Mark trips over his own feet and nearly drops the tray of food that he just spent an hour preparing. After he was just thinking about drawing attention to the house, dropping the tray would have done just that. He wouldn't even have had to step out of the house at the wrong moment to be discovered. After gaining his composure from the very thought of sending out the dinner call to the deadheads, he swears at himself for being so damned clumsy and proceeds to head for the basement.

Balancing the tray with his right hand, Mark opens the studio door with his left hand swinging the door open, while focused on the tray so not to drop it, as was almost the case upstairs. Stepping through the doorway, focusing on the tray more so than where he is going, he almost trips over Nathan standing at the doorway and almost dropping the tray once again. Mark gains control of the tray and closes the door behind him.

Exhaling through his mouth, Mark scruffs the top of Nathan's hair, while saying to the boy, "That was a close one, buddy." Nathan just stares up at the tray in anticipation of what treats lay before him.

Nathan follows closely as his father walks over and sets the tray on the folding card table that's set up in the middle of the studio. Pulling out the chair with the booster seat, Mark hoists him up setting the excited boy into the booster seat. Nathan squeals with excitement.

Mark places a plate of nuggets in front of Nathan and his squealing drops to a hum, while he bobs up and down from kicking his legs. Mark opens the bag of potato chips and Nathan stops with a chicken nugget in his right hand, looks at the bag and then to Mark, "Mm-mm" Nathan hums.

Part way through eating his meal, Mark begins to feel that tightness and cramping discomfort in his abdomen, warning him to start for the toilet or else. Putting a hand on his gut, "Oh boy, I better hit the can, buddy. I'll be right back." Nathan doesn't even acknowledge his father's statement, while stuffing another nugget in his mouth. Getting up from the table, Mark hurries over to what was once the vocal recording booth that he converted into a bathroom.

Before rushing through the vocal booth's doorway, he glances over at his son sitting at the table enjoying his potato chips. He smiles and then winces to the pains of impending doom if he doesn't hit the throne immediately. Mark steps in and shuts the door behind him.

Nathan finishes the last potato chip on his plate and grabs his sippy cup. He gives the cup a shake and holds it up in the air in front of him with great admiration as if he just found the coveted cup of Christ. Nathan mumbles to himself, brings the cup to his lips, tilts it up, and drinks the wonderful liquid of immortality quickly. After consuming all of the cups contents, he holds it up in the air in front of him once more, gives it a shake, "All gone" he says and slams the cup down on to the table.

Mark sits down on the campsite portable toilet that he never got to use for an actual camping trip. While thinking about how things used to be before all hell broke loose in the world, his bowels broke out a hell of their own. With the release of what may be the closest a man feels as far as menstrual pains are to a woman, he also reflects on how thankful Nathan and himself are, alive and safe in their soundproof room.

After finishing off the few chicken nuggets and potato chips that were left behind on his father's plate, Nathan looks around the room. He pushes the plate away and begins to squirm himself around in his seat.

Once he is turned around with his back somewhat facing the table, he slides down between the chair and table as if he was descending into the small access door of an Army tank. Now on the floor, he is free.

Nathan crawls out from under the table and starts about his usual routine of running around the studio, yelling, hooting, and squealing. Nathan stops at the make shift bathroom and slaps the glass window literally scaring the shit out of his father. Mark looks up to his left and sees a small hand and a pair of eyes looking in at him. Mark smiles and waves. Nathan takes off running again.

Mark picks up from the floor an old issue of 'Musician's Friend' magazine and flips through the pages of various musical instruments and audio recording equipment. He thinks to himself of how it is most unfortunate that he can't go out and purchase new equipment, let alone order any of the goodies within the pages of this magazine. With a sigh, Mark also thinks of how nice it would be to just take Nathan to the school playground at the end of their street again. "God, this sucks" he says aloud to himself, dropping the magazine to the floor and grabs a roll of toilet paper.

Opening the vocal booth door Mark immediately hears the sound of Nathan laughing and squealing, along with a lot of banging and pounding. He looks toward where the noise is coming from and sees the studio door open. "Oh shit!" Mark now realizes that he forgot to lock the studio door when he brought the food down. He runs for the door.

Running up the basement stairs he can hear pounding and breaking glass coming from all around the house. Nathan got the attention of the deadheads wondering around outside and now they were all converging on the house, adding more noise in the process, and drawing more attention to the house.

Mark gets to the top of the stairs and sees Nathan in the living room laughing, while pounding back to his friends standing on the porch just on the other side of the boards covering the picture window in the living room. Mark runs over and picks Nathan up just as the boards covering the window start to break and splinter.

Running back toward the basement door, the panicked father looks back to see the boards breaking away from the picture window and deadheads falling through. The sound of glass and wood breaking are heard elsewhere on the first floor of the house.

Rushing through the doorway leading to the basement stairs, Mark trips on the deadbolts lying on the top step like he did earlier in the day, nearly losing his hold on Nathan. Grabbing the basement door, he slams it shut and runs down the stairs wishing he had got the deadbolt locks installed on the basement doors. He runs into the studio, sets Nathan down, and closes the door locking the doorknob.

Mark stands looking around the studio for something to barricade the studio door. All he really has is a couple of guitar amplifiers and the folding card table, which won't do any good. He begins to think about how they're trapped down here and that they may have a chance getting away upstairs. That's when he noticed all the vibration coming from upstairs from the growing number of unwanted visitors that are just letting themselves into his home. Panic really begins to set in.

Mark runs into the engineer room where all the recording gear is and grabs his 9mm pistol off of the top shelf running along the back wall. He pulls the clip out to make sure it's loaded, restores the clip into the handle, pulls the slide bar back to put a round into the chamber, and checks that the safety is on. He stuffs it into the back of his pants like he's seen many an actor in the movies do and runs back out into the studio.

Nathan is running around making his usual noises and laughter. Mark stops and watches his son and begins to feel an overwhelming feeling of sorrow as he tries to hold back the tears. He begins to realize that the situation is most likely not going to have a good outcome. The pounding on the door begins.

Mark rushes over to Nathan, snatches the boy up and runs back into the recording room. Setting the boy down, Nathan looks up at his father and smiles. Nathan is unaware of the grave danger they are in. Tears begin rolling down Mark's face as he smiles back at his son and he places a hand on the boy's face. Nathan giggles and starts to head toward the door. Mark turns, shuts and locks the door separating the two rooms before the boy makes his escape.

Mark begins to pace the small area staring out of the double pain glass window looking out into the studio. He focuses on the studio door, just waiting for it to burst open. He keeps trying to think of any way to escape, but there isn't any possible way other than through that door. The basement windows he had blocked up when he built the studio to prevent noise from entering and escaping. Now sound is not the only thing that can't escape.

Nathan begins to walk alongside his father laughing and giggling at the amusing march they're doing. Mark looks down at Nathan and watches as the boy marches next to him. Bursting into tears once again, Mark stops and kneels down hugging his son. Nathan returns the hug and rests his head on his father's chest. Mark begins to cry uncontrollably and holds Nathan tightly.

"I'm sorry, son, so very sorry. I tried my best to keep you safe, but I failed you. I failed" Mark says as he leans his son back by the shoulders. Mark then puts his hands to Nathans cheeks, "I love you, son".

Thud Thud Thud

Mark is jolted by the noise and looks to the glass window where there is a group of deadheads in various stages of decomposition staring back at him. Mark can see the audience growing behind the crowd at the window as they file in through the door.

"You fucking bastards!" he yells at the deadheads pounding and clawing at the glass window. "God damn you all! God damn you all to hell!" Mark exclaims.

More deadheads start gathering at the window. The pounding keeps getting louder, more frequent, and the pounding has started at the door as well.

Mark grabs Nathan by the arm and pulls him over to the corner of the room. Mark sits down on the floor and plops Nathan down to his left holding him close with his left arm while holding the gun in his right hand. He flips the safety off with his thumb.

The pounding is almost deafening and Mark watches as the first pane of glass begins to crack. He can hear the sounds of wood cracking as the pounding on the door escalates. The first pane of glass shatters and the next pane is already beginning to crack as well.

"Forgive me, son, please forgive me son" Mark begins to say over and over.

The glass gives way with a crash and the odor immediately engulfs the room, causing Mark to gag as he begins to yell in anger. As the deadheads push on each other desperately trying to get into the room, the group in the front of the crowd are becoming eviscerated on the shards of glass sticking up from the bottom of the window frame.

Mark points the gun at the group trying to make their way in through the window. He keeps wishing that this is all just a bad dream and that he is about to wake up at any minute. One deadhead manages to fall through and disappears behind the mixing board. A hand missing the middle and ring finger pops up grasping the top of the board. Fluid that resembles sour cream, guacamole and black coffee swirled together begins to ooze out of where the fingers used to be as pressure is applied from the deadhead pulling himself up off of the floor.

Just then, the door bursts open. Mark begins to yell and shoots the first rotten bastard falling through the doorway in the temple. Immediately Mark's ears begin to ring and Nathan starts screaming and kicking. Mark points his pistol at the deadhead crawling over the mixing board directly in front of him and Nathan. He squeezes the trigger and the back of the festering intruder's head explodes all over the upper part of what's left of the window. Swinging the pistol back towards the door, he fires off two more shots hitting one in the shoulder and missing the other one coming up from behind all together.

During the whole time Mark is trying to hold off the inevitable, he is trying to remember how many shots he has left in the pistol. That inevitability is tearing him apart more than what these putrid sons of bitches want to do to him and his son. He can't stand the thought of it and he becomes angrier the more he thinks about it. Then Mark thinks, Damn it! How many shots do I have left?

Mark hated himself for having to waste two bullets just for missing in the first place. Mark shoots three more at the door way and two more that fell through the window. The smell from cracking these rotten eggs open is becoming overwhelming and Marks eyes are beginning to water from trying to keep down his supper. Nathan is freaking out at this point.

"God, why!" Mark screams up at the ceiling. "Why, why, why?" Mark begins to cry once again and squeezes Nathan tighter with his arm wrapped around him while putting his hand over Nathans eyes. Nathan is screaming and kicking frantically. Mark puts the gun to Nathan's temple and says, "I'm so sorry, son."

Just then, a deadhead who made it through the doorway and over the pile collecting on the floor grabs Nathan's ankle. Nathan squeals even louder and kicks even more violently. Mark yells, "Fuck you!' and blasts it in the head just before it bites Nathan in the shin.

Mark quickly puts the gun back to Nathan's temple, "Please forgive me, I love you buddy" and pulls the trigger. Nathan goes limp.

The rapport from the pistol is the loudest explosion to ever come across Mark's ears. This one sound has taken away any will that remained within himself to even think of survival, for the only thing worth living for is now gone and worst of all, it was done by his own hands. Mark screams and spits at the ceiling, "Damn you! You ignorant motherfucker! Fuck you! Fuck you!"

Mark's now crying uncontrollably holding Nathan's head to his chest as his son's blood pours down his chest into his lap. He watches as the deadheads make their way into the room and fall over the bodies on the floor. As they crawl closer to him he yells, "Motherfuckers, you motherfucking bastards. I'm not going to give you the satisfaction of ripping my ass apart alive!"

A deadhead missing its legs clawed its way around the mixing board and reaches Mark grabbing his leg. Mark holds the gun under his chin, looks his stalker in the eyes and says, "Fuck you!" and pulls the trigger.

CLICK

THE END

###

Low~Carb Diet
By R.R. Alexander

It's not easy being a zombie. Brian was barely three days dead and already he was unable to recognize his own face in the mirror. His skin was turning green in some places, purple in others, and blisters were beginning to swell and break. The palms of his hands and fingers were shriveled, as if he'd been soaking in the bathtub for approximately an eternity. Without question, he'd been a bit of a fat bastard before he'd met his untimely death, but now he was bloated to the point of looking like he might have just eaten a small horse... or two. He found himself wondering how the undead fiends in the Romero movies managed to stay so contrastingly fit.

Among the worst of it all was the maggot situation. Brian had been deceased for just over half an hour when the first of the flies had begun to show up. He'd put forth a noble effort to fend them off, but after a while it had become a losing battle. The eggs had started to hatch a day or so later, and now thousands of the little white larvae squirmed throughout his flesh. Mercifully, he was unable to actually *feel* them crawling around inside of him but their presence was nonetheless impossible to ignore.

The most important thing to consider now was his hunger. Never in life had Brian felt so incredibly ravenous as he did in death. He had ransacked his secluded one-story lakeside cabin in a desperate search for something to satisfy his craving, but had found nothing of interest. The thought of consuming anything from his kitchen repulsed him almost as much as his own posthumous decay. It wasn't until his dry, unblinking eyes had caught the movement of a mouse scurrying across the hardwood floor that he'd finally realized that the object of his fervid obsession was, to his astonishment, the flesh of the living.

After hours spent in a futile struggle to capture the mouse, Brian had ventured outside to try his luck with the wildlife in the forest surrounding the lake. However, he was forced to limit his time outdoors, as the woods were swarming with an immeasurable variety of worms, insects, and flying things, most of which would delight in ravaging him to the bone. There was the possibility of larger predators lurking about as well: cougars, coyotes, perhaps even bears – all were better equipped to make a meal of Brian than he was of them.

After day three of snacking only on frogs and snakes, Brian's starvation was a rabid monster, which clawed away at the remnants of his sanity. His despair was absolute. He had to end this. According to the movies, the best way to destroy the living dead was by a gunshot to the head, or by fire. Brian didn't own a firearm, but he did have plenty of matches, and a half a fifth of flammable tequila in the kitchen cupboard.

He held the bottle over the top of his head and poured slowly, being sure to douse as much of his naked body as possible. As the liquid rushed down his swollen, blistered legs and pooled on the floor, he struck a single match against the striker strip on the side of the matchbox.

The match failed to ignite.

Before he could attempt a second strike, the sound of a car engine caught his attention. Louder, then terminating abruptly near the front of the cabin. The *clunk* of a door shutting. Keys jingling.

Someone knocked at the front door.

Brian dropped the matches; he wasn't going to need them after all. He staggered to the entryway leaving a trail of tequila and body fluids. His lips stretched into a grisly smile as he opened the door. Bile leaked from his mouth and formed yellow-green rivulets on his chin. His voice was hardly a whisper, weakened by decaying vocal cords and muffled by the squirming mass of parasites behind his teeth.

"Hello Mother"

THE END

###

Klondike
By Keith Carpenter

T he icy crunch of newly fallen snow is all that could be heard in the dark gloom of the shrouded mountain. The night was frozen on the mountain and the man, running for his life, had long since lost his snowshoes and his every labored step was sinking into the white blood-soaked snow. The blood that ran down his arm and painted a trail through the snow was his and he was losing it fast and the deep layer of fresh snow was slowing him down, but it didn't seem to be slowing down the 'thing' that was pursuing him.

***

August 16, 1896, the Skookum party discovered gold deposits in the icy waters of Bonanza Creek and the Klondike River, which winds its way through the mountainous tundra of the Yukon. There are many stories about the discovery that was made that fateful year and it's not clear who actually made it. Some say it was Kate Carmack and others say it was Skookum Jim Mason, but the one thing nobody seems to dispute was the fact that Gold wasn't the only thing that was found there... near the banks of the Klondike.

***

Seth had only caught a glimpse of the creature in the grotto. He thought it was dead at first but soon realized that whatever death had stilled its rotting corpse was like nothing he had seen, for the moment his lamp-light shone on its twisted gnarled face, it lurched forward and wrapped its gaping maw around his forearm. His gun had jammed and he had dropped his buck-knife into the snow, leaving behind it a knife shaped impression descending several feet into the white crunchy ice. There was no 'reaching into the hole' to find the knife. It was gone and there just wasn't time.

Seth knew his friend had to be dead. There was no way a person could survive having his face eaten off and his throat pulled out like someone gutting a trout. Exposed tendons and nerves and a blood soaked esophagus was all he could remember. That and the expression on his friends face when the creature began to rip out his organs and shove them into its mouth. Seth dropped his lantern and ran like hell.

"Oh dear God, what have I done?" Seth mumbled to himself, as he crashed through the snow spackled trees. "What Hell have I uncovered... what demon have I awakened?"

Just below its branches, at the base of an old pine that was in the path in front of him, Seth saw the abnormally large opening to a burrow of some sort. It seemed the perfect place to hide in hopes that the creature would push past him in the knee-high snowdrift.

He quickly dove into the small cave and curled into a ball, trying to take up as little room as possible. His teeth chattering and his heart racing and the bite on his arm throbbing with a burning sensation like nothing he had ever felt. His body writhed in pain and trembled as his stomach knotted up like a twisted rope being pulled to its breaking point. His heart pounded in his chest as he tried to control his breathing. The last thing he wanted was to give away his position, but he had little control over the state of his throbbing body.

"Mother Mary, deliver me from this demon that pursues me like a rabid animal." Seth repeated the prayer under his breath over and over again. It was all he could hear as it rang in his ears, when suddenly there was a loud 'CRACK' just outside the burrow entrance.

The moonlight beamed through the burrow's two-foot wide opening, casting shadows all around, but Seth could only pray that the sound had come from some angry badger or mongoose or, hell, even a skunk. He was hoping beyond hope that it was anything but that fiend that had chased him here.

Suddenly, there it was again, the noise outside the burrow entrance. Again Seth prayed under his breath, asking God to let it be the small fuzzy animal that owned the burrow. All had gone quiet for a moment, when suddenly he heard a faint gurgling sound. He tried to tell himself the sound could have come from any number of sources, but in his heart he knew better… it was too familiar to be just anything.

He got his wits about him enough to shift his weight so he was able to see just outside the small opening. He could see nothing but the shadow-riddled snow bank on the other side of the neighboring trees. The space was cramped but there was just enough room in the burrow for Seth to fold his legs and stretch out his body so he could lie on his stomach. Elbows folded tight under his chest, he inched his way toward the opening, hoping to see a clear path of escape. He knew he could not hide in there forever.

A small voice in his head told him to wait… just a little bit longer. He put his face in his hands and began to cry, muttering some unintelligible words to God, when out of the blue he was overwhelmed by the smell of death. The aroma was not only recognizable but it burned his nostrils like acid. He trembled like a scared rabbit and he dared not peek out from his cupped hands.

He could feel something moving into place just over his head, stretching and craning its way into the opening of the burrow. Was it the creature? Was it possible that it could not see him lying there in the shadows, covered in snow? Why hadn't it attacked him? Whatever loomed above him was inches away from his head, that was facedown cupped in his hands pushed into the snow.

Seth separated two fingers and peeked out. He could see a shadow on the wall next to him that was cast there by the moonlight. The foreboding shadow spread itself across the stone in the shape of a human. It slowly and methodically moved as someone or something craned its head into the opening of the burrow and it was literally inches away from the back of Seth's skull. He could only hope that by some miracle of God... the 'thing' didn't see him.

The gurgling sound was louder now and Seth could feel something cold and sticky dripping down the back of his neck. The thing that was hovering over him didn't seem to be able to smell him and he began to think that if he waited it out it might just go away.

Suddenly Seth's heart leapt in his chest. A wisp of hope washed over him. He could hear footsteps in the snow. They seemed to come from behind whatever was looming over him in the burrow entrance. Had help come to rescue him from this nightmare? Had his friends from the camp followed him up the mountain out of curiosity and were now there to come to his aid? After a few heart-stopping moments his answer came.

After what seemed like an eternity, the low wet gurgling sound was accompanied by a faint airy moan. It was the kind of sound someone might make if their esophagus had been ripped out. Seth squeezed his eyelids tight and let out a soft moan of his own, because he knew. He realized that the "person" who had joined the creature was Warren, his partner who had been killed back in the grotto.

The time had come. Seth had summoned enough courage to take a look, so he slowly opened his eyes and tilted his head upward, but the moment his eyes adjusted to the darkness, it overwhelmed him. The creature instantly lunged on top of Seth, joined by what had once been his friend Warren. There was only time enough to let out a blood-curdling scream before they both had hold of him and drug him kicking and screaming from the burrow entrance.

Without warning or without any reservation, Warren and the ghoul ripped out Seth's throat, putting an abrupt end to his screams. The wicked sensation of jagged teeth ripping into his throat and the razor sharp claws of the creature thrusting deeply into his abdomen, tearing the flesh effortlessly, were the last sensations Seth ever felt.

The pain was more than he could take... everything went black as he tried to cry out with nothing more than the gurgling sound of his own blood gushing from his open gaping throat. It was over... Seth was dead, but only for the time being.

***

FIVE HOURS EARLIER:

"Goddamit Seth, we're gonna freeze out here if you don't get your ass up this mountain."

Seth Berdgis and Warren Garver had been living in camp Rabbit Creek with the rest of their party for just over six months. The cold had become relentless and the winter had taken its toll. The population of the camp had dwindled from sixty men to just fewer than twenty over the months, due to a number of reasons. Sickness and death had thinned out the population substantially not to mention the disillusionment of claim holders who never found the huge mountains of gold they had unrealistically expected.

The men that were left in camp were greedy for the most part, but Seth Berdgis took the cake. Rumors of other kinds of treasures had traveled to the Klondike and they had definitely gotten his attention. A traveling merchant who came through every few weeks told Seth of a hidden grotto not far from the camp where there was rumored to be an ancient stash of all sorts of ancient native Indian artifacts and handicrafts that could be worth a small fortune. The rumor of artifacts and valuables was accompanied by the whisperings of an ancient Indian curse but that part of the legend had a tendency to fall on deaf ears. Most of the men, even the superstitious ones, were more inclined to be driven TOWARD riches rather than AWAY from the rumor of native Indian curses. But in this instance, Seth Berdgis and Warren Garver were the only two men in camp who believed the legend enough to spend their hard-earned gold on a map of its alleged location.

"The grotto is supposed to be just through these trees."

Seth pointed and yelled over the howling wind that had picked up just moments earlier. It looked like a blizzard was heading their way, so they made for the grotto with urgency. The gusting wind painted everything in sight with an ever-deepening blanket of snow, so Seth and Warren ducked under an outcropping of rock to try and stay warm.

Seth pressed his buckskin mittens that were lined with rabbit fur against his face to muffle the sound of his chattering teeth.

"Where the fuck is this secret cave, Seth? Warren grumbled. "You're the one with the goddamned map!"

"According to this," he fumbled to stretch out a crumpled piece of muslin cloth so he could view the markings scribbled on it, "We're there, but with this blizzard, who knows if we'll ever find it."

The two men sat huddled together, as the snow relentlessly pounded against their skin, stinging it with every flake. Red and chapped from the freezing temperatures, their lips began to crack and get frozen together, making talking a chore.

Hugging himself tight for warmth, Seth closed his eyes and drifted away to thoughts of his family and all the things he was going to provide them with once he found his illustrious treasure. As his mind raced, a chuckled emerged from deep in his gut as he thought of the ridiculous notion of curses and bogeymen.

Before Seth realized how much time had gone by, he noticed that storm had subsided. In the blink of an eye, two hours had passed. Warren had dozed off and the snow had covered him like a blanket. The blizzard was over and they could now search for the grotto but how they would find it under several feet of freshly fallen snow seemed like an impossible task.

"Why did you let me fall asleep?" Warren grunted as he pulled a cigar from his coat and lit it. "I could have frozen to death."

He began pushing the fresh snow away in hopes of finding solid ground. In the recess of the small outcropping, Warren uncovered a pile of rocks that were concealing an opening of some sort. The two men brushed all the snow away and began pulling down the pile of rocks, revealing the entrance to a long since abandon cavern.

"Oh my God, this has to be it, Warren."

Seth eagerly threw the stones aside, like an excited child.

"I'm telling you, Warren, whatever is in here is going to change our goddamned lives…. FOREVER!"

Seth took a small kerosene lamp that he had stowed in his satchel and lit it and sat it in the snow. Then, to be on the safe side, he pulled out his revolver and opened the chamber to make sure it was fully loaded.

"You never know…. There may be a bear in there." Jim said, as he holstered his gun and grabbed the lantern.

"Yeah, a bear that rocks up the door when it leaves?" Warren rolled his eyes and threw aside the final stone.

The sun was going down and it was dusk out, and the lantern instantly provided them a small circle of light that illuminated the cave entrance just enough for them to see several feet inside.

The cavern was large and smelled of bittersweet rot that permeated their nostrils. The stone walls all around the entrance were covered with strange writing that neither Seth nor Warren could read. It seemed to be some sort of ancient text that was written there by who or whatever had sealed up the cavern.

"Do you really think there could be anything worth a damn in this place?"

Warren ran his fingers along the drawing of a rough stick figure of a man that looked like it was eating the other stick figures around it. The closer they looked at the pictographs, the more gruesome they seemed to get, but there was no sign in any of the gruesome pictures that indicated anything about treasure or valuables.

"This all looks like a bunch of superstitious hogwash. All these pictures look like some sort of ritual killing spree, but there ain't a damn thing about anything valuable." Warren grumbled through his cigar. "I just hope we didn't come all this way for nothing."

Seth held his lantern up to another picture that seemed to depict one single figure kneeling as it ate something. Holding the lantern even closer, Seth could make out what it was the figure was eating. The drawings all around the lone figure seemed to represent severed body parts and they were strewn all around the figure. The men thought it very sickening that anyone would draw such things but neither Seth nor Warren had any idea what sort of significance the drawings might hold.

"Seth, you remember that old medicine man that used to come into camp and trade his pelts for food and supplies?"

Seth thought for a moment and nodded his head.

"Yeah, I remember that crazy old bastard. Why do you ask?"

Warren rubbed his finger along a few of the drawings and turned to Seth with a very intense look in his eyes.

"That old bastard used to tell stories about some ancient Indian curse that caused an entire tribe to be killed off."

"Yeah so, that sort of shit happens all the time around here." Seth replied. "You got one tribe killing off another and so on and so on and before ya know it, the whole damned Indian tribe is extinct. So?"

"Yeah, but the legend says they didn't stay dead."

Warren pulled his buck knife from its sheath punctuating the uneasiness in his voice.

"Well, all we're going to find in here are a bunch of old Indian artifacts that will hopefully bring us a pretty penny, so stop acting like a baby and let's get going."

Seth rolled his eyes, held up the lantern and continued into the cavern. He was determined to find something valuable no matter what the legends said.

As they made their way deeper into the cavern, Seth and Warren could see all manner of Indian relics that had been left behind by some long since extinct tribe. For thousands of years the northern territories of the Canadian Yukon, especially around the Klondike River, had been home to dozens of native people who had made the cold icy tundra their home for many generations. To see a cavern such as this, which was probably some sort of burial ground, was not at all out of the ordinary, but to have it sealed away so tightly was strange. It was obvious that the people that had sealed it up wanted to keep unwelcomed visitors out, but the thought that was kicking around in Warren's head was, 'What if they really wanted to keep something in?'

The first room of the cavern, a very large area with a dome-shaped ceiling, was cluttered with broken clay pots, rotten buckskins and all manner of Indian beadwork and other forms of art. It was as if they had been placed there as some sort of sacrificial gift to a heathen god, but as Seth braved the deeper darker recesses of the strange gloomy cavern, he couldn't help but think this was a place no 'god' would ever reside in.

"Here, help me move this." Seth said, grabbing the edges of a large flat stone that marked the end of the large room they had walked through. He motioned for Warren to grab the other side so they could attempt to push it aside.

"I don't like this…"

Warren pulled Seth's lantern up to the markings on the stone. It appeared to be a door that sealed off another portion of the cavern and it was adorned with markings even more sinister then the last ones.

"God damn, these Injuns sure liked to draw some gruesome shit." Warren grunted as he pushed.

The huge flat stone was just over six feet in height and weighed hundreds of pounds, but with a bit of leverage in the right direction, Seth and Warren were able to push it aside, making a gap wide enough to squeeze through.

"This has to be it, my friend." Seth smiled. "Whatever wonderful secrets this place is hiding, they have to be hidden in here."

The stone had been sealed to the wall with a layer of thick clay that cracked and fell away as they pushed the stone aside.

The moment the seal was broken there was a hiss of putrid air that rushed from the hidden room within. As Seth entered the chamber, his lamp filled the small dark space with light. The walls glistened with what seemed like sparkling gems at first, but upon closer examination Seth and Warren could see that what they had thought to be gems was actually a shiny layer of dripping tar-like goo that covered almost every inch of the jagged inner walls. It was obvious to them that the tar-like goo was the source of the rancid smell in the room.

As they moved in further, they were greeted with a horrible sight. There, littering the floor, were dozens of corpses. All of which had been bound tightly, wrapped in what appeared to be buckskin straps and each and every one of them were frozen in a horribly distorted pose. It was as if they had been buried alive and had fought relentlessly to free themselves from their buckskin restraints.

"Good Lord, Seth, what in the hell is this horrible place?" Warren got the words out just before turning away to vomit.

"I'm guessing a burial chamber, but like nothing I've ever seen."

The closer Seth looked, the more disgusting the scene before him became. The corpses, which after decades of decomposition, should have been dried and mummified, but they were nothing of the sort. Each one of them seemed to be oozing the same tar-like slime that was covering the walls and causing the horrific odor in the room.

All the corpses were withered and twisted and obviously lifeless, but they still seemed moist and soft with a putrid aroma coming from them, but none of them were nearly as decomposed as they should have been given the amount of time they had been hidden away in their tomb.

Seth was closely examining each and every cadaver, looking for any valuables might have been buried with them, when suddenly he saw something curious. Between two of the bodies was a pile of the same buckskin wrapping that the other corpses were bound in, but these seemed to have been shed like a cocoon. Suddenly, it dawned on him. Seth stopped and looked around, putting his finger to his mouth motioning Warren to not make a sound. Had one of the corpses been freed from its restraints by another looter? Certainly it didn't escape on it's on…. It was dead, or was it?

Without warning a sound echoed though the room. Seth looked at Warren and Warren looked at Seth. They both wondered which of them had made the noise, but it soon became obvious that it was neither of them… it had come from something else. Being a cave and the way sound travels, it was impossible to know where it had come from. Then, there it was again. It was a soft gurgling growl, almost like an animal would make when it was warning you that you had invaded its space. They were not alone in the tomb… something or someone was in there with them. Seth pulled out his revolver.

"Seth, I don't give a flyin' fuck-all if there is anything in this godawful place worth money, I want to get the hell out of here, NOW!

With that, Warren yanked the lantern out of Seth's hand and made for the opening, but there it was, standing between him and freedom. It was the most horrifying remnant of what once had been a man that Warren had ever seen. The much sought-after secret. The thing they had braved the mountainous tundra and the stinging blizzard to find. The thing they both were sure was going to change their lives, and it did. But not the way they thought it would. Not the way they wanted it to. But change their lives.... It did!

THE END

###

One Last Shot
By Wayne Hood

I don't need to bore you with the details of the NC-401 virus and how the contamination began. Any of you left reading this have already witnessed the apocalypse from its origin. I don't need to reiterate the attempted government cover up, or the ensuing plague that was believed to be "under control". We all remember where we were when we heard the newscast, much like Kennedy being shot or the Challenger blowing up, the image of that day is burned into our memories like some recurring nightmare that awakens us every night in tremors and cold sweats. It doesn't matter if you've spent the last thirty years in a cave or even under a rock, one look outside and you see the massive hordes of the undead as they stagger about, wandering aimlessly fueled only by the most basic animal instinct, and even that may be a stretch; and an insatiable appetite for the human flesh.

No, I won't bore you with the details of how we arrived at this God-awful existence; this purgatory for the damned. Just like me, you too have seen the undead walking amongst the living, eliminating all life at every opportunity, feeding upon, not only our flesh and our bodies, but devouring our souls as well. I will however, tell you my story of survival, as I feel my time is drawing near.

Almost a year has passed since my wife's hand was last clutching mine; shouting horrified as she was being pulled away; the moans and gnawing at her body were momentarily drowned out by our screams. I would've jumped on top of her, I would've sacrificed myself if only to save her for a brief second longer, I would've but I couldn't. As I shouted her name, trying with every ounce of my strength to pull her back from the mass of undead bodies engulfing her, I felt the cold, slimy grip of the undead creature clutch my shoulders. Call it panic, call it fear, or call it instinct (God knows I still don't know what it was), maybe I was simply too weak at that point, but in that moment when that thing grabbed my shoulder, my grasp upon her hand released as I was knocked to the side, spinning halfway around as I stumbled to catch my balance. I turned so fast my eyes could not even keep up. With a shifting, blurry sense of vision, like a drunk man spinning in circles, I swung at the first thing I saw, and with a soft grunt the staggering corpse stumbled enough to the side that I was able to refocus and dart in the opposite direction, putting maybe eight feet between me and it. I returned my gaze to where I was just clutching my wife's hand, where not even ten seconds ago, the chorus of our screams echoed through the air, now, only the sounds of carnage remained. I couldn't speak, I couldn't shout, I couldn't move…there I stood frozen, paralyzed like a deer staring at the headlights as they burrow towards it, aware of its impending doom, but unable to react. Those bastards, among all the blood and innards that were being torn apart and ripped into by rotting teeth, while her entire body was engulfed, trapped under a pile of ravenous carnivores; even with all this, I could see only her face. Her face… those things had to do it on purpose, leaving her face in plain view for me to see, to look at the terror and the pain and agony of her final seconds, as if at that moment they're only intention was to brag about they're conquest to me, too add insult to injury. They had taken her, ravished her body, eaten her alive while she writhed in agony. Yet, they left her face untouched, left it to look back at me, as if she was shouting from her grave "You failed me". That was all I could see…zombies eat brains…my ass zombies eat brains. And if they do, it must be the last thing they eat, like some sweet dessert they savor for the end of their unholy feast. Or perhaps they just did that to me.

I barely noticed the geek that I had just knocked from my shoulders staggering back towards me with its arms out. That hollow, empty moan seemed to echo through my head, until it snapped me out of my trance, and took my eyes back off my wife and back upon him. I looked into its eyes, those empty, lifeless eyes; they didn't even seem to be looking back at me. At that moment I felt a rage build inside me the likes that I had never experienced before. Being a peaceful man most all my life, my last fight being with Howard Nelmore in the sixth grade, I was not one prone to violence. But seeing this abomination slowly limping towards me, poised to attack while its friends devoured the only thing in this world I truly loved, I felt a rage and a hatred that overwhelmed me. Almost before I could even think, I pulled my arm back like a rock in a slingshot, and released with such velocity, I can't be sure that at that moment a bullet fired from the long barrel of this here Colt 45 could've done much more damage. I could never have imagined just how frail these creatures could be…hard to kill, but easy to hurt.

The moment my fist connected with the rotten, bloody flesh already barely clinging to the hollow skull on the side of the creatures face, I could feel it shatter under the impact. To this day I'm shocked my fist did not go clean through and out the other side. In one continuous motion the geek fell to the ground, and for a split second laid there, motionless like a corpse is supposed to do. At that moment, I didn't know what to do; I stood there over my opponent like that famous photo of Ali after knocking out Frazier. I swore to God I had just killed it, and just when I thought it was down for the count, it began to move, like some bad horror movie where the killer is not dead, and just when you think it's safe, he begins to rise. Lucky for me, this thing lacked the coordination and strength to be able to pick itself up off the ground. While it began to struggle, I quickly glanced around, and seeing a rock within a couple feet about the size of a football, I hastily grabbed it. He was now almost to his knees, so without hesitation, I raised the rock with both hands as high as I could manage and, with all my strength, threw it onto the creatures head. I'll never forget the sound; it's an almost indescribable crunch as the bone shatters and the skull cracks open like a peanut being stepped on at the ballpark. I saw a small line of blood shoot out from under the rock. The creature was finally motionless. I felt a sense of relief; I almost allowed myself to crack a smile as I looked at this once undead monster that I had just KILLED.

In my moment of triumph, I almost failed to realize that the remaining horde had made short work of my wife and began to turn their focus on me. The commotion of my recent struggle had alerted them to the fresh meat available; and believe me they wanted it. Although I was still high from my murderous accomplishment thirty seconds earlier, I was in no mood to attempt a kamikaze mission of trying to take out the remaining group. I estimated there were about eight of them, a task much too big for me to reasonably expect to be able to pull off. So, I ran. To my wife, I'm sorry, to this day I pray you're looking down with forgiveness on me; I ran away from them, and I ran away from you.

It must have been a mile or so before I saw the beat up red Ford truck barreling down the road, kicking up so much dust you could hardly even see it, swerving to avoid the dips and potholes in the road, occasionally hitting one causing the truck to bang with a sound that made me swear the front axles were just going to break right off. I ran out to the middle of the road and raised my arms, waving them shouting "HEY!!" "HEY!!!" I thought to myself, "I don't think he's going to stop" but just before I was ready to give it up and jump out of the way, I heard the brakes lock, as the truck began to skid to a stop. At this point, I began to wonder if I even really wanted this truck to stop after all. Although, the news reports had given us warnings, signs and symptoms of these creatures and what they are and aren't capable of (driving obviously not being one of their skills), I still didn't know what to think. I half expected one of those bastards to hop out of the truck and come at me, staggering and moaning, drooling blood from its vile, flesh encrusted mouth.

As I stood there attempting to catch my breath, struggling with every inhalation, feeling as if my lungs wanted to collapse; I squinted my eyes, hoping to peer through the sunlight blinding me as it beamed off the windshield. My heart was pounding, my legs were shaking, my lungs felt as though they were going to burst, and just as I began to notice all these agonizing things, the driver's side door swung open, making me forget about them once again. The first thing I saw was the pistol pointing out the open window. "Don't shoot, please!" I shouted. The man slowly stepped completely out from behind the cover of his pick-up. I noticed the way he cocked his head back, giving me a look like he was pondering whether to kill me anyway. I almost thought he was going to, as a matter of fact, I'm almost positive he was. But instead he hesitantly lowered his gun, and asked "You okay?" Still trying desperately to breathe, let alone think, I bent over resting my hands on my knees, and managed to gasp out a short "Yeah." After a brief moment that felt like an eternity, the man scolded and, like a father ordering his teenage son, he ordered me to get in the truck; I had never been so grateful in all my life.

As I sat down on the flat bench seat, I exhaled a long breath, and leaned my head back, resting it against the rear window. My body was sore, my lungs still felt as if they wanted to explode. The man, who had made his way to bed of his truck, returned to the driver side door and hopped in with a bottle of water in his hand, "Here". I grabbed the bottle, said a quick "thank you" and, without a moment hesitation, twisted the cap off and drank nearly half in one long gulp. I proceeded to continue struggling to catch my breath. "I'm Jim," he said, extending his right hand towards me. I glanced at his face, hoping to catch a friendly smile; instead he still had that stone cold, almost grimacing look. "Thomas," I answered back, shaking his hand, still too weak to grasp with a firm grip. "Thanks again," I said, and with a slight nod of acknowledgement, he threw the truck in drive and punched the gas, the back tires spinning in place for a few seconds before finally catching the dirt road and speeding off.

"These fucking things are everywhere. I thought you were one to be honest, I was going to run your ass right over and not even think twice, until I saw you waving your arms" I looked at Jim, for the first time, really stopping to take notice of what he looked like. He was an older man, I guessed around fifty or so, his salt-n-pepper hair was uncombed and blowing backwards from the wind. His black t-shirt had been ripped, exposing his right arm and the tattoo that he displayed like a badge of honor. The words '62nd Infantry' wrapped around an eagle clutching the flag in one talon, and the standard issue M16A2 in the other. He continued to babble, cursing the dead and bragging about the ones he killed while he bravely managed to narrowly escape, like a war veteran recalling his story from the Korean civil war of 2016 that we for some reason felt we had to be a part of. I assumed that's where he served; I simply nodded my head and gave the occasional recognition like I was impressed. I had barely noticed his ramblings fade off when I realized I had not said a word in response. Not wanting to be rude, I chimed in with my recent tale of conquest as well. I refused to mention my wife though, not wanting to relive that horror within myself. He let out a laugh, "Good job, man, I wish I coulda seen that bastards head explode!" while patting my left arm with his right. I cracked a small forced smile. I wish I could've been as happy as he was about the whole thing.

"So, where ya headed?" he asked me. After a couple seconds of silence, I responded, "I don't really know." "Well, where's your family? You wanna try to make your way to any of them?" He looked over at me, while I stared ahead, and then slowly twisted my head to the right, looking out the window. All he said was, "Oh, I'm sorry." There was a moment of awkwardness following that exchange, me not having much to say, and Jim obviously feeling some mix of embarrassment and compassion. After what I believed was much deliberation to himself, he snapped at me "Well, you can ride along with me then, give ya someplace safe," I looked at him, "Thank you," then looked down at the floor, feeling almost a burden at this point, but not prepared to decline the offer. He slapped at the controls on the dash, "Goddamn radio ain't had shit on for days, fuckin' government spoutin' all that bullshit about isolated incidents, and the situation being contained and all that nonsense, can't trust them fuckers either, for all we know they set this shit off on purpose." "What is the latest?" I asked, not having heard a word on television or radio myself in about four days. "The latest?" he looked sharply at me, "The latest is fuckin' walkin' around outside, the latest is what's attackin' everybody." I looked down, almost ashamed that I had asked the question. "Fuck, the latest is what did this shit," he said rolling up his left sleeve as far as he could, and still grasping the steering wheel with his left hand, twisted his arm enough to show me the bite on his bicep, the blood beginning to dry and form a crust around the torn, bruised edges. "You like that shit?" He asked, his eyes widening with a gleam of some crazy pride he felt. "Bastard got a nice little taste of me before I blew his fuckin' head off!" He let out a laugh, that horrible sounding laugh, like an old man that spent a lifetime smoking cigarettes, almost wheezing out every joyless syllable. I stared in shock, and upon him returning his arm to its natural state, I looked at his face, staring, not knowing what to think. I don't know if he was simply ignoring it, not wanting to accept the truth or he truly did not think there was anything wrong, but I knew this was not good.

As we pulled into the long dirt driveway, I saw the house. The two-story farmhouse looked as if it hadn't been maintained in 50 years. There were broken shingles overlapping cracked siding next to dirty windows, trees overgrown almost covering the entire front of the decaying residence. I remember thinking to myself, "Yup, this is pretty much what I expected."

"Help me grab this shit, will ya?"

"Of course,"

Upon exiting the truck I felt a rush of anxiety as I quickly looked around. I noticed the overgrown bushes lining the trees all around the property. I kept expecting one of those things to come staggering out. But I quickly ignored my fears and turned my attention to the bed of the truck, where Jim had obviously scrounged up more than a few supplies. He grabbed the cooler and a few small boxes of canned goods, and he instructed me to grab the bags and the rope. I obliged, and we made our way into the house.

"Have a seat," he ordered me as he motioned to the kitchen, the lifeless room held only a small table with two chairs, and an ashtray. "Oh, thank God," he proclaimed, as he grabbed a pack of smokes and lit one up. "My dumbass forgot these earlier, I'll never make that mistake again," he offered me one, which I quickly but politely refused. He laughed, "What, afraid it'll kill ya?" He continued to laugh as he opened up a cabinet and pulled out a bottle of Jack Daniel's. "Don't tell me you don't drink either!" I looked at him, and with a chuckle, I responded "No, that I do,"

While he poured two glasses strait up, I looked around his lonely home. There were no pictures of family on the walls, no signs of loved ones ever visiting, not even a dog, out of everything else, that's what I most found odd. I don't know why, I had just always pictured a rough old man like him as having a dog. He set my glass down on the table, then with a long grunt and soft moan, slouched into his adjacent seat at the empty table. He leaned back and took a puff of his cigarette, then quickly sat forward and returned his focus to me. He grabbed his glass and raised it. "Cheers". I quickly reached for my glass, like some awkward reaction to an event that I should have already been prepared for. "Oh, yes, cheers, thank you," I lightly tapped my glass against his; after taking a sip, there was an awkward silence that Jim thankfully and expectantly broke.

We sat and conversed for a while, mostly him continuing his conspiracy theories and militant rants regarding our current situation. I occasionally responded with a few insignificant facts that I had recalled from prior news stories, which he quickly shot down with responses of government lies and cover-ups. I will be honest, if at any other normal point in time, I had met Jim, I would not have been very fond of him, but given this current situation, I felt safe sitting in his quiet, empty home, sipping Jack Daniel's listening to him go on and on. He motioned to his arm "Well, lemme go clean this shit up, you hurt at all, need any first-aid?' "Umm, no thanks, I'm okay. Hey does that hurt at all?" I asked, trying to figure out if I should be worried or not. "Nah, burns like a bitch though, I had worse in Korea," He opened the cabinet once again, and grabbed the bottle of Jack, setting it on the table and looking at me, "Don't be shy, help yourself," "Thanks," I felt an uneasiness settle in, as I looked once more at his arm, while he stepped away from the table. Was he oblivious to his arm? Did he really not know what he was on the verge of becoming? Or was he simply choosing to ignore it; not wanting to face the God-awful truth? He hastily made his way upstairs. I contemplated running. But I didn't.

About 15 minutes later he returned downstairs brandishing a beautiful, shiny Colt 45 revolver. He extended it towards me, "Here, take this," I looked at him almost confused. "Just in case, you never know, I've got mine on me at all times," He lifted his shirt, revealing the butt of his gun tucked securely in the waist of his faded jeans. I grabbed the gun slowly, staring at it in disbelief, almost amazed with it. I had never even held a gun before, let alone shot one. "You know how to use that thing?" Jim asked with a smirk and a hint of sarcasm in his tone. "Uhh, which end's the dangerous one?" I jokingly responded, trying to lighten the mood and avoid having to actually answer with the truth. "Ha-ha, c'mon, let's go shoot something," He quickly knocked back his double shot of Jack and started out the front door.

We stood on the porch, and enjoyed the fading sunshine as it was slowly creeping away towards dusk. There was a slight breeze, and the sound of the birds chirping actually made me forget for a second the apocalypse that was going on just over the hill past those trees that I still anxiously watched. Jim motioned over to the far right of the yard, where he had set up a makeshift target with some hay bales and a piece of plywood with a crude bull's eye painted onto it. "Show me what ya got!" I looked at him, my heart pounding with excitement and anticipation, I wanted to say, "I don't know how to shoot," but, although I knew he already knew that, I didn't want to admit it. I raised the barrel of the Colt 45 while squinting my left eye and cocking my head to the right. I aimed for the bull's eye and squeezed. Upon pulling the trigger, the gun kicked back with such velocity I thought for a second my arms had jumped out of their sockets. I was almost knocked on my backside, and I probably would have been had Jim not caught me. I missed the target, and with a roaring laugh he patted my back and proclaimed, "It's okay, soldier, try again,"… So, I did.

I suppose in many ways I owe my life to that man. Jim the rugged old army-vet; he was crude, he was rude, and he cursed to make a sailor blush. But had he not picked me up and brought me here, or given me that gun and showed me how to use it that day, then I would not be sitting here writing to you now. I also would not have been able to put a bullet in between his eyes later that night. While I slept on the downstairs couch, the revolver still clutched in my hands, I was awakened by the sounds of moaning and feet dragging heavily across the old wooden flooring. I awoke and jumped up, looking face to face with my fears. I knew it was going to happen… Jim had converted; he was now consumed with the virus, now walking amongst the dead; now walking towards me. I raised the Colt 45 that he had previously handed me, and remembering what he taught me earlier, I once more pulled the trigger… After a few seconds, I dropped to my knees and broke down in tears.

In one day I had lost everything; I witnessed my wife's ungodly death and had to shoot the last person that I could consider a friend. That's all I have to say about Jim, he's buried in the backyard of his home; may he rest in peace.

I decided to remain at Jim's house after his death. I decided that with his stock of food, water, guns and ammo, to leave would just be plain stupid. I didn't think he would mind too much either.

The first six months flew by fairly uneventfully; I would run into the occasional staggerer on my various trips to scrounge supplies. One quick shot and it was time to move on. I had become a survivor, a lone survivor, feeling as if I was the last person alive in this world of the dead.

In early February, I ran out of gas while driving my normal route to head into town. Although most everything had already been scoured and picked, it was the only place I had ever seen with anything useful in the way of supplies. I was approximately halfway between my refuge and the town, which was about three miles. I got out of the truck, and looked around. The wind was especially cold that day, and the bitter chill of every sharp breeze seemed to rip right through me. This was as nervous as I had been since my first voyage into town alone. But I got through that, so I calmed my nerves and told myself I'll get through this. I muttered to myself, "Shit!" Bundling my coat a little tighter, lowering my head to tuck my chin as close to my chest as I could, I began to walk back; shivering with every step.

I was almost a mile closer to home when I noticed the staggering corpse ahead in the distance. It was alone, as I had come to expect, so I saw no reason to worry and just continued walking in stride. I removed my glove and unzipped my coat, not missing a step, reaching into my waist and grabbing my last remaining friend. I pulled the Colt from out of my jeans and held it firmly by my side in my right hand. I could see the creature, which had been previously limping along blindly finally take notice of me as I closed to within a hundred yards. The bitter cold wind almost seemed to increase, carrying with it the smell of rotting flesh. Something felt different, something felt wrong. I ignored these feelings and never took my eyes off it. The closer I got, the quicker my pace became, until I was close enough that I could hear it moaning, the stench of its decaying flesh growing stronger. I was now within about 20 yards of it when I raised my right arm, aiming the gun at the creatures head. I never missed a step, never missed a stride, I had become a pretty good shot, and this appeared normal.

As I approached within the final 10 yards, I could see that he was focused on me, the same as I was focused on him, raising his arms and slightly picking up his pace, about as close to running as these things are capable of. Five feet was close enough, I pulled the trigger and watched as the creature instantaneously fell silent to the ground. The only problem was there was no silence; I could still hear the moans echoing through the air, as the wind continued to carry the overwhelming stench of death alongside it. I stood confused for a second before quickly turning around and realizing…I had been outsmarted; I'll be damned these bastards actually got smart. While I had focused my attention on the one lonely corpse that staggered pathetically alone in front of me, fixating my gaze solely on it, I had failed to notice the horde that crept out of the field behind me.

I suppose at this point in time, most people would naturally stop and ask themselves what went wrong and why they hadn't grabbed a better gun for this type of situation. Perhaps I never thought I would need more than eight shots, I supposed I would never run into the day where an entire horde would manage to sneak out behind me while I trudged carelessly along, oblivious to the impending doom that staggered behind me. Well, whatever the reason was that I only ever carried my trusty little Colt 45, it wasn't enough anymore.

I quickly raised my arm and shot the first two creatures before telling myself that I was currently engaging in a futile activity. There were too many to shoot. I turned back around and began running towards my house. I didn't dare slow down, I would occasionally turn around just to make sure that they hadn't also learned how to run as well. I mean, at this point, I didn't know what these things were now capable of. But no, they just continued to stumble and stagger like they always did. As I looked back and watched the ravenous mob grow smaller and smaller in the background, I felt relieved, extremely anxious, but relieved nonetheless.

I ran the remaining mile or so until I returned to my house. I quickly charged up the steps and slammed the front door, locking all the locks I had installed and throwing the giant 2x8 board into its braces across the door. I had long since boarded up the first story windows and chained the cellar doors outside, so I immediately checked those off the list inside my mind. I stood inside at the door for a minute, catching my breath and waiting. I peered outside and upon seeing nothing, I ran upstairs to grab Jim's old Colt. I had never fired it, I kept it on the bed in what was once his bedroom, as my show of respect. But now, I needed it. Grabbing it, I made my way to the other front bedroom, my room, and sat down at the small table by the front window, watching the road and the adjoining driveway.

I always kept my ammo on that table. This room is where I spent most of my time anyway. I always watched the road, always waiting for the day when the undead would come staggering into the driveway and turn this house into "Night of the Living Dead" I pulled the three boxes of ammo from the left edge and placed them in the middle of the table. I reloaded the three bullets into mine, and loaded Jim's, as his was still empty from the day we met. Eight bulls-eyes he hit, I kid you not. After loading the two revolvers, I returned my focus outside, returning my watchful eye to the driveway.

It wasn't long until the first staggerer made his way to my driveway. I could see him on the road and thought, "Please just keep walking". But unfortunately he did not oblige my request. As he turned and began stumbling down my driveway, I swear he was looking right at me, those black empty eyes peering at me through the window. I stood there watching him, debating to myself if and how I wanted to shoot it. That's when the remaining horde caught up. My eyes became wide as the initial shock made me jump back from the window. There must have been 25 by now, all walking close in some strange tight-knit mob, all with the same goal, all wanting me.

My first reaction was natural, open up the window and start shooting. So, with a Colt in each hand that's precisely what I did. Sixteen shots later, I managed to drop eight. For some reason, they're harder to hit from a half-opened second story window. I decided that firing one from each hand like some wild-west gunslinger was not the way to go. So I reloaded my trusty Colt and recollected myself. Leaning back out the window, I steadied my aim, and this time managed to drop six more with eight shots. The remaining ten or so continued to make their way towards my house and by the time I reloaded, they were already on the porch, blocked by the roof, I was unable to shoot at them.

I stopped for a second then loaded the other gun. I tucked that into my waist while I hastily went downstairs. From the bottom of the steps I could see and hear the remaining zombies as they tried to make their way inside however they could. Not being the strongest or smartest creatures in the world, they would have a pretty hard time getting past my locks and boards. The problem was I had no way to shoot them without going outside; or opening the front door, but that option seemed to be more counter-productive than anything.

The longer I waited inside, the worse I knew my chances became. As I looked out of the window I could see more coming. My heart almost sank into my stomach, as I watched another small horde come staggering towards my house. I didn't know what to do. If I opened the door I was dead. My only thought was to somehow make it out of the house and take off through the woods. But almost as soon as I thought of that plan I noticed them making their way around the sides of the house towards the back.

So, here I sit, writing you. This is my story, I've made it as long as I can, I've fought as hard I could. My house is surrounded, and I feel my time is up. I suppose all I can do anymore is load up and go out in a blaze of glory, saving one last bullet for myself. I can't make it to the woods; I don't have enough ammo to take them all out.

I sit here and think about her. I suppose I always had hope that this would all one day come to an end. I always wanted to believe that whoever was responsible for this destruction would come in and clean it up, fix everything and make life normal again. I fought for her; I stayed alive because I knew she wouldn't want me to give up. But now, I just want to see her again. I've all but given up hope on any salvation for mankind. This is the world. This lonely, empty house surrounded by ravenous carnivores attempting to eat me. This is reality, and this is a world I no longer want to live in.

I hope if you are reading this that mankind has been restored. I hope that the undead have been returned to the ground, and life as we once knew it is restored. I wish I could have left a better legacy, but I hope you enjoyed my story. I hope my tale of survival is either inspirational or educational, depending on what the current state of affairs is.

Goodbye…I will take out as many of these bastards as I can… then with my final bullet, I shall return to my wife. I will finally be at peace.

THE END

###

the adventures of Daddy's Lil Girl

By Matt Ficner

About Keith Carpenter

Keith Carpenter has been a diehard zombie fan since he watched his first Romero film at the tender age of 14. Growing up a dyslexic kid, he loved to watch horror movies and dream up stories but having a hard time as a young reader, finishing an entire novel was always more of a chore than a delight. Despite this battle with dyslexia, he loved to write as a kid and was always penning his own fantasy adventure stories that tended to get creepier and creepier the older he got. He has spent most of his life watching every zombie movie he could get his hands on but it was only in the last decade or so that he got a hold of his first zombie horror novel, *Reign of the Dead* by Len Barnhart, which he couldn't put down and flew through in a few hours. Today he has a large collection of zombie anthologies, novels and graphic novels that he loves to read again and again. *"I don't consider myself a great writer,"* he says, *"But I can't help having stories to tell and I just have to write them down or my head will explode. I just hope someone out there will enjoy reading them."* As a result of having a secret passion to someday produce his own zombie movie, Keith collaborated with his dear friend Matt Ficner and came up with a fresh new zombie story that he later wrote in the form of a full-length movie screenplay by the title of *Zombie Circus*. The movie has yet to be made, but to date he has taken the movie script and adapted it into novel form, which is available on Amazon.com. After writing the novel version of *Zombie Circus*, the bug bit him hard and he began work on the book you just read, *Freeze Dried*. He also plans sequels for both of these books, so keep your eyes open for them.

Check out this other great zombie title by:

Keith Carpenter

Zombie Circus Available at:
Amazon.com
Createspace.com
Smashwords.com (In digital form)
www.keithcarpenter.biz

www.ingramcontent.com/pod-product-compliance
Lightning Source LLC
Chambersburg PA
CBHW072212170626
46813CB00003B/898